The LOXLEYS and CONFEDERATION

Written by
Mark Zuehlke

With
Alexander Finbow

and
Niigaanwewidam James Sinclair

Illustrated by
Claude St. Aubin

Colour Artist
Christopher Chuckry

Letters
Todd Klein

Editor
Alexander Finbow

Published by Renegade Arts Canmore Ltd trading as Renegade Arts Entertainment Ltd
Office of publication: 25 Prospect Heights, Canmore, Alberta T1W 2S2 Canada

RENEGADE
ARTS ENTERTAINMENT

Renegade Arts Entertainment is
Alexander Finbow   Luisa Harkins John Finbow
Alan Grant   Doug Bradley   Emily Pomeroy
Nick Wilson and Jennifer Taylor.

Visit our website for more information on our titles: renegadeartsentertainment.com

ISBN: 9780992150891   First edition printed May 2015

Graphic Novel written by
Mark Zuehlke
with Alexander Finbow & Niigaanwewidam James Sinclair
Illustrated by Claude St. Aubin
Colours by Christopher Chuckry
Letters, logo and cover design by Todd Klein
Editor and publisher Alexander Finbow
Additional Editing by Alan Grant
Printed in Canada by Friesens

Also available now is *The Loxleys and the War of 1812.*

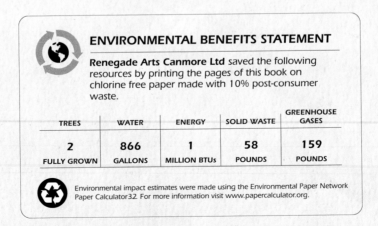

ENVIRONMENTAL BENEFITS STATEMENT

Renegade Arts Canmore Ltd saved the following resources by printing the pages of this book on chlorine free paper made with 10% post-consumer waste.

TREES	WATER	ENERGY	SOLID WASTE	GREENHOUSE GASES
2	866	1	58	159
FULLY GROWN	GALLONS	MILLION BTUs	POUNDS	POUNDS

Environmental impact estimates were made using the Environmental Paper Network Paper Calculator 3.2. For more information visit www.papercalculator.org.

FSC
www.fsc.org

MIX
Paper from
responsible sources
FSC® C016245

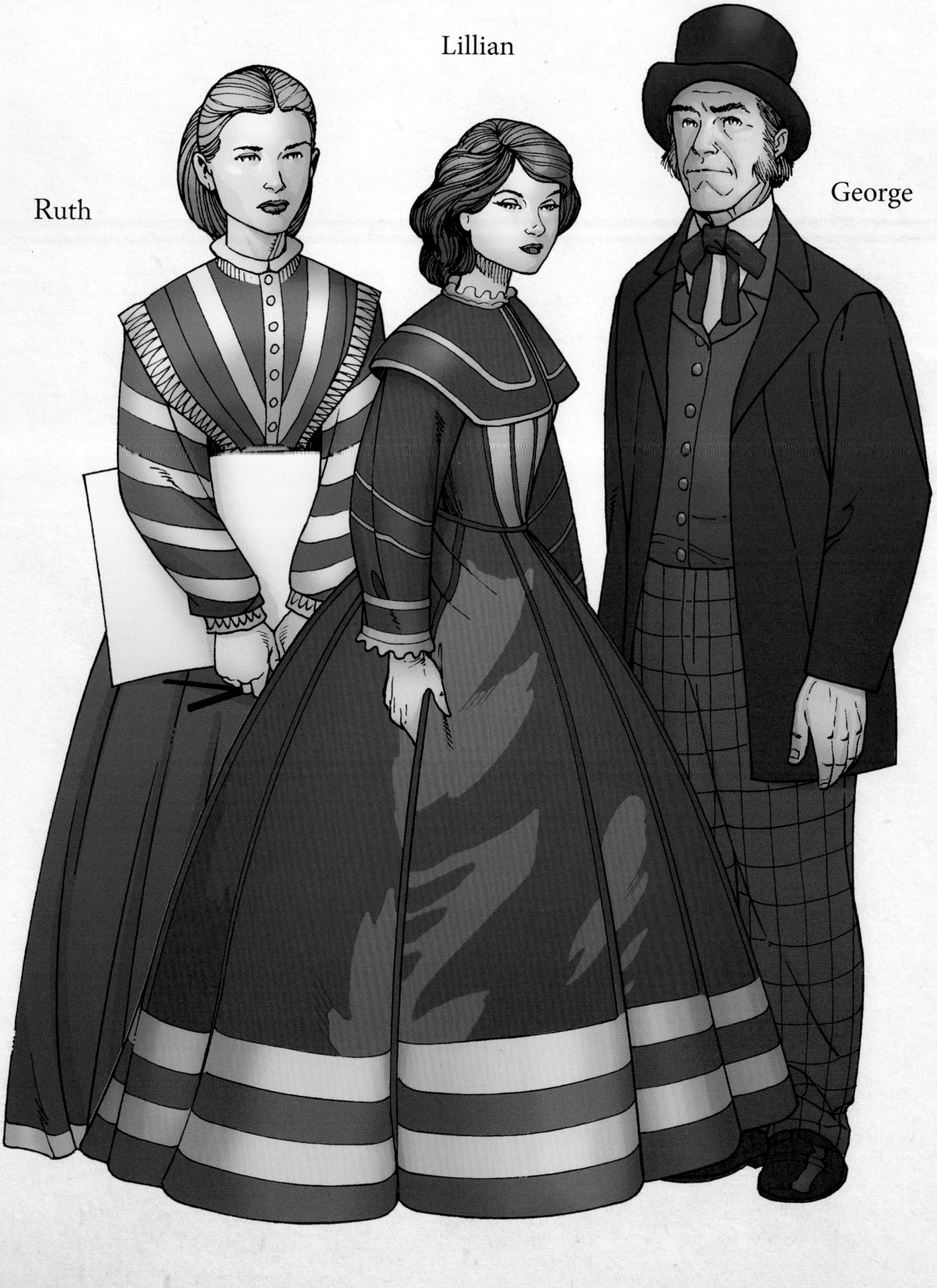
Lillian
Ruth
George

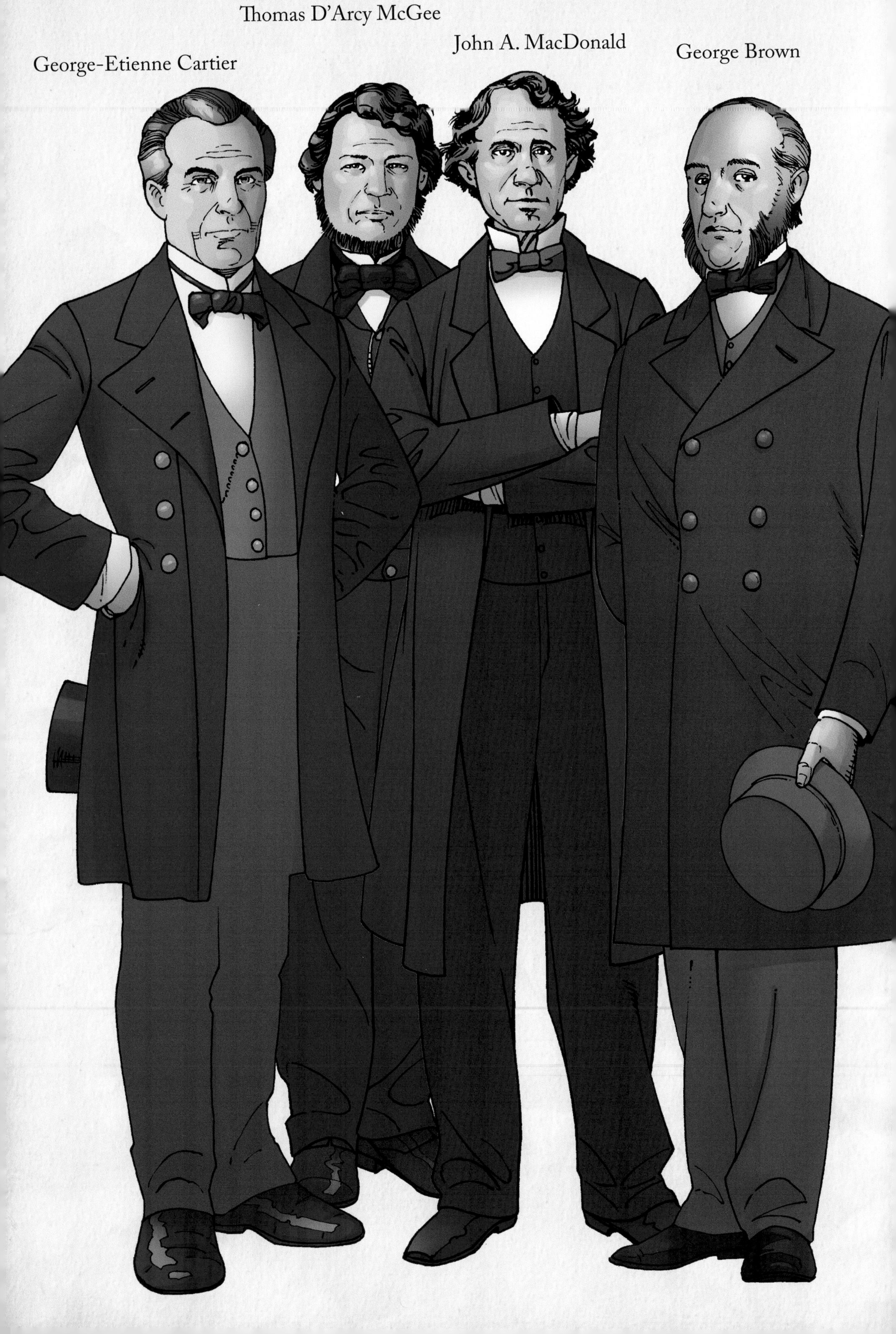
George-Etienne Cartier
Thomas D'Arcy McGee
John A. MacDonald
George Brown

Contents

Foreword

Last week I sat in a Citizenship and Immigration classroom in Calgary with a twenty question citizenship test before me. This event was exciting and terrifying in equal measure. Exciting, as it meant that my knowledge of Canadian history, politics and geography would have a chance to prove itself. Terrifying, because it was the first written exam I'd had to sit since high school and, having spent the last 5 years immersed in Canadian history for the two Loxley books, to fail this test might shatter my confidence to talk about Canadian history ever again.

As the adrenaline coursed through my body, I read the first question; 'Which provinces originally joined together to form the Dominion of Canada?'

The Loxleys and Confederation was born from my desire to create more books that would invite Canadians into their history in the same way we achieved with The Loxleys and the War of 1812, whilst we were working on the definitive Canadian World War One graphic novel.

As we wrestled with 1914-1918, Mark Zuehlke and Claude St. Aubin found gaps in their schedules that a book about 1864-1867 wanted to fill. The history of how the British North American colonies took the first steps to becoming a country in its own right didn't instantly appear to be the adventure filled thrill ride that other historical episodes did. But, when you join the Loxleys as they again find themselves in the middle of history, you quickly realise that Confederation is a story about people and their struggle for identity and prosperity against the backdrop of a rapidly transforming United States of America.

Lillian Stock, the fifteen year old granddaughter of one our 1812 heroes, George Loxley, asked to take on the role of storyteller for this book. We of course agreed to her request and see the rapidly changing world through her eyes as she grows and falls in love for the first time. Her personal journey takes place as the American Civil War rages, Abraham Lincoln meets his untimely end and the colonies once again have to defend against invasion from America.

Mark has done a wonderful job of distilling the events leading to Confederation into a compelling human story, ably taking on the lead writer's role from 1812's Alan Grant. This is his first graphic novel script and Mark proved adept at switching from prose to the more collaborative process needed for comic books. His work ethic and dedication to Canada's history is without fault, as his many awards and accolades demonstrate. Winning the 2014 Pierre Berton award for his books about Canadian servicemen and women in the two world wars was richly deserved. I worked closely with Mark on Lillian's story as we found her personal moments within the bigger narrative.

I was also thrilled when Niigaanwewidam James Sinclair accepted my invitation to join our writing team. I knew Niigaan was a comic book writer alongside his role as Professor of Native Studies at the University of Manitoba, and a fan of The Loxleys and the War of 1812. He brought the indigenous point of view to Confederation that I felt we needed to understand and address in this book. One of Niigaan's most telling contributions was to suggest that we started the story back in 1534 as Cartier first discovered Canada. This initial meeting between the indigenous people of Canada and the European settlers sets the pattern for their troubled relationship moving into the future.

Claude once again took up the mantle of realising every person, place and object in the story. The amount of effort and time a great comic book artist has to commit to researching and then creating pages for a historical story should not be underestimated. Even with having to juggle DC Comics' demands to draw both Green Arrow and Superman at the same time, Claude has beautifully given life to the world of The Loxleys and Confederation.

Another team change from the 1812 book was welcoming Chris Chuckry as colour artist, replacing Lovern Kindzierski who was tied up with his writing commitments. Like Lovern, Chris is a Winnipegger with a long line of colour art credits to his name, including one of my favourite series, The Unwritten by Mike Carey and Peter Gross. Chris has delivered sumptuous colour to complement the clean and flowing inked lines from Claude.

Todd Klein returned once more to bring his many years at the top of the lettering profession to Confederation. Again he took on the role of my production mentor, helping to shape the overall look of the book from cover to cover.

I am very proud of the work everyone has produced for The Loxleys and Confederation, and hope sincerely that our book helps to open up more of Canada's rich history.

Now, back to that test.

Which provinces originally joined together to form the Dominion of Canada?

Hopefully, once you've read this book you will be able to easily answer this question yourself!

Happily, I can report, that both my wife Karen and I passed the Citizenship test with 100% scores. As you read this, we should now both have become citizens of Canada.

Enjoy this journey through history with The Loxleys and Confederation.

Alexander Finbow
Canmore, Alberta
May 4th 2015

Matthew Loxley

Aaron Loxley

William Loxley

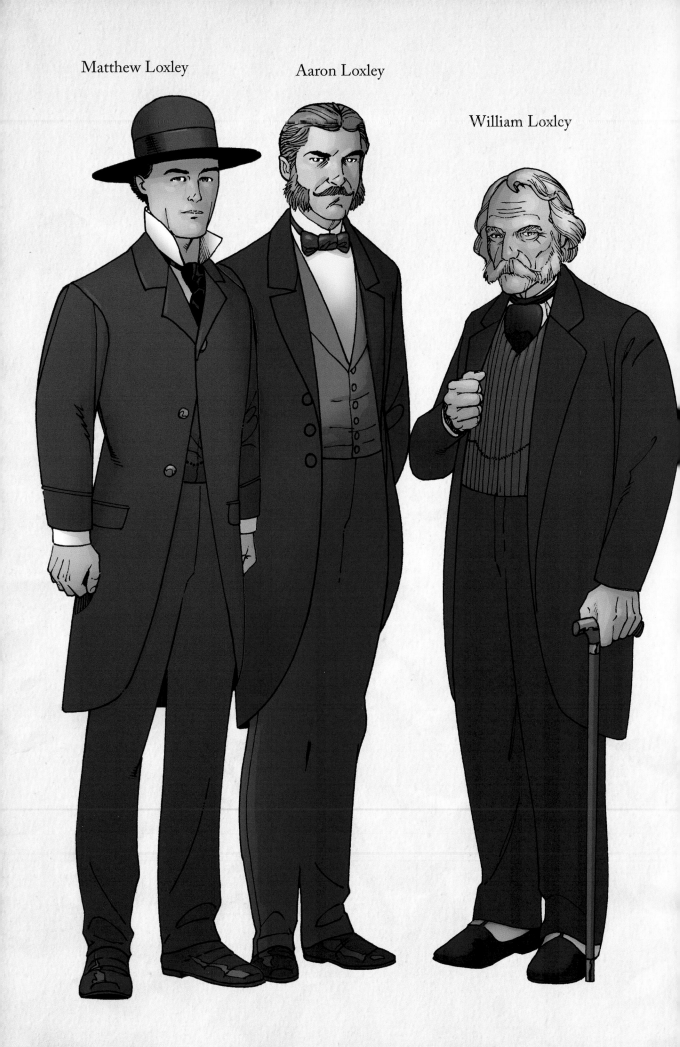

Prologue

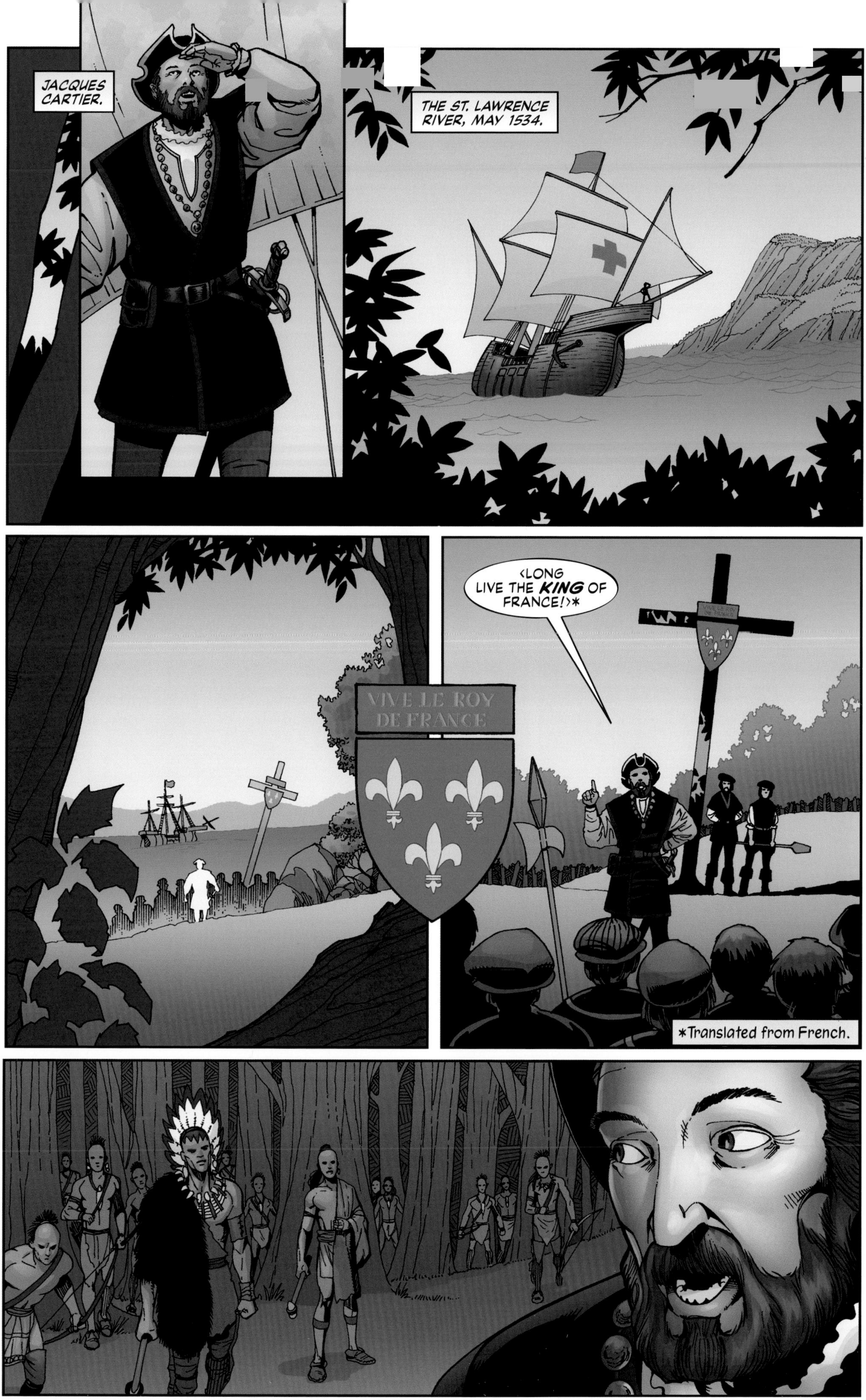
JACQUES CARTIER.
THE ST. LAWRENCE RIVER, MAY 1534.
VIVE LE ROY DE FRANCE
<LONG LIVE THE KING OF FRANCE!>*
*Translated from French.

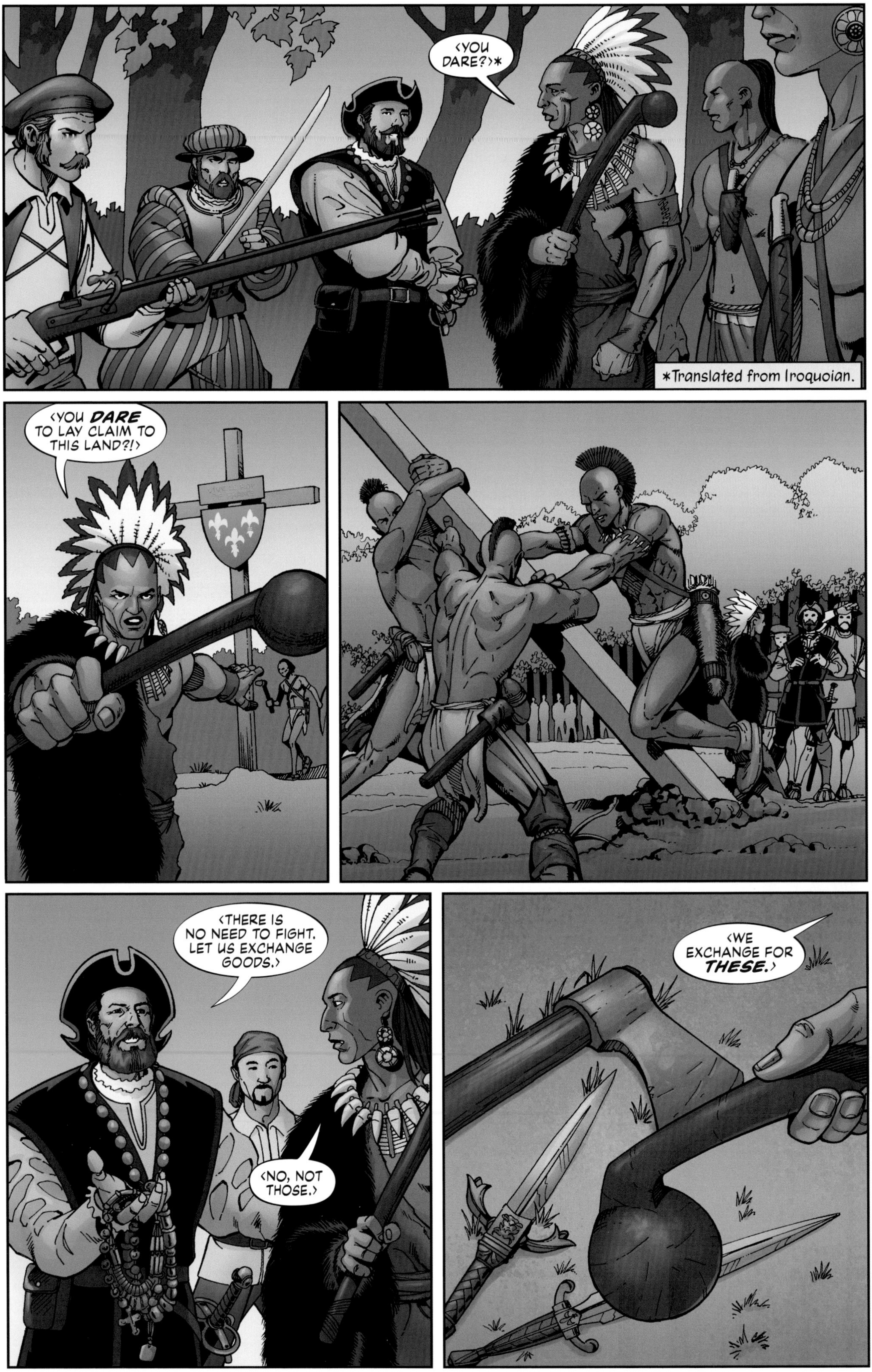
‹YOU DARE?›*
*Translated from Iroquoian.
‹YOU DARE TO LAY CLAIM TO THIS LAND?!›
‹THERE IS NO NEED TO FIGHT. LET US EXCHANGE GOODS.›
‹NO, NOT THOSE.›
‹WE EXCHANGE FOR THESE.›

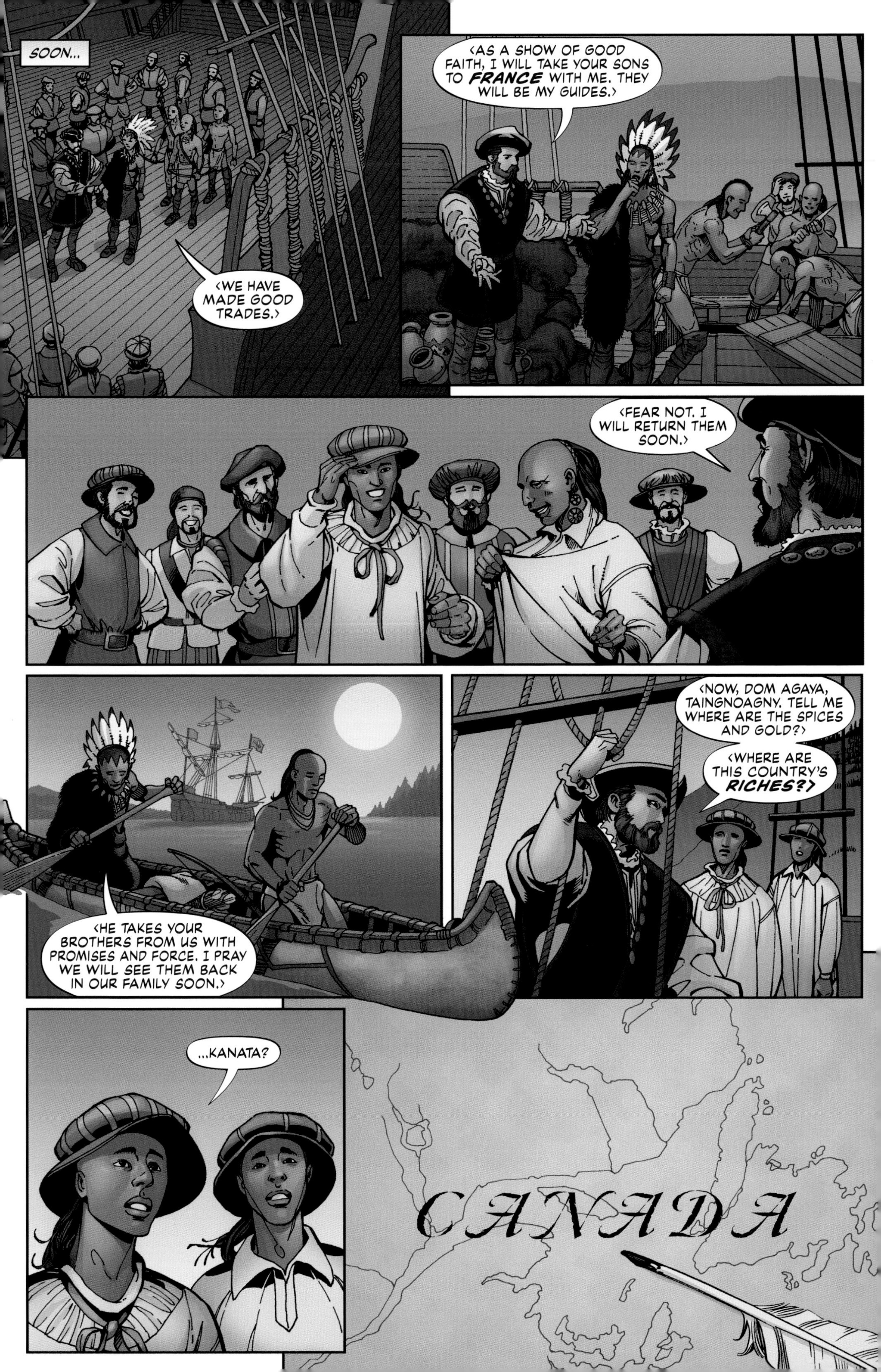
SOON...
‹AS A SHOW OF GOOD FAITH, I WILL TAKE YOUR SONS TO FRANCE WITH ME. THEY WILL BE MY GUIDES.›
‹WE HAVE MADE GOOD TRADES.›
‹FEAR NOT. I WILL RETURN THEM SOON.›
‹HE TAKES YOUR BROTHERS FROM US WITH PROMISES AND FORCE. I PRAY WE WILL SEE THEM BACK IN OUR FAMILY SOON.›
‹NOW, DOM AGAYA, TAIGNOAGNY. TELL ME WHERE ARE THE SPICES AND GOLD?›
‹WHERE ARE THIS COUNTRY'S RICHES?›
...KANATA?
CANADA

The LOXLEYS and CONFEDERATION

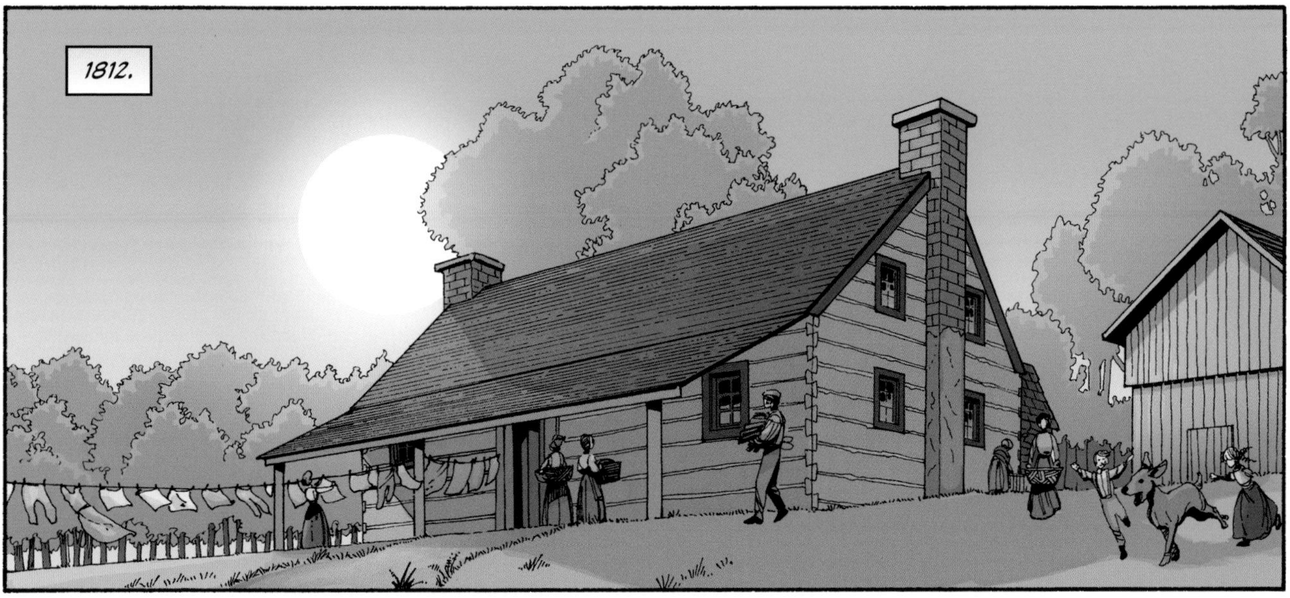
1812.

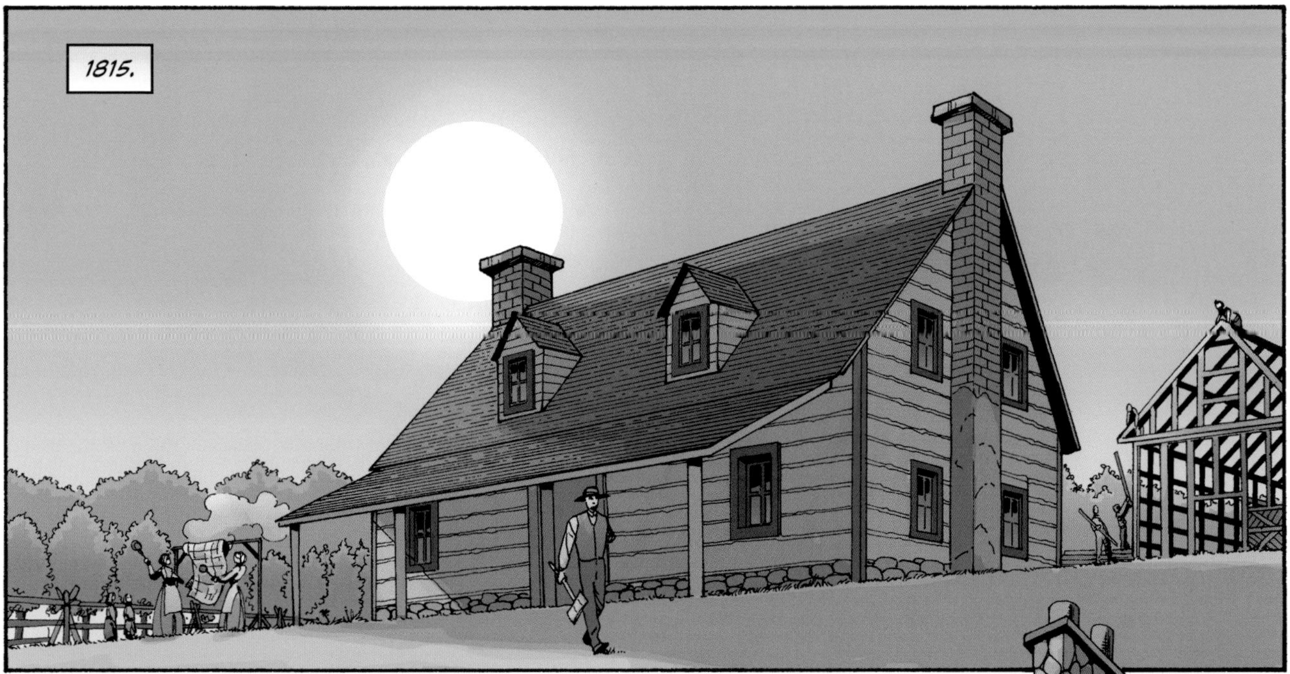
1815.

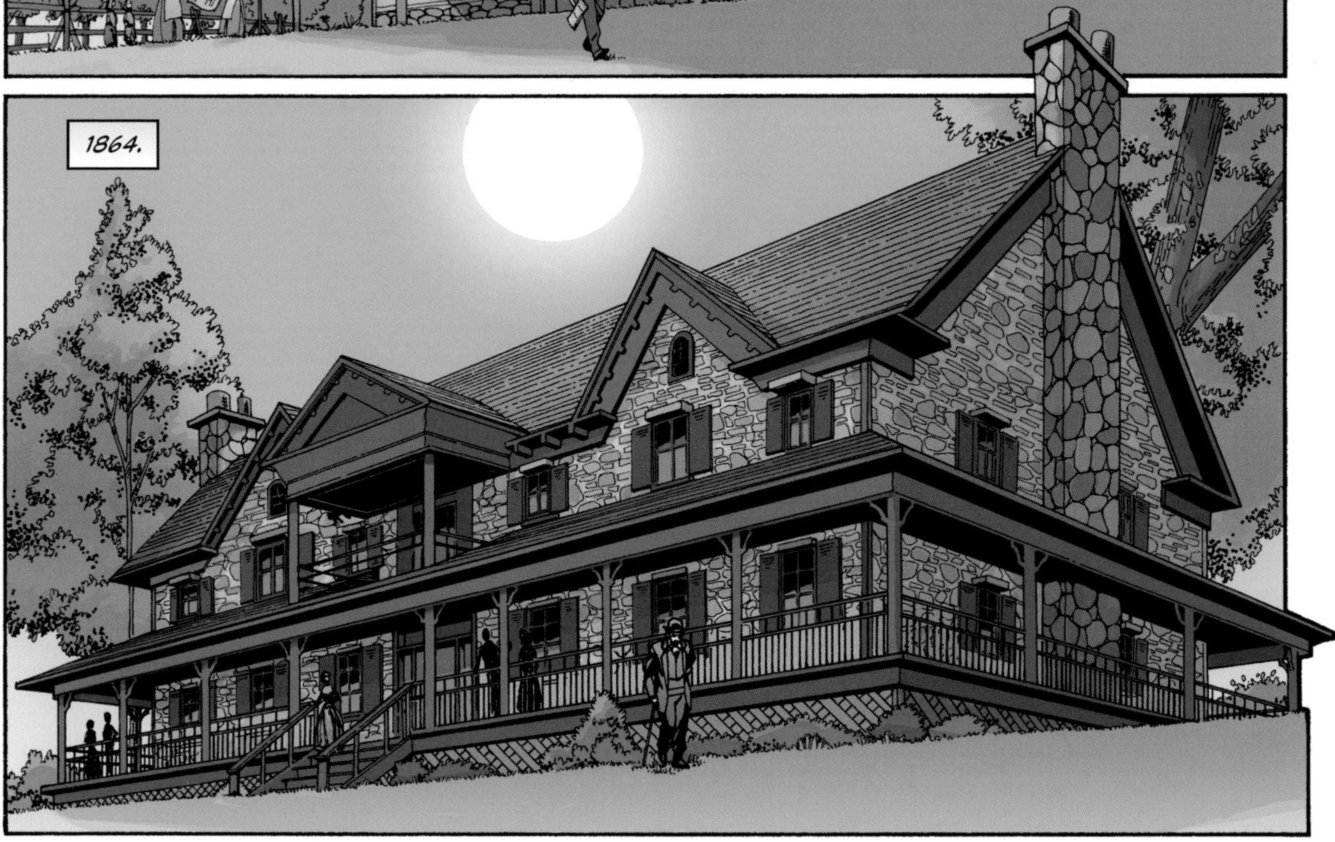
1864.

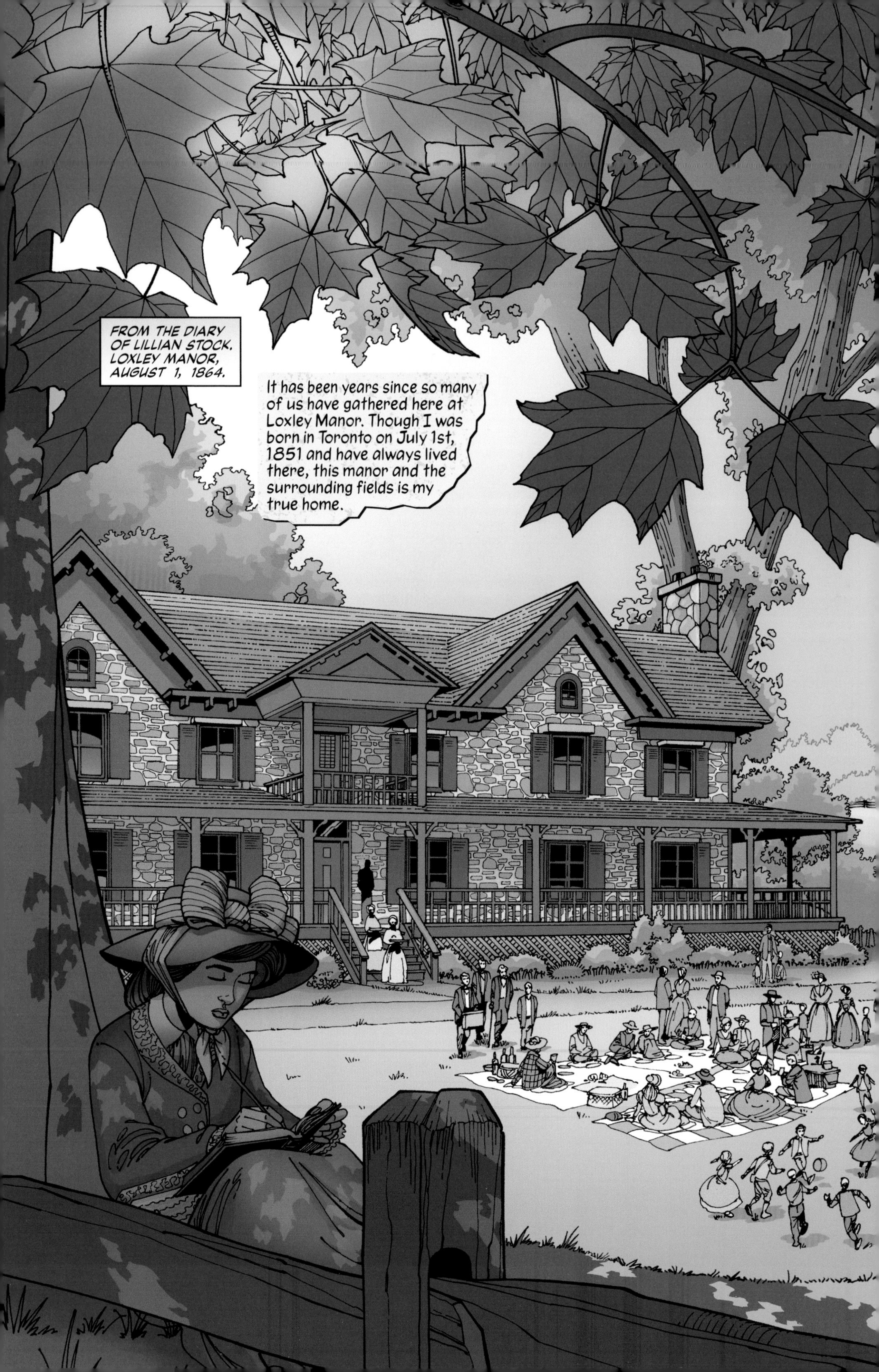
FROM THE DIARY OF LILLIAN STOCK. LOXLEY MANOR, AUGUST 1, 1864.
It has been years since so many of us have gathered here at Loxley Manor. Though I was born in Toronto on July 1st, 1851 and have always lived there, this manor and the surrounding fields is my true home.

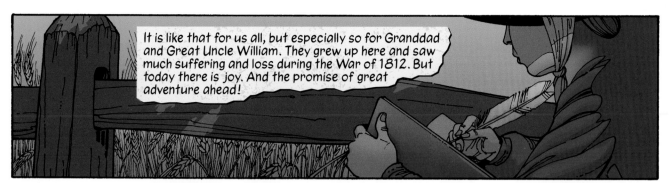

It is like that for us all, but especially so for Granddad and Great Uncle William. They grew up here and saw much suffering and loss during the War of 1812. But today there is joy. And the promise of great adventure ahead!

LILLIAN! GET YOUR HEAD OUT OF YOUR DIARY AND COME JOIN US!

COMING, MAMA!

My Diary 1864

A TOAST TO THOSE WHO ARE TOO FAR AWAY TO BE HERE TODAY...

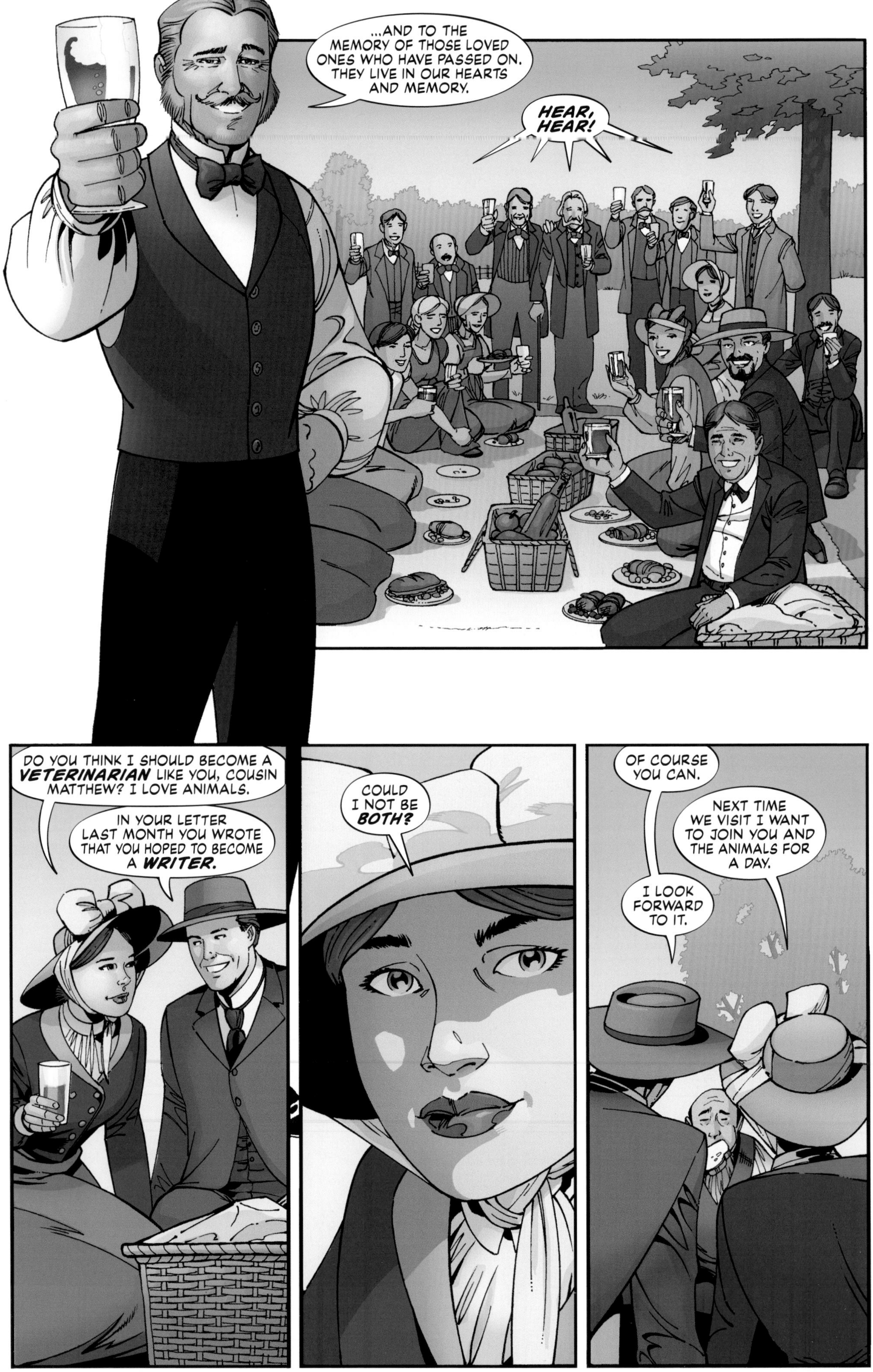
...AND TO THE MEMORY OF THOSE LOVED ONES WHO HAVE PASSED ON. THEY LIVE IN OUR HEARTS AND MEMORY.
HEAR, HEAR!
DO YOU THINK I SHOULD BECOME A VETERINARIAN LIKE YOU, COUSIN MATTHEW? I LOVE ANIMALS.
IN YOUR LETTER LAST MONTH YOU WROTE THAT YOU HOPED TO BECOME A WRITER.
COULD I NOT BE BOTH?
OF COURSE YOU CAN.
NEXT TIME WE VISIT I WANT TO JOIN YOU AND THE ANIMALS FOR A DAY.
I LOOK FORWARD TO IT.

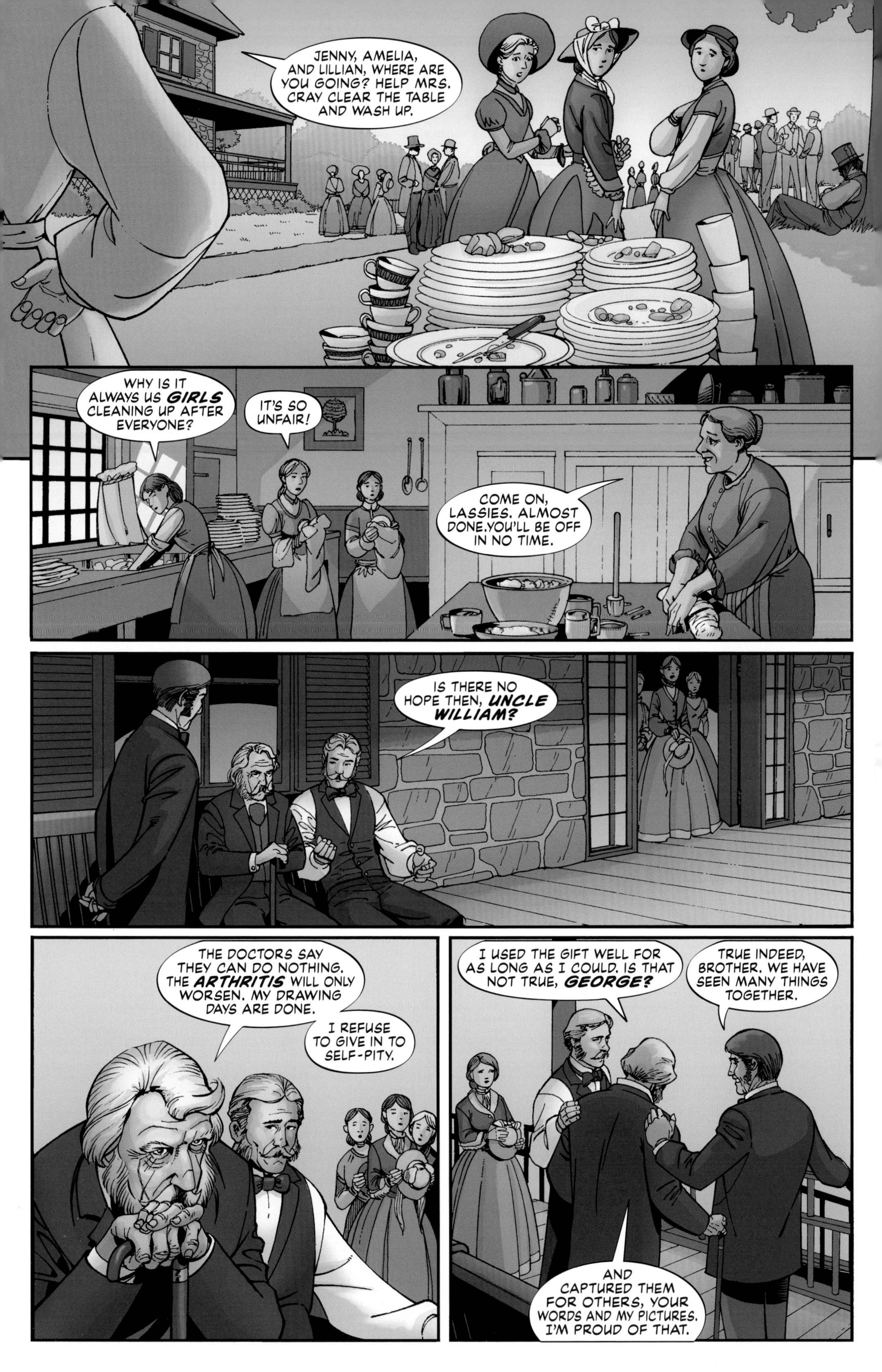
JENNY, AMELIA, AND LILLIAN, WHERE ARE YOU GOING? HELP MRS. CRAY CLEAR THE TABLE AND WASH UP.
WHY IS IT ALWAYS US GIRLS CLEANING UP AFTER EVERYONE?
IT'S SO UNFAIR!
COME ON, LASSIES. ALMOST DONE.YOU'LL BE OFF IN NO TIME.
IS THERE NO HOPE THEN, UNCLE WILLIAM?
THE DOCTORS SAY THEY CAN DO NOTHING. THE ARTHRITIS WILL ONLY WORSEN. MY DRAWING DAYS ARE DONE.
I REFUSE TO GIVE IN TO SELF-PITY.
I USED THE GIFT WELL FOR AS LONG AS I COULD. IS THAT NOT TRUE, GEORGE?
TRUE INDEED, BROTHER. WE HAVE SEEN MANY THINGS TOGETHER.
AND CAPTURED THEM FOR OTHERS, YOUR WORDS AND MY PICTURES. I'M PROUD OF THAT.

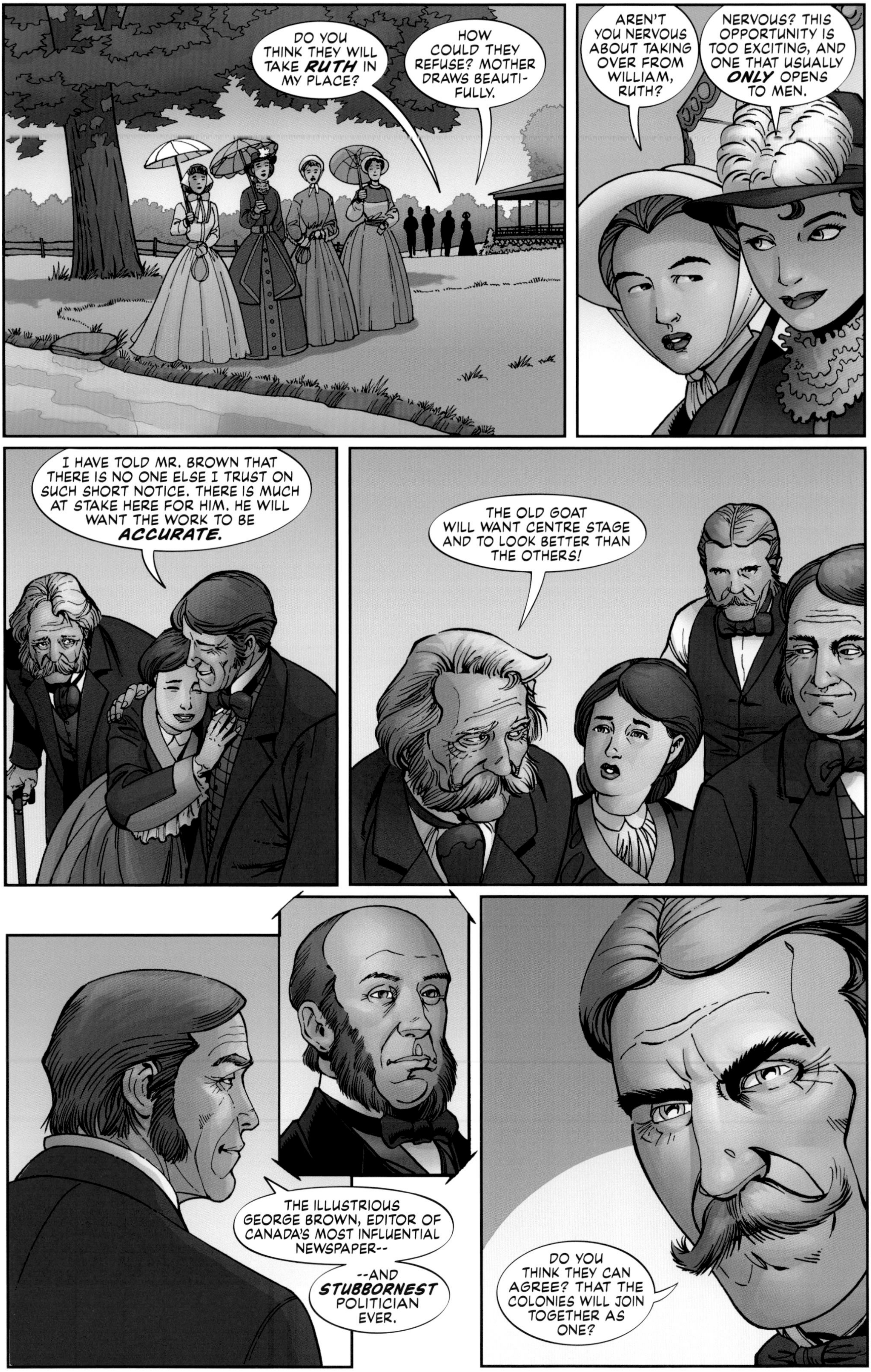
DO YOU THINK THEY WILL TAKE RUTH IN MY PLACE?
HOW COULD THEY REFUSE? MOTHER DRAWS BEAUTI-FULLY.
AREN'T YOU NERVOUS ABOUT TAKING OVER FROM WILLIAM, RUTH?
NERVOUS? THIS OPPORTUNITY IS TOO EXCITING, AND ONE THAT USUALLY ONLY OPENS TO MEN.
I HAVE TOLD MR. BROWN THAT THERE IS NO ONE ELSE I TRUST ON SUCH SHORT NOTICE. THERE IS MUCH AT STAKE HERE FOR HIM. HE WILL WANT THE WORK TO BE ACCURATE.
THE OLD GOAT WILL WANT CENTRE STAGE AND TO LOOK BETTER THAN THE OTHERS!
THE ILLUSTRIOUS GEORGE BROWN, EDITOR OF CANADA'S MOST INFLUENTIAL NEWSPAPER--
--AND STUBBORNEST POLITICIAN EVER.
DO YOU THINK THEY CAN AGREE? THAT THE COLONIES WILL JOIN TOGETHER AS ONE?

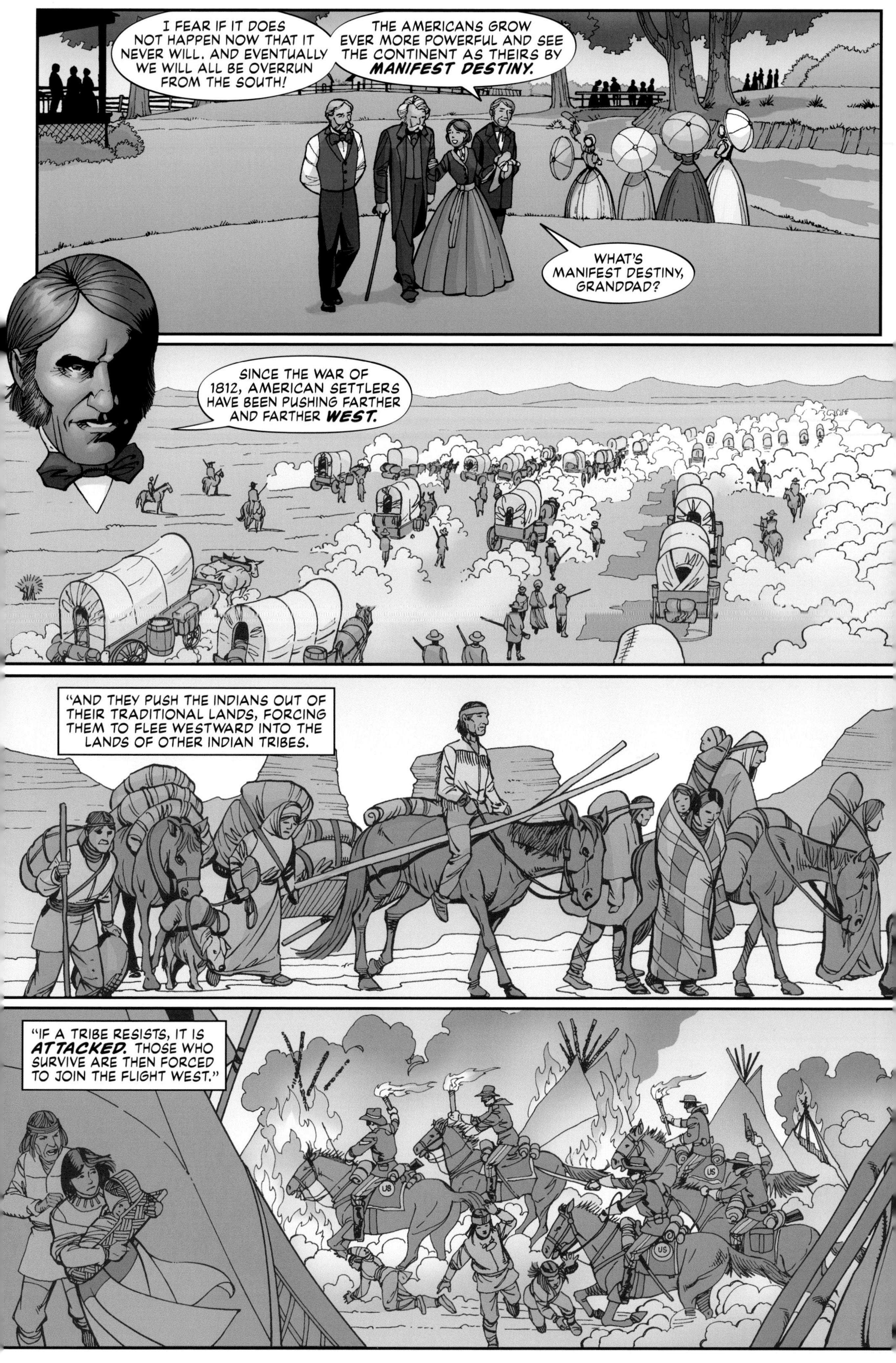
I FEAR IF IT DOES NOT HAPPEN NOW THAT IT NEVER WILL. AND EVENTUALLY WE WILL ALL BE OVERRUN FROM THE SOUTH!
THE AMERICANS GROW EVER MORE POWERFUL AND SEE THE CONTINENT AS THEIRS BY ***MANIFEST DESTINY.***
WHAT'S MANIFEST DESTINY, GRANDDAD?
SINCE THE WAR OF 1812, AMERICAN SETTLERS HAVE BEEN PUSHING FARTHER AND FARTHER ***WEST.***
"AND THEY PUSH THE INDIANS OUT OF THEIR TRADITIONAL LANDS, FORCING THEM TO FLEE WESTWARD INTO THE LANDS OF OTHER INDIAN TRIBES.
"IF A TRIBE RESISTS, IT IS ***ATTACKED.*** THOSE WHO SURVIVE ARE THEN FORCED TO JOIN THE FLIGHT WEST."
US
US
US
US

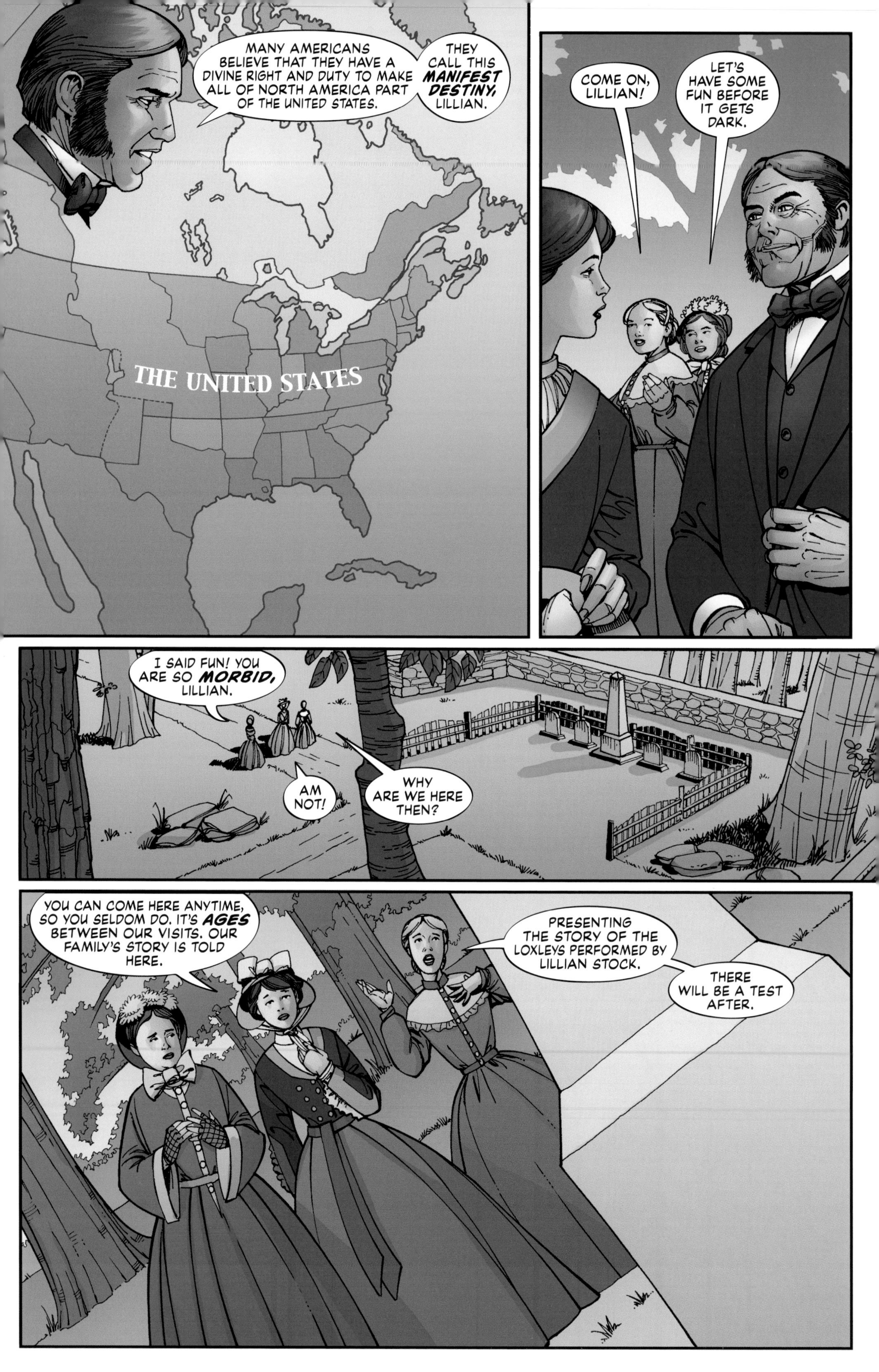
MANY AMERICANS BELIEVE THAT THEY HAVE A DIVINE RIGHT AND DUTY TO MAKE ALL OF NORTH AMERICA PART OF THE UNITED STATES.
THEY CALL THIS MANIFEST DESTINY, LILLIAN.
THE UNITED STATES
COME ON, LILLIAN!
LET'S HAVE SOME FUN BEFORE IT GETS DARK.
I SAID FUN! YOU ARE SO MORBID, LILLIAN.
AM NOT!
WHY ARE WE HERE THEN?
YOU CAN COME HERE ANYTIME, SO YOU SELDOM DO. IT'S AGES BETWEEN OUR VISITS. OUR FAMILY'S STORY IS TOLD HERE.
PRESENTING THE STORY OF THE LOXLEYS PERFORMED BY LILLIAN STOCK.
THERE WILL BE A TEST AFTER.

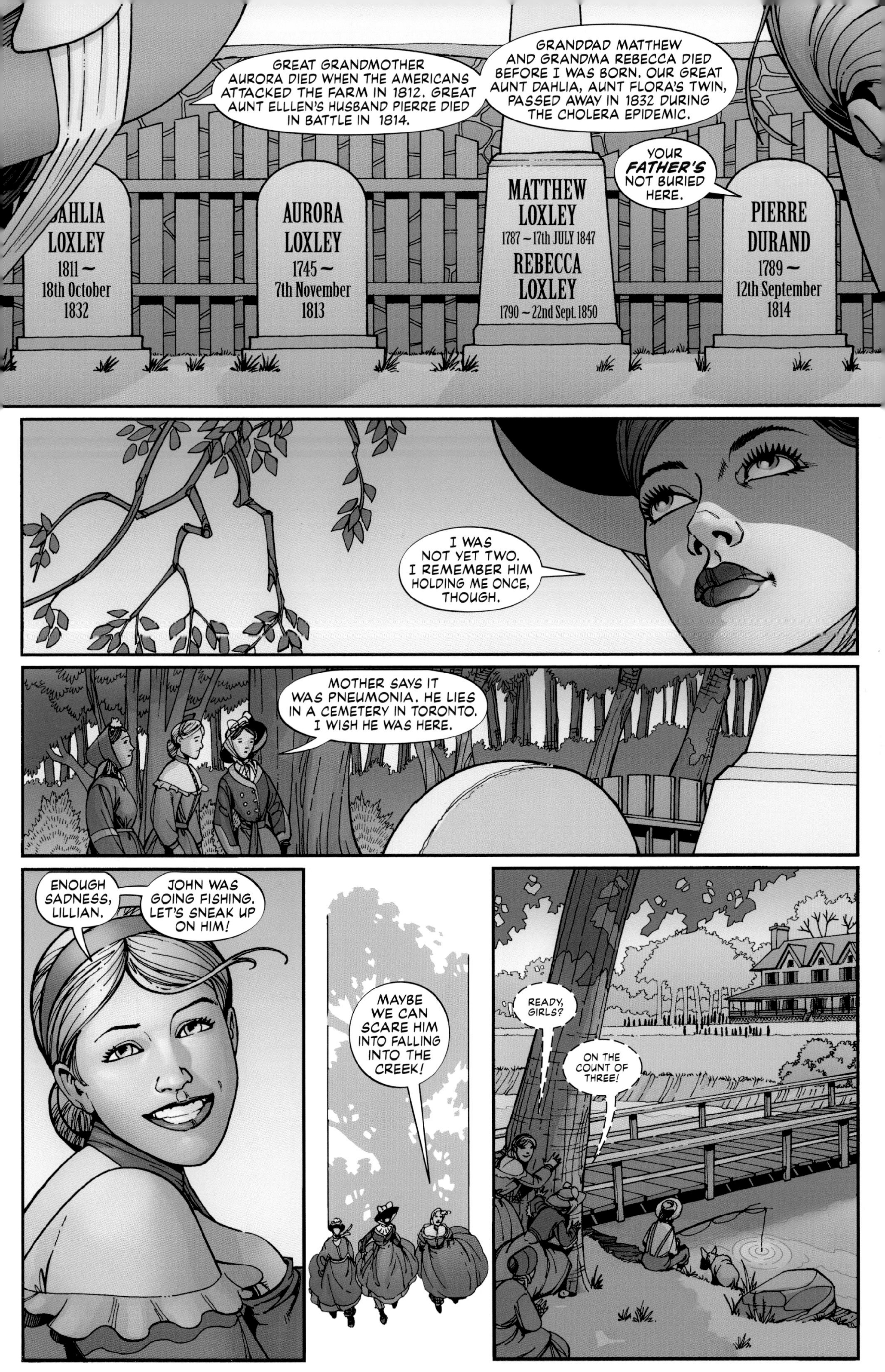
GREAT GRANDMOTHER AURORA DIED WHEN THE AMERICANS ATTACKED THE FARM IN 1812. GREAT AUNT ELLLEN'S HUSBAND PIERRE DIED IN BATTLE IN 1814.
GRANDDAD MATTHEW AND GRANDMA REBECCA DIED BEFORE I WAS BORN. OUR GREAT AUNT DAHLIA, AUNT FLORA'S TWIN, PASSED AWAY IN 1832 DURING THE CHOLERA EPIDEMIC.
YOUR FATHER'S NOT BURIED HERE.
DAHLIA LOXLEY 1811 ~ 18th October 1832
AURORA LOXLEY 1745 ~ 7th November 1813
MATTHEW LOXLEY 1787 ~ 17th JULY 1847
REBECCA LOXLEY 1790 ~ 22nd Sept. 1850
PIERRE DURAND 1789 ~ 12th September 1814
I WAS NOT YET TWO. I REMEMBER HIM HOLDING ME ONCE, THOUGH.
MOTHER SAYS IT WAS PNEUMONIA. HE LIES IN A CEMETERY IN TORONTO. I WISH HE WAS HERE.
ENOUGH SADNESS, LILLIAN.
JOHN WAS GOING FISHING. LET'S SNEAK UP ON HIM!
MAYBE WE CAN SCARE HIM INTO FALLING INTO THE CREEK!
READY, GIRLS?
ON THE COUNT OF THREE!

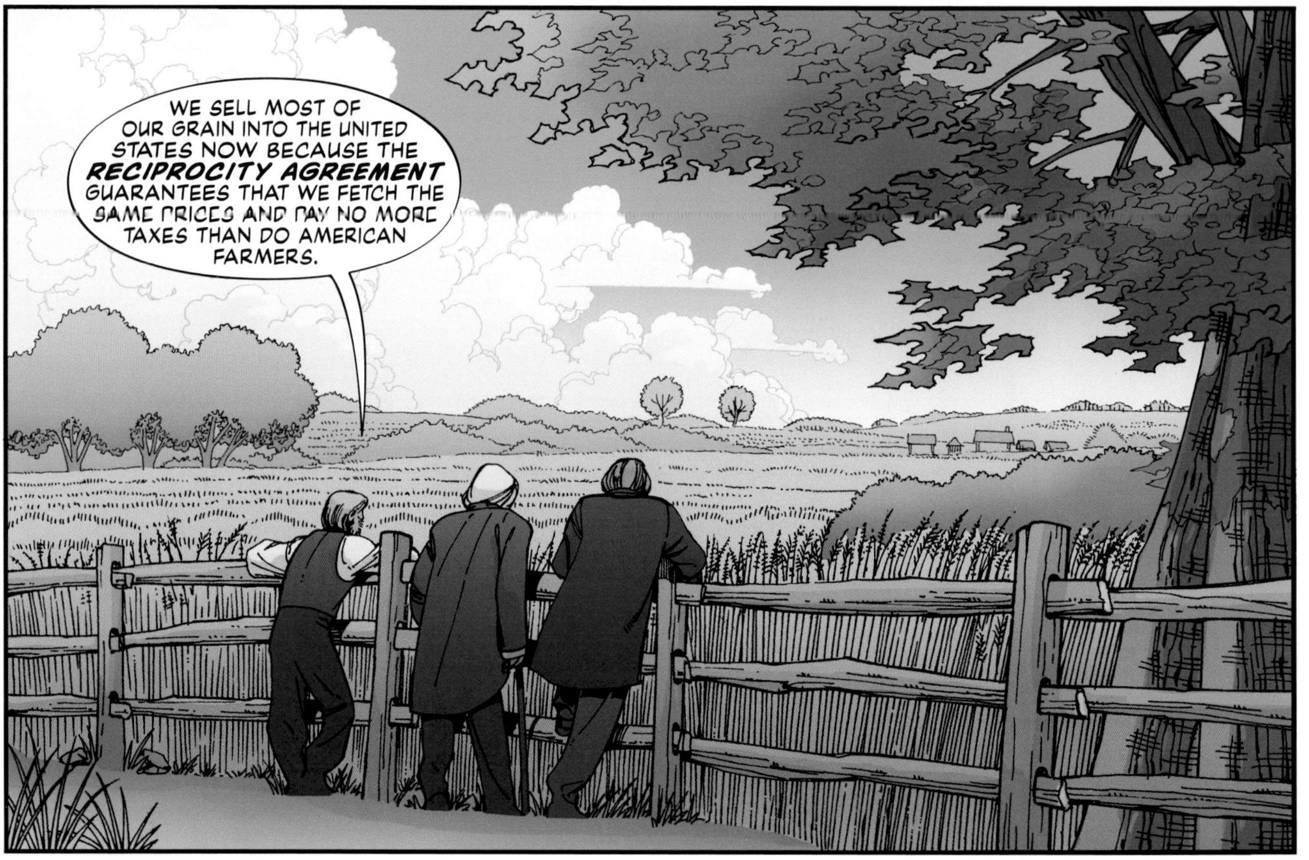
WE SELL MOST OF OUR GRAIN INTO THE UNITED STATES NOW BECAUSE THE RECIPROCITY AGREEMENT GUARANTEES THAT WE FETCH THE SAME PRICES AND PAY NO MORE TAXES THAN DO AMERICAN FARMERS.

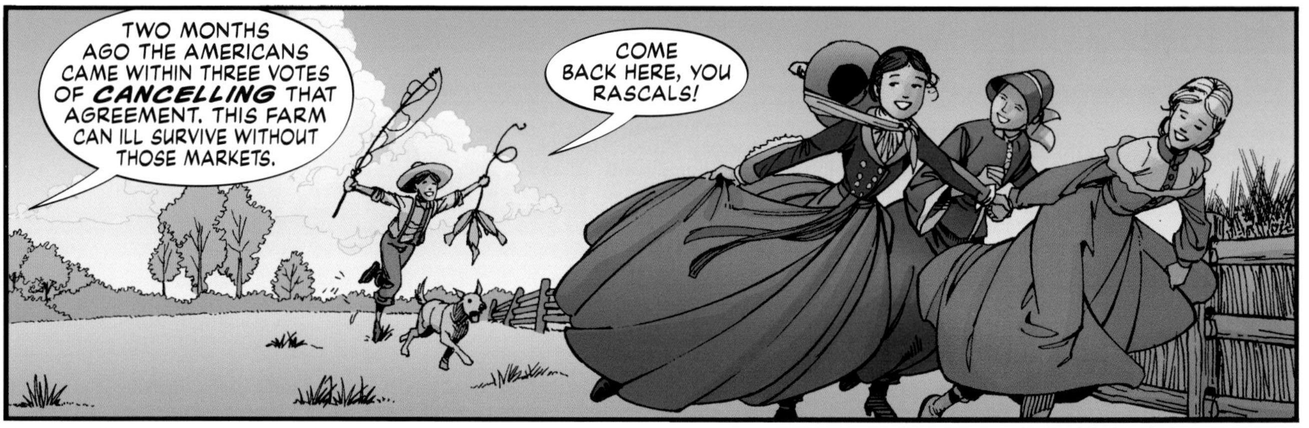
TWO MONTHS AGO THE AMERICANS CAME WITHIN THREE VOTES OF CANCELLING THAT AGREEMENT. THIS FARM CAN ILL SURVIVE WITHOUT THOSE MARKETS.
COME BACK HERE, YOU RASCALS!

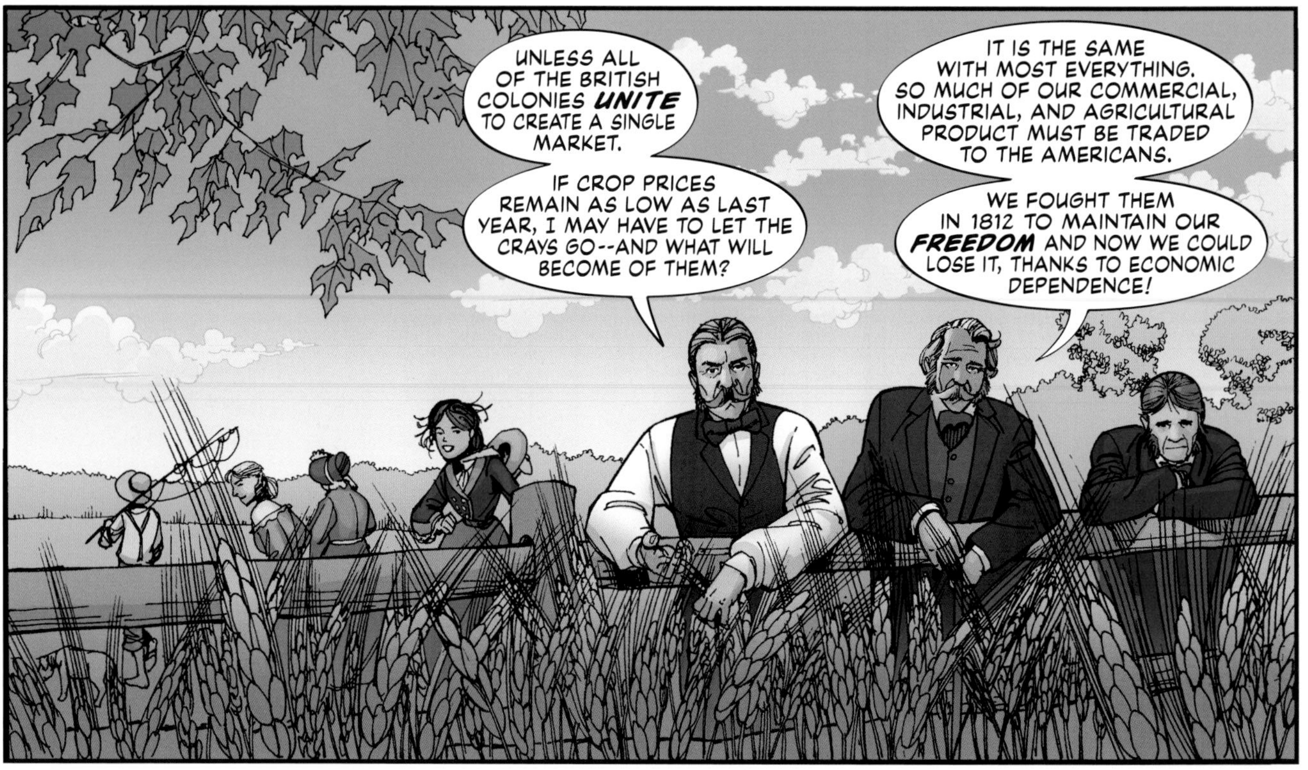
UNLESS ALL OF THE BRITISH COLONIES UNITE TO CREATE A SINGLE MARKET.
IF CROP PRICES REMAIN AS LOW AS LAST YEAR, I MAY HAVE TO LET THE CRAYS GO--AND WHAT WILL BECOME OF THEM?
IT IS THE SAME WITH MOST EVERYTHING. SO MUCH OF OUR COMMERCIAL, INDUSTRIAL, AND AGRICULTURAL PRODUCT MUST BE TRADED TO THE AMERICANS.
WE FOUGHT THEM IN 1812 TO MAINTAIN OUR FREEDOM AND NOW WE COULD LOSE IT, THANKS TO ECONOMIC DEPENDENCE!

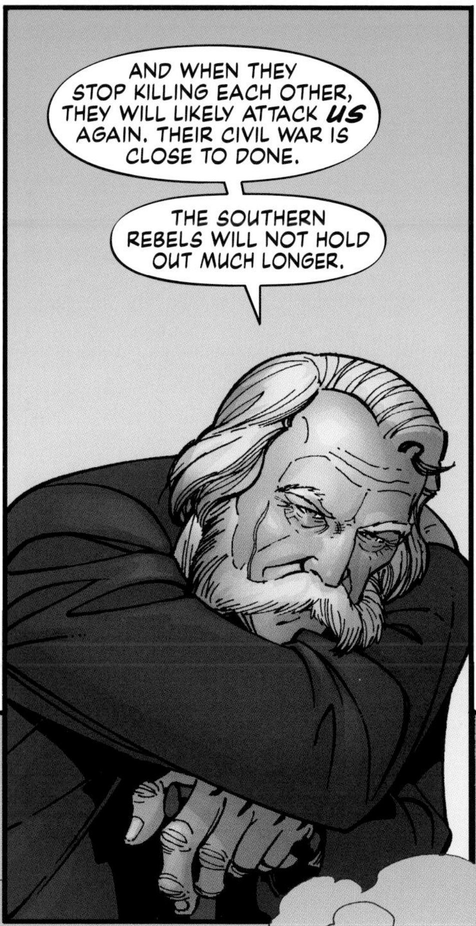
AND WHEN THEY STOP KILLING EACH OTHER, THEY WILL LIKELY ATTACK *US* AGAIN. THEIR CIVIL WAR IS CLOSE TO DONE.
THE SOUTHERN REBELS WILL NOT HOLD OUT MUCH LONGER.

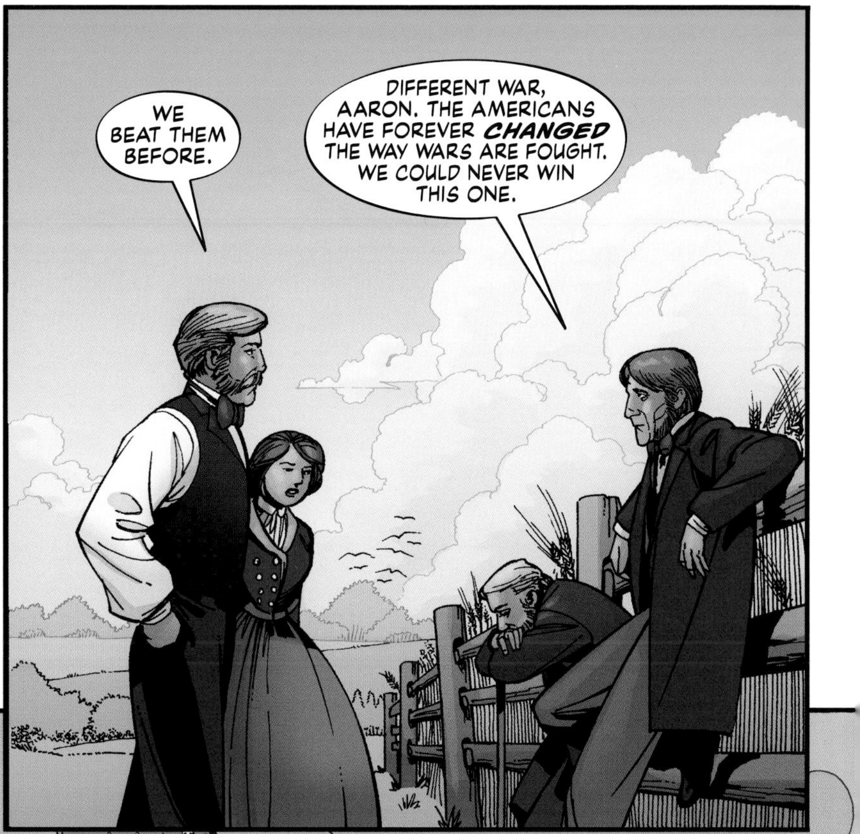
WE BEAT THEM BEFORE.
DIFFERENT WAR, AARON. THE AMERICANS HAVE FOREVER *CHANGED* THE WAY WARS ARE FOUGHT. WE COULD NEVER WIN THIS ONE.

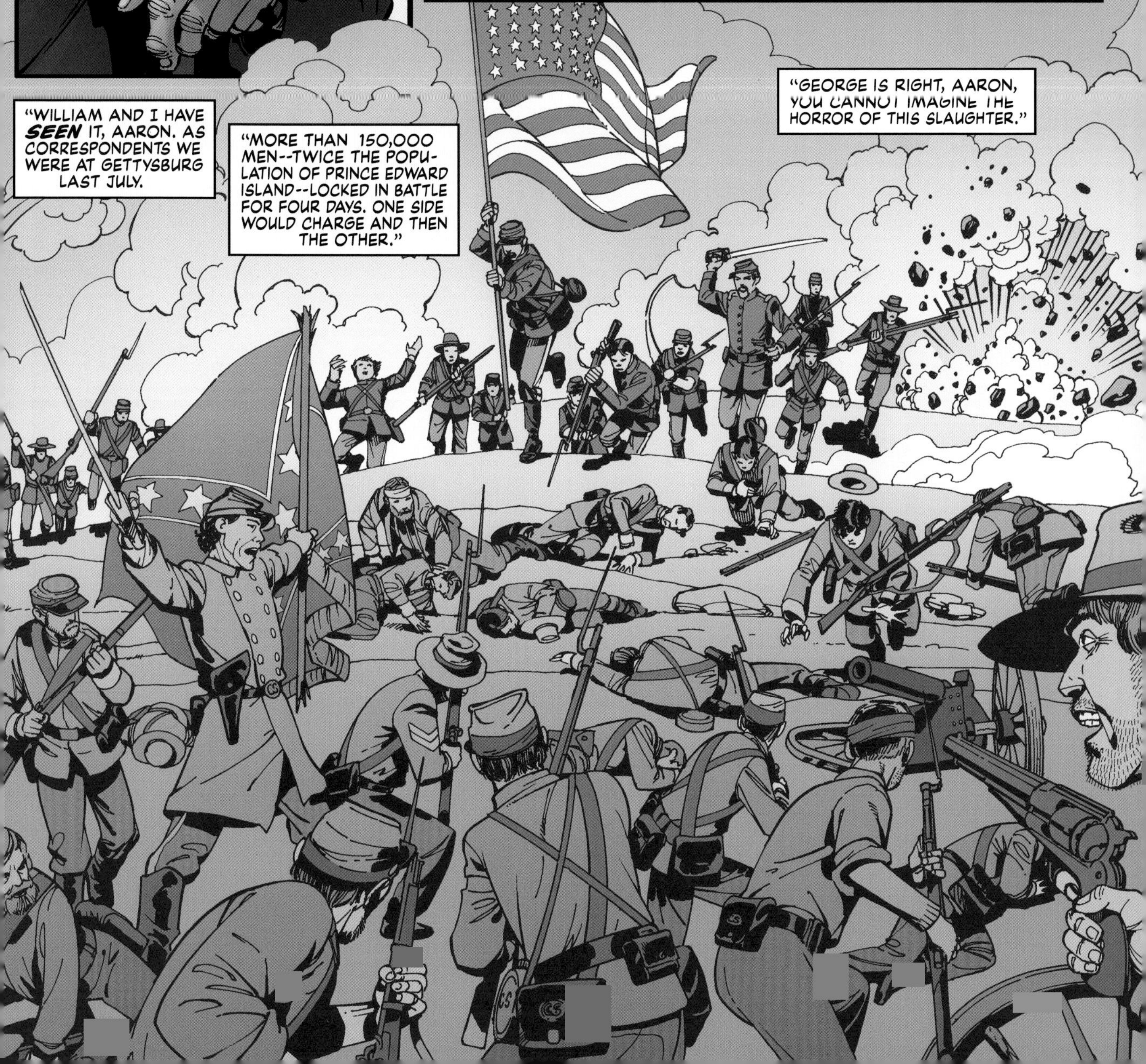
"WILLIAM AND I HAVE *SEEN* IT, AARON. AS CORRESPONDENTS WE WERE AT GETTYSBURG LAST JULY.
"MORE THAN 150,000 MEN--TWICE THE POPULATION OF PRINCE EDWARD ISLAND--LOCKED IN BATTLE FOR FOUR DAYS. ONE SIDE WOULD CHARGE AND THEN THE OTHER."
"GEORGE IS RIGHT, AARON, YOU CANNOT IMAGINE THE HORROR OF THIS SLAUGHTER."

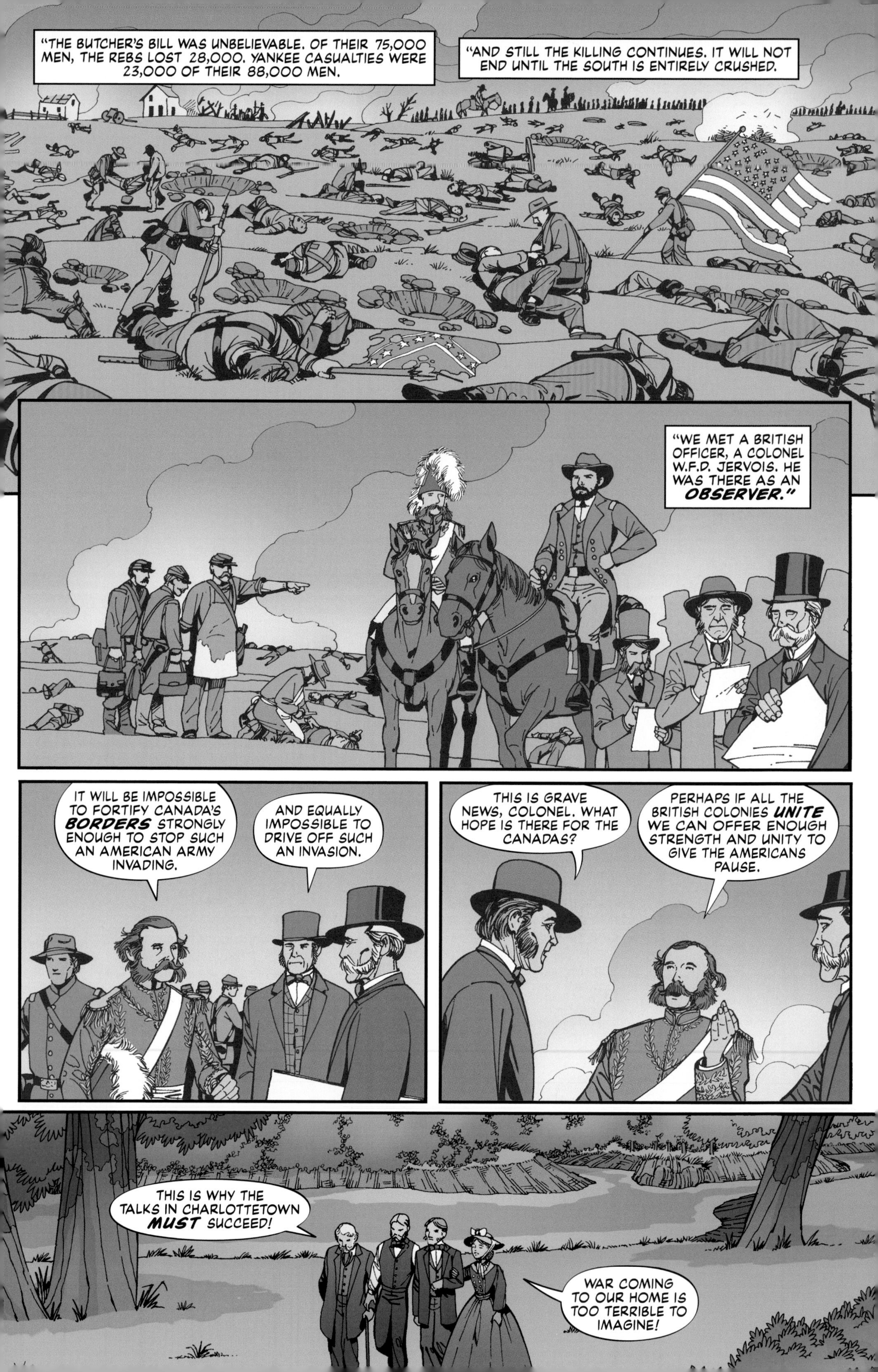
"THE BUTCHER'S BILL WAS UNBELIEVABLE. OF THEIR 75,000 MEN, THE REBS LOST 28,000. YANKEE CASUALTIES WERE 23,000 OF THEIR 88,000 MEN.
"AND STILL THE KILLING CONTINUES. IT WILL NOT END UNTIL THE SOUTH IS ENTIRELY CRUSHED.
"WE MET A BRITISH OFFICER, A COLONEL W.F.D. JERVOIS. HE WAS THERE AS AN OBSERVER."
IT WILL BE IMPOSSIBLE TO FORTIFY CANADA'S BORDERS STRONGLY ENOUGH TO STOP SUCH AN AMERICAN ARMY INVADING.
AND EQUALLY IMPOSSIBLE TO DRIVE OFF SUCH AN INVASION.
THIS IS GRAVE NEWS, COLONEL. WHAT HOPE IS THERE FOR THE CANADAS?
PERHAPS IF ALL THE BRITISH COLONIES UNITE WE CAN OFFER ENOUGH STRENGTH AND UNITY TO GIVE THE AMERICANS PAUSE.
THIS IS WHY THE TALKS IN CHARLOTTETOWN MUST SUCCEED!
WAR COMING TO OUR HOME IS TOO TERRIBLE TO IMAGINE!

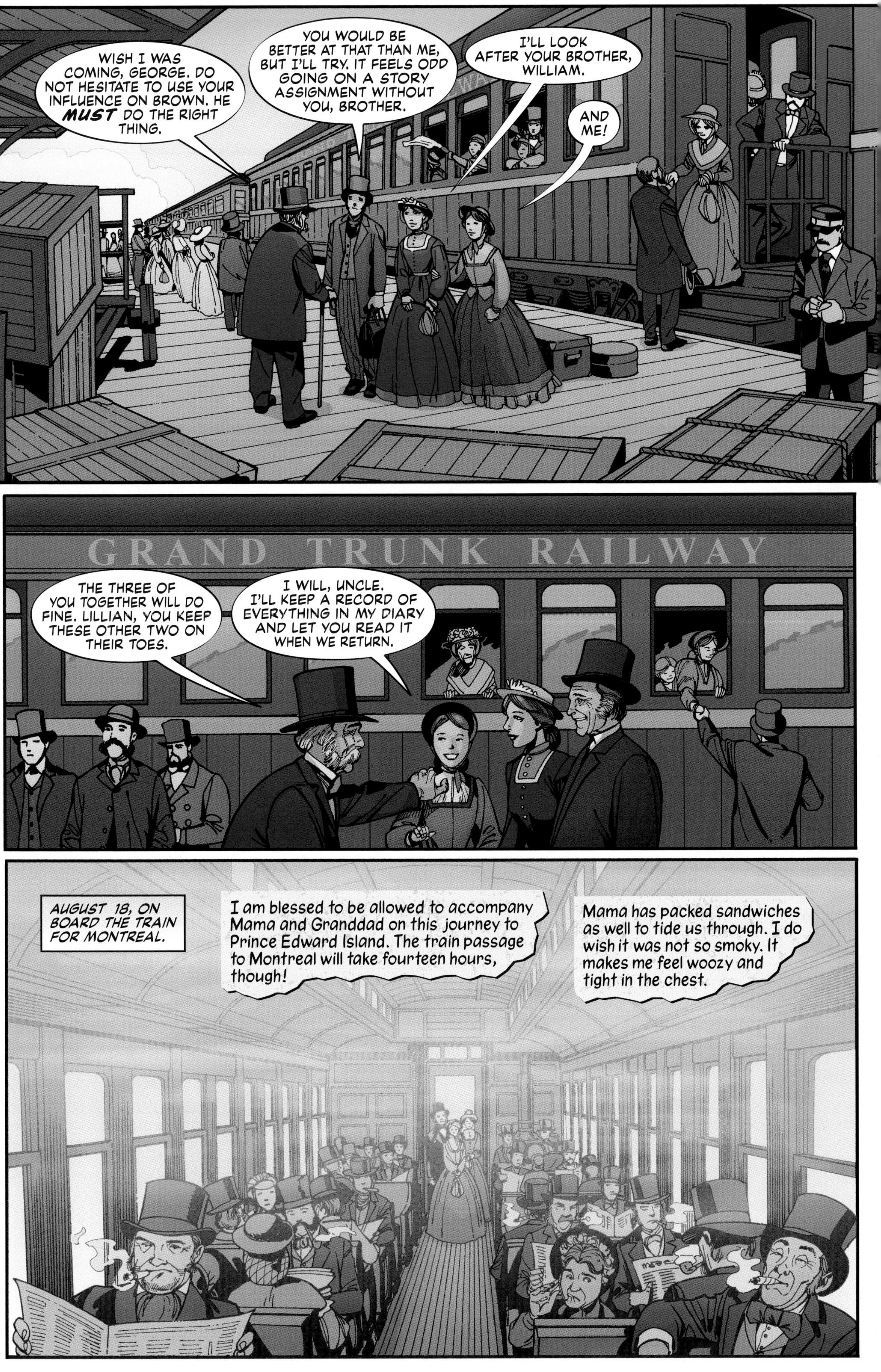
WISH I WAS COMING, GEORGE. DO NOT HESITATE TO USE YOUR INFLUENCE ON BROWN. HE MUST DO THE RIGHT THING.
YOU WOULD BE BETTER AT THAT THAN ME, BUT I'LL TRY. IT FEELS ODD GOING ON A STORY ASSIGNMENT WITHOUT YOU, BROTHER.
I'LL LOOK AFTER YOUR BROTHER, WILLIAM.
AND ME!
GRAND TRUNK RAILWAY
THE THREE OF YOU TOGETHER WILL DO FINE. LILLIAN, YOU KEEP THESE OTHER TWO ON THEIR TOES.
I WILL, UNCLE. I'LL KEEP A RECORD OF EVERYTHING IN MY DIARY AND LET YOU READ IT WHEN WE RETURN.
AUGUST 18, ON BOARD THE TRAIN FOR MONTREAL.
I am blessed to be allowed to accompany Mama and Granddad on this journey to Prince Edward Island. The train passage to Montreal will take fourteen hours, though!
Mama has packed sandwiches as well to tide us through. I do wish it was not so smoky. It makes me feel woozy and tight in the chest.

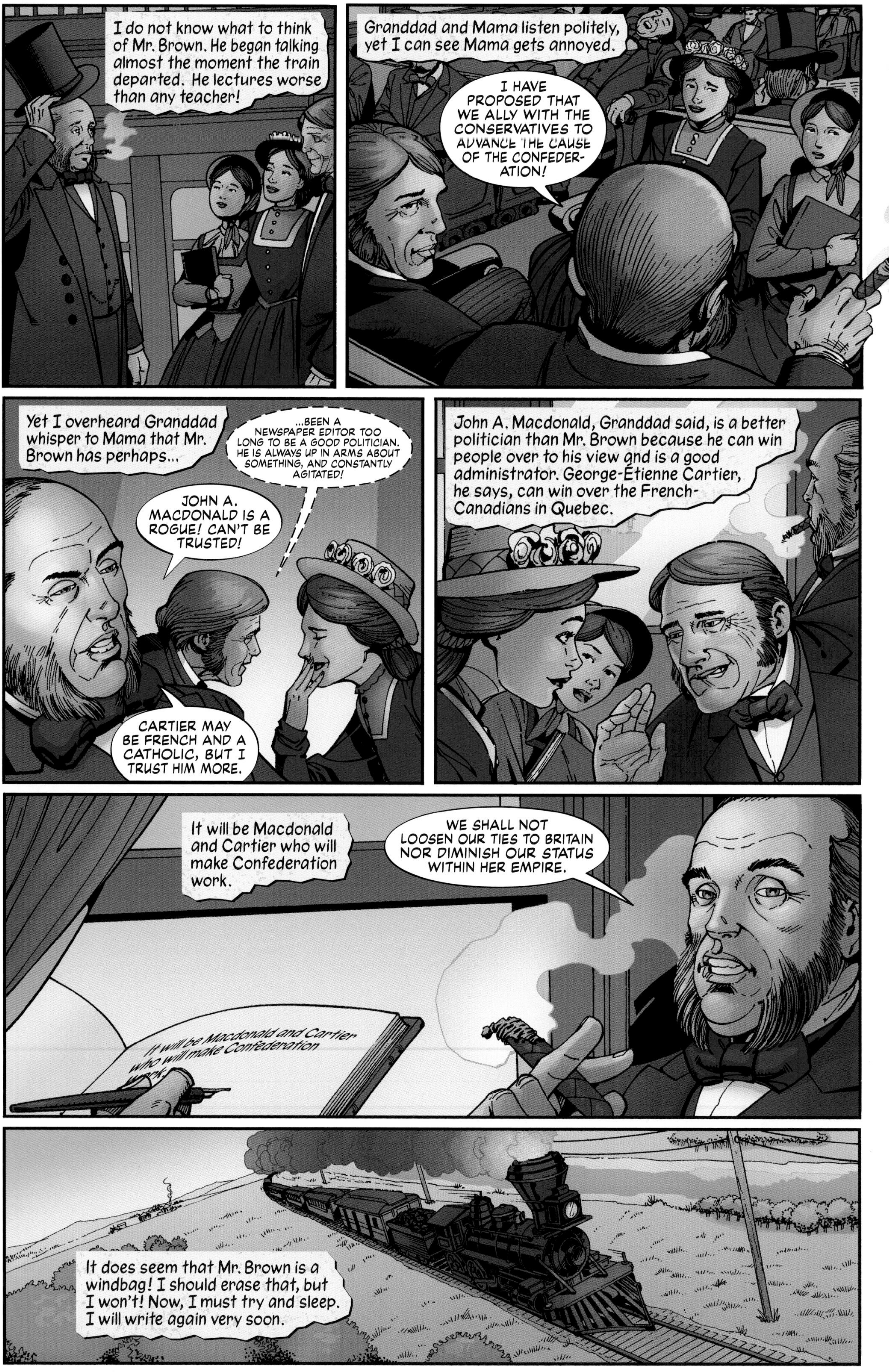
I do not know what to think of Mr. Brown. He began talking almost the moment the train departed. He lectures worse than any teacher!
Granddad and Mama listen politely, yet I can see Mama gets annoyed.
I HAVE PROPOSED THAT WE ALLY WITH THE CONSERVATIVES TO ADVANCE THE CAUSE OF THE CONFEDER-ATION!
Yet I overheard Granddad whisper to Mama that Mr. Brown has perhaps...
...BEEN A NEWSPAPER EDITOR TOO LONG TO BE A GOOD POLITICIAN. HE IS ALWAYS UP IN ARMS ABOUT SOMETHING, AND CONSTANTLY AGITATED!
JOHN A. MACDONALD IS A ROGUE! CAN'T BE TRUSTED!
CARTIER MAY BE FRENCH AND A CATHOLIC, BUT I TRUST HIM MORE.
John A. Macdonald, Granddad said, is a better politician than Mr. Brown because he can win people over to his view and is a good administrator. George-Étienne Cartier, he says, can win over the French-Canadians in Quebec.
It will be Macdonald and Cartier who will make Confederation work.
WE SHALL NOT LOOSEN OUR TIES TO BRITAIN NOR DIMINISH OUR STATUS WITHIN HER EMPIRE.
It will be Macdonald and Cartier who will make Confederation work.
It does seem that Mr. Brown is a windbag! I should erase that, but I won't! Now, I must try and sleep. I will write again very soon.

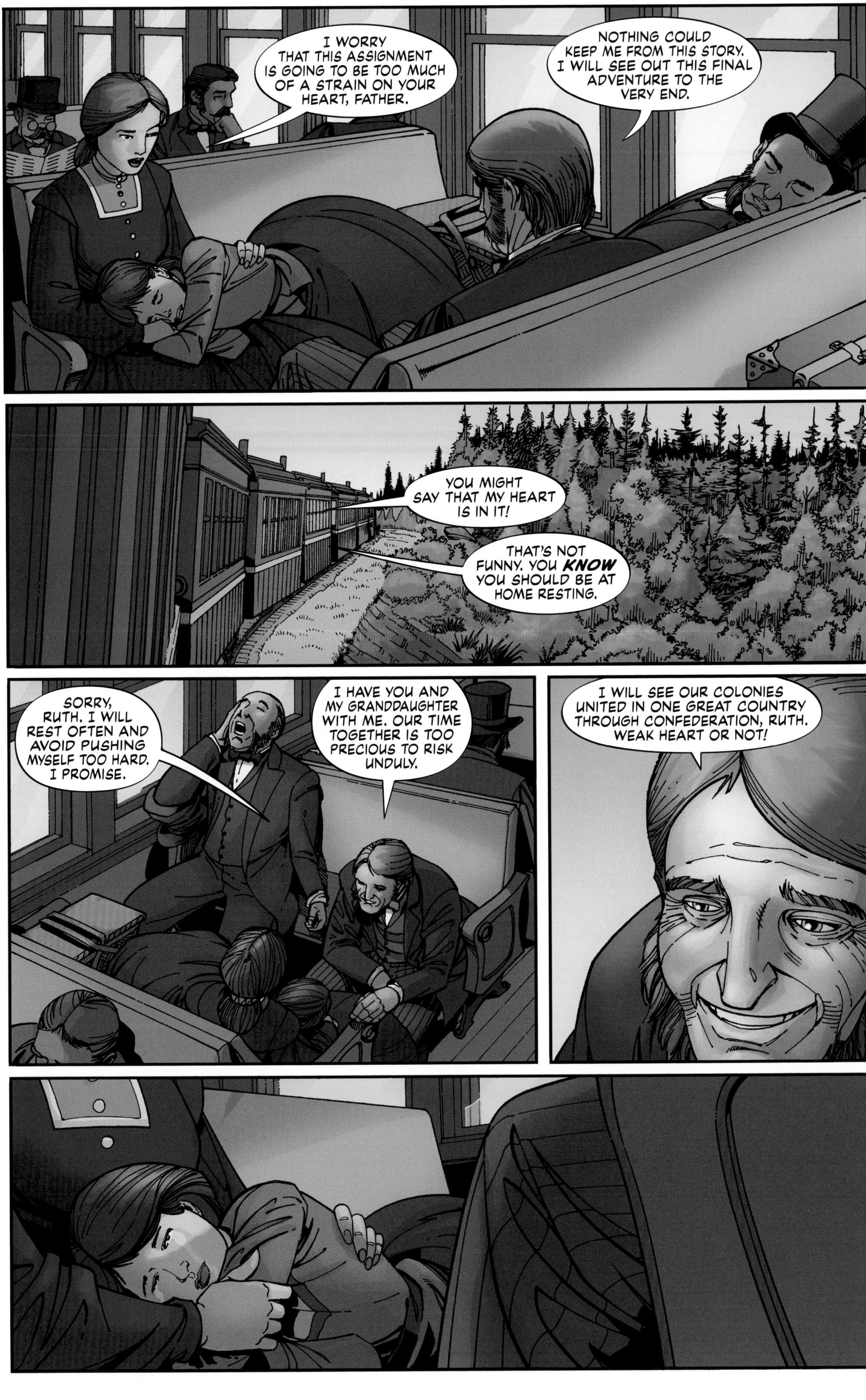
I WORRY THAT THIS ASSIGNMENT IS GOING TO BE TOO MUCH OF A STRAIN ON YOUR HEART, FATHER.
NOTHING COULD KEEP ME FROM THIS STORY. I WILL SEE OUT THIS FINAL ADVENTURE TO THE VERY END.
YOU MIGHT SAY THAT MY HEART IS IN IT!
THAT'S NOT FUNNY. YOU ***KNOW*** YOU SHOULD BE AT HOME RESTING.
SORRY, RUTH. I WILL REST OFTEN AND AVOID PUSHING MYSELF TOO HARD. I PROMISE.
I HAVE YOU AND MY GRANDDAUGHTER WITH ME. OUR TIME TOGETHER IS TOO PRECIOUS TO RISK UNDULY.
I WILL SEE OUR COLONIES UNITED IN ONE GREAT COUNTRY THROUGH CONFEDERATION, RUTH. WEAK HEART OR NOT!

ALL OF THE WORKERS IN THAT FIELD ARE CHILDREN!

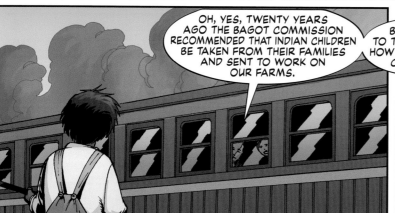

OH, YES, TWENTY YEARS AGO THE BAGOT COMMISSION RECOMMENDED THAT INDIAN CHILDREN BE TAKEN FROM THEIR FAMILIES AND SENT TO WORK ON OUR FARMS.

BEST WAY TO TEACH THEM HOW TO BECOME CIVILIZED.

BUT WHAT OF THEIR *PARENTS,* MR. BROWN?

DON'T WORRY, MY DEAR GIRL. THEY ARE BACK ON THE RESERVES, FAR AWAY FROM *POISONING* THEIR CHILDREN. THAT IS THE ONLY WAY THESE CHILDREN WILL LEARN.

I WONDER IF THEY MISS HOME?

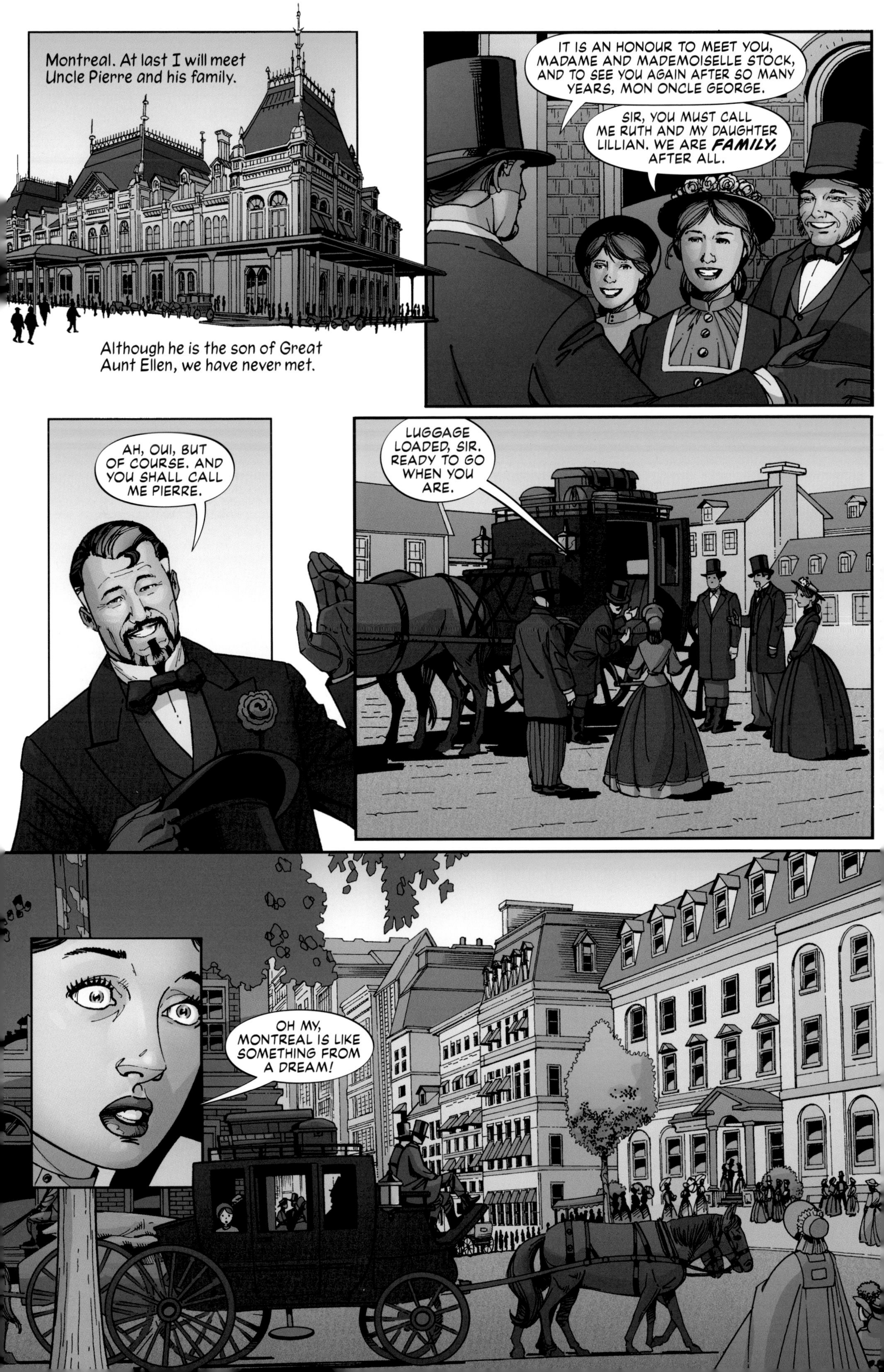
Montreal. At last I will meet Uncle Pierre and his family.
Although he is the son of Great Aunt Ellen, we have never met.
IT IS AN HONOUR TO MEET YOU, MADAME AND MADEMOISELLE STOCK, AND TO SEE YOU AGAIN AFTER SO MANY YEARS, MON ONCLE GEORGE.
SIR, YOU MUST CALL ME RUTH AND MY DAUGHTER LILLIAN. WE ARE ***FAMILY,*** AFTER ALL.
AH, OUI, BUT OF COURSE. AND YOU SHALL CALL ME PIERRE.
LUGGAGE LOADED, SIR. READY TO GO WHEN YOU ARE.
OH MY, MONTREAL IS LIKE SOMETHING FROM A DREAM!

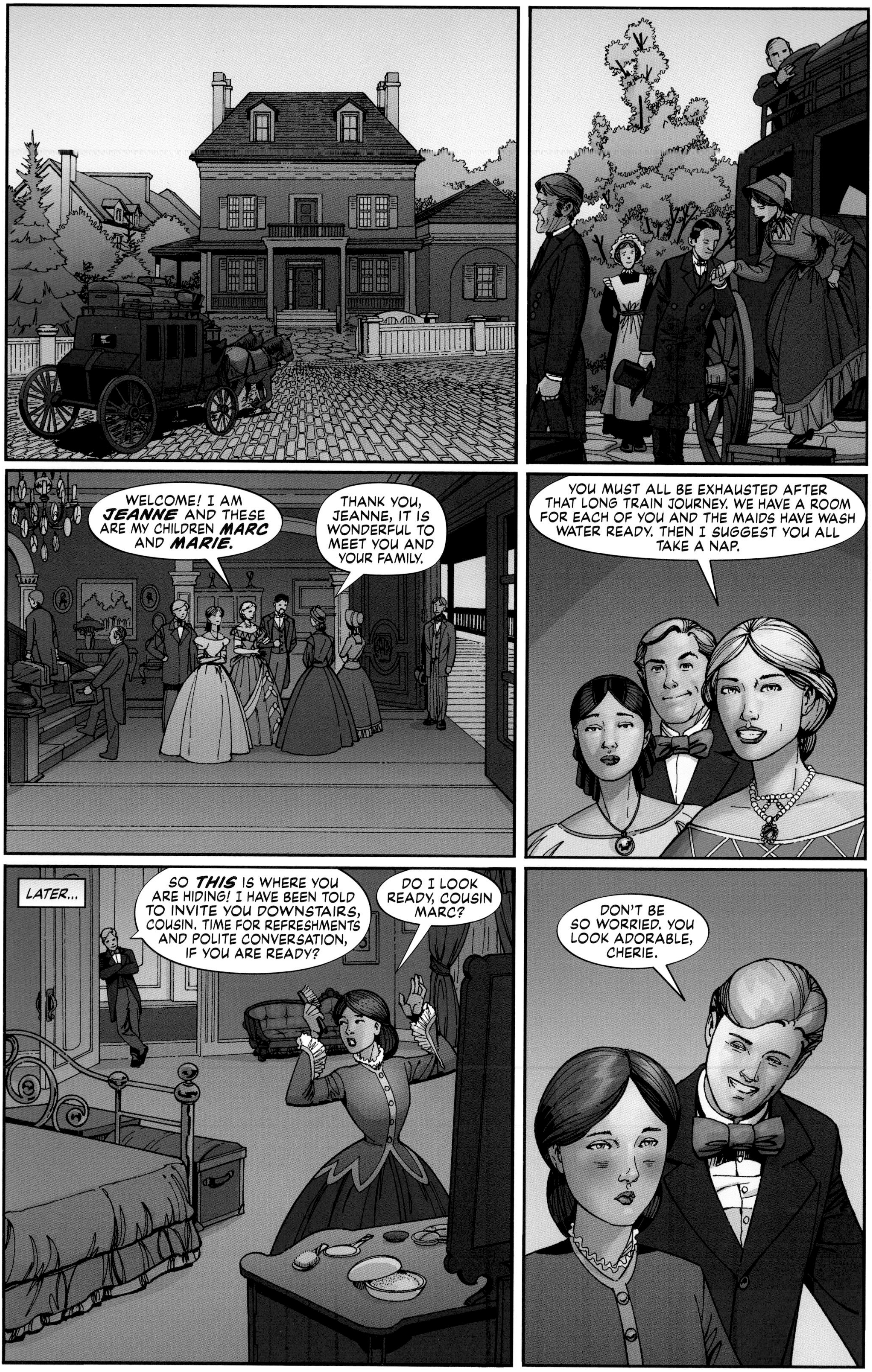
WELCOME! I AM **JEANNE** AND THESE ARE MY CHILDREN **MARC** AND **MARIE.**
THANK YOU, JEANNE, IT IS WONDERFUL TO MEET YOU AND YOUR FAMILY.
YOU MUST ALL BE EXHAUSTED AFTER THAT LONG TRAIN JOURNEY. WE HAVE A ROOM FOR EACH OF YOU AND THE MAIDS HAVE WASH WATER READY. THEN I SUGGEST YOU ALL TAKE A NAP.
LATER...
SO **THIS** IS WHERE YOU ARE HIDING! I HAVE BEEN TOLD TO INVITE YOU DOWNSTAIRS, COUSIN. TIME FOR REFRESHMENTS AND POLITE CONVERSATION, IF YOU ARE READY?
DO I LOOK READY, COUSIN MARC?
DON'T BE SO WORRIED. YOU LOOK ADORABLE, CHERIE.

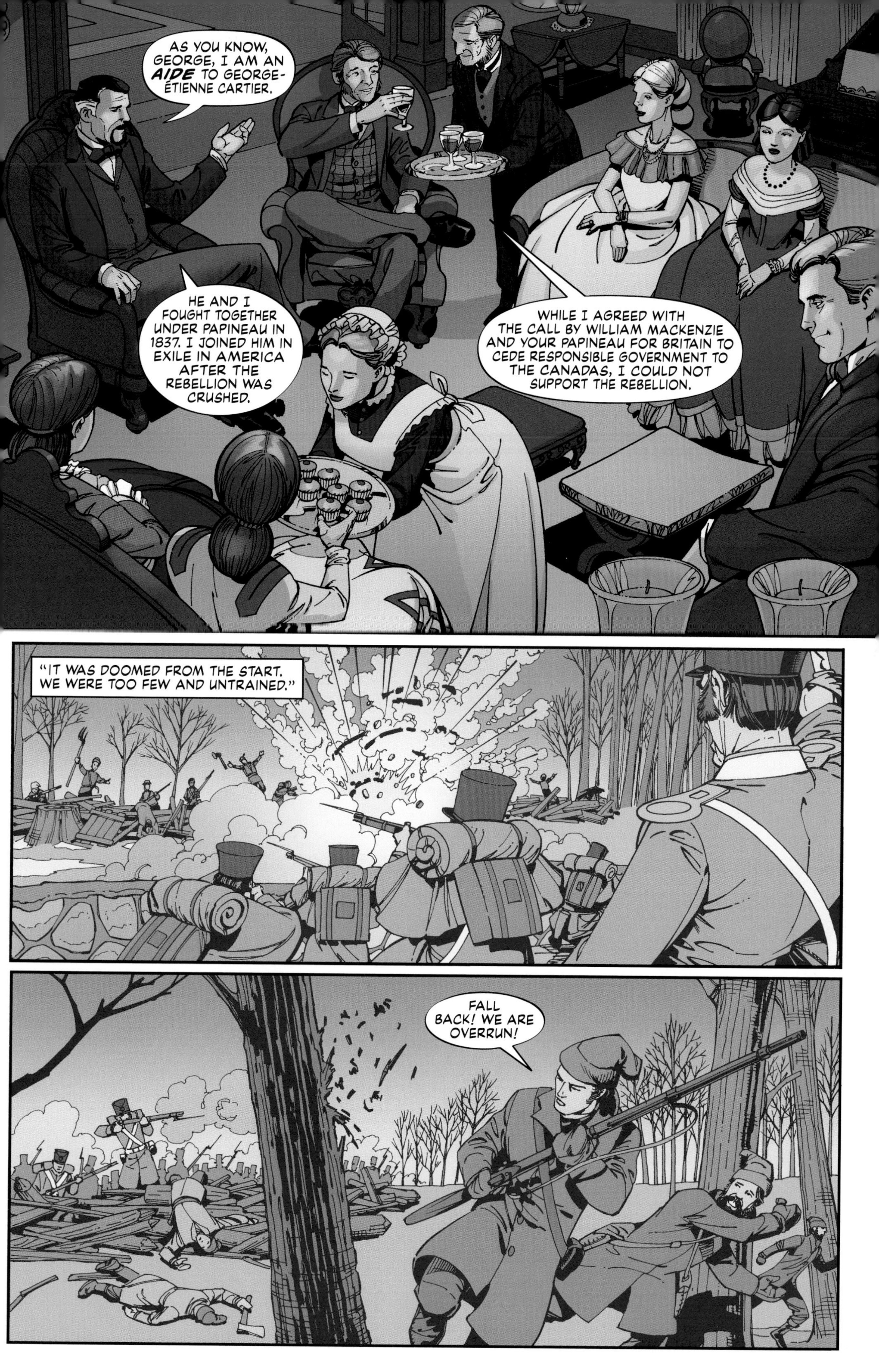
AS YOU KNOW, GEORGE, I AM AN AIDE TO GEORGE-ÉTIENNE CARTIER.
HE AND I FOUGHT TOGETHER UNDER PAPINEAU IN 1837. I JOINED HIM IN EXILE IN AMERICA AFTER THE REBELLION WAS CRUSHED.
WHILE I AGREED WITH THE CALL BY WILLIAM MACKENZIE AND YOUR PAPINEAU FOR BRITAIN TO CEDE RESPONSIBLE GOVERNMENT TO THE CANADAS, I COULD NOT SUPPORT THE REBELLION.
"IT WAS DOOMED FROM THE START. WE WERE TOO FEW AND UNTRAINED."
FALL BACK! WE ARE OVERRUN!

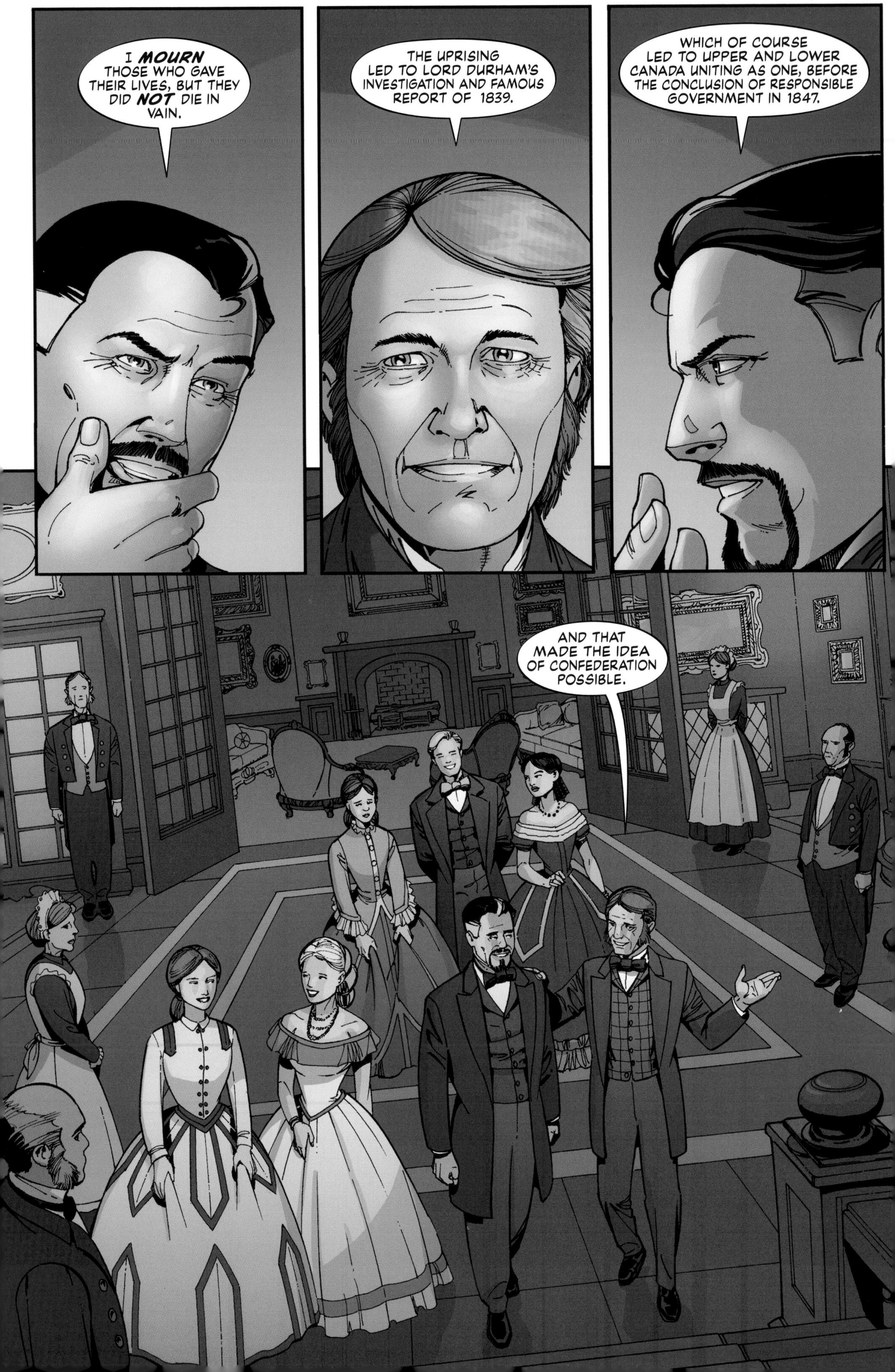
I MOURN THOSE WHO GAVE THEIR LIVES, BUT THEY DID NOT DIE IN VAIN.
THE UPRISING LED TO LORD DURHAM'S INVESTIGATION AND FAMOUS REPORT OF 1839.
WHICH OF COURSE LED TO UPPER AND LOWER CANADA UNITING AS ONE, BEFORE THE CONCLUSION OF RESPONSIBLE GOVERNMENT IN 1847.
AND THAT MADE THE IDEA OF CONFEDERATION POSSIBLE.

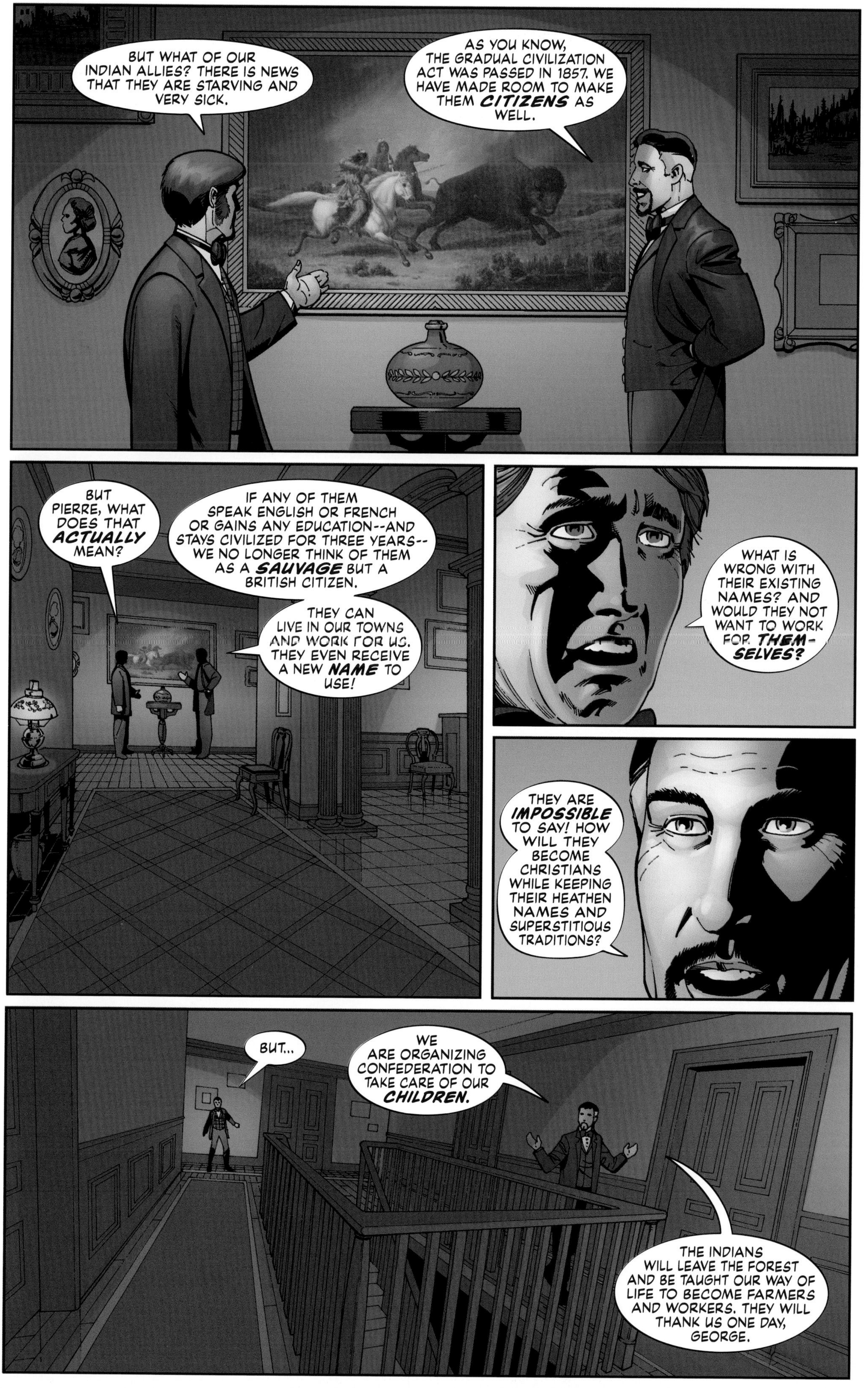
BUT WHAT OF OUR INDIAN ALLIES? THERE IS NEWS THAT THEY ARE STARVING AND VERY SICK.
AS YOU KNOW, THE GRADUAL CIVILIZATION ACT WAS PASSED IN 1857. WE HAVE MADE ROOM TO MAKE THEM CITIZENS AS WELL.
BUT PIERRE, WHAT DOES THAT ACTUALLY MEAN?
IF ANY OF THEM SPEAK ENGLISH OR FRENCH OR GAINS ANY EDUCATION--AND STAYS CIVILIZED FOR THREE YEARS--WE NO LONGER THINK OF THEM AS A SAUVAGE BUT A BRITISH CITIZEN.
THEY CAN LIVE IN OUR TOWNS AND WORK FOR US. THEY EVEN RECEIVE A NEW NAME TO USE!
WHAT IS WRONG WITH THEIR EXISTING NAMES? AND WOULD THEY NOT WANT TO WORK FOR THEM-SELVES?
THEY ARE IMPOSSIBLE TO SAY! HOW WILL THEY BECOME CHRISTIANS WHILE KEEPING THEIR HEATHEN NAMES AND SUPERSTITIOUS TRADITIONS?
BUT...
WE ARE ORGANIZING CONFEDERATION TO TAKE CARE OF OUR CHILDREN.
THE INDIANS WILL LEAVE THE FOREST AND BE TAUGHT OUR WAY OF LIFE TO BECOME FARMERS AND WORKERS. THEY WILL THANK US ONE DAY, GEORGE.

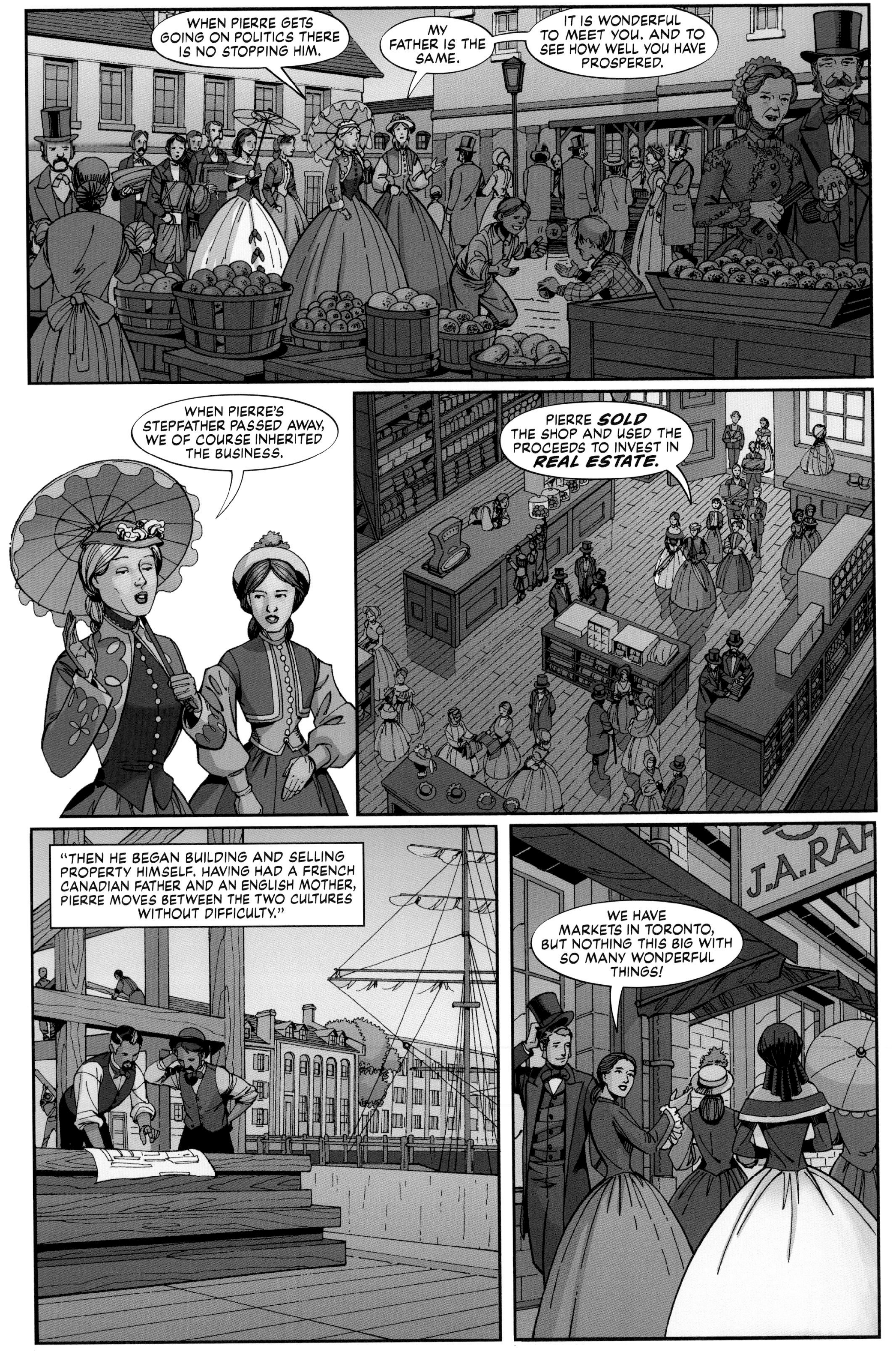
WHEN PIERRE GETS GOING ON POLITICS THERE IS NO STOPPING HIM.
MY FATHER IS THE SAME.
IT IS WONDERFUL TO MEET YOU. AND TO SEE HOW WELL YOU HAVE PROSPERED.
WHEN PIERRE'S STEPFATHER PASSED AWAY, WE OF COURSE INHERITED THE BUSINESS.
PIERRE SOLD THE SHOP AND USED THE PROCEEDS TO INVEST IN REAL ESTATE.
"THEN HE BEGAN BUILDING AND SELLING PROPERTY HIMSELF. HAVING HAD A FRENCH CANADIAN FATHER AND AN ENGLISH MOTHER, PIERRE MOVES BETWEEN THE TWO CULTURES WITHOUT DIFFICULTY."
WE HAVE MARKETS IN TORONTO, BUT NOTHING THIS BIG WITH SO MANY WONDERFUL THINGS!

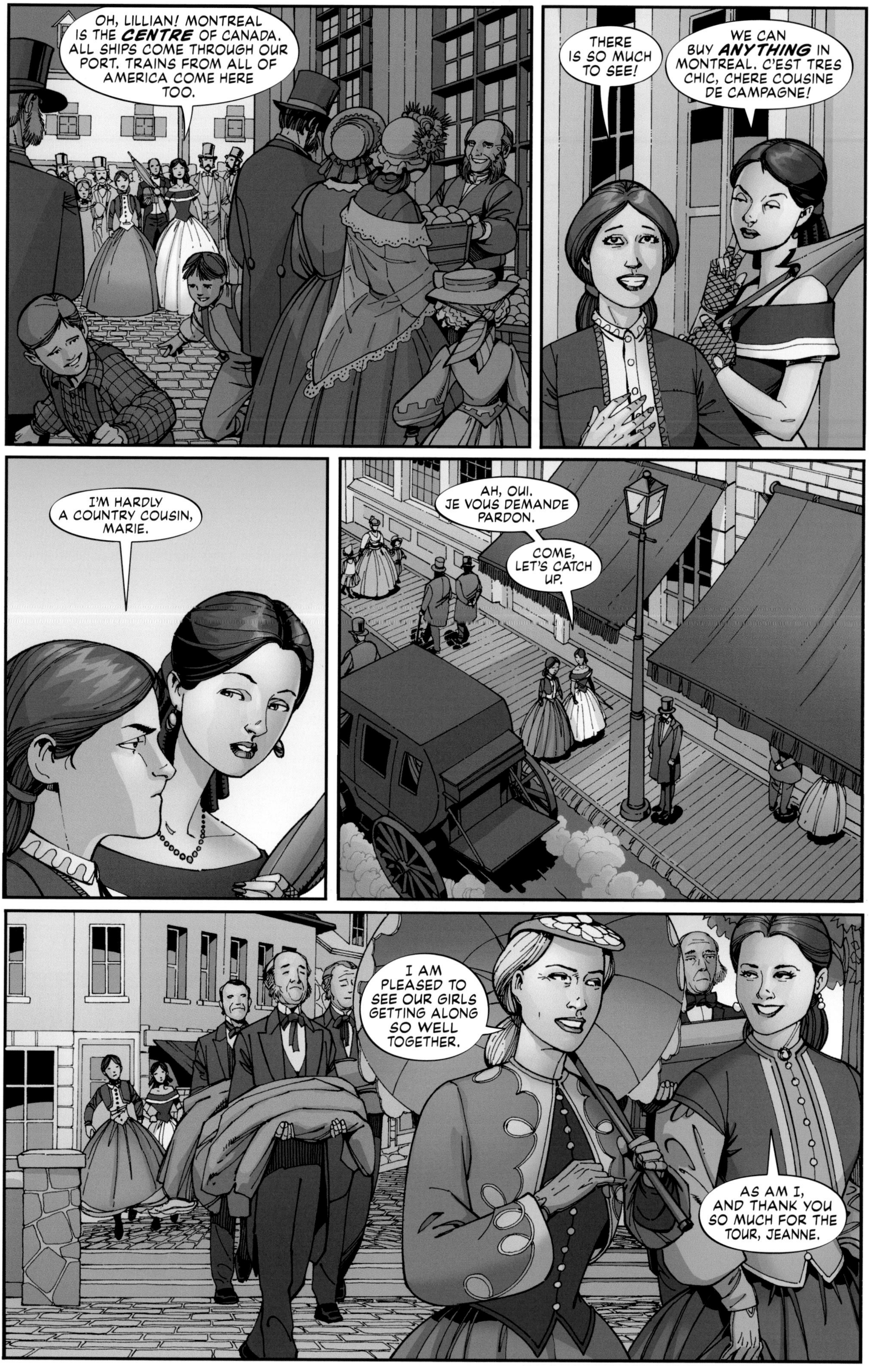
OH, LILLIAN! MONTREAL IS THE ***CENTRE*** OF CANADA. ALL SHIPS COME THROUGH OUR PORT. TRAINS FROM ALL OF AMERICA COME HERE TOO.
THERE IS SO MUCH TO SEE!
WE CAN BUY ***ANYTHING*** IN MONTREAL. C'EST TRES CHIC, CHERE COUSINE DE CAMPAGNE!
I'M HARDLY A COUNTRY COUSIN, MARIE.
AH, OUI. JE VOUS DEMANDE PARDON.
COME, LET'S CATCH UP.
I AM PLEASED TO SEE OUR GIRLS GETTING ALONG SO WELL TOGETHER.
AS AM I, AND THANK YOU SO MUCH FOR THE TOUR, JEANNE.

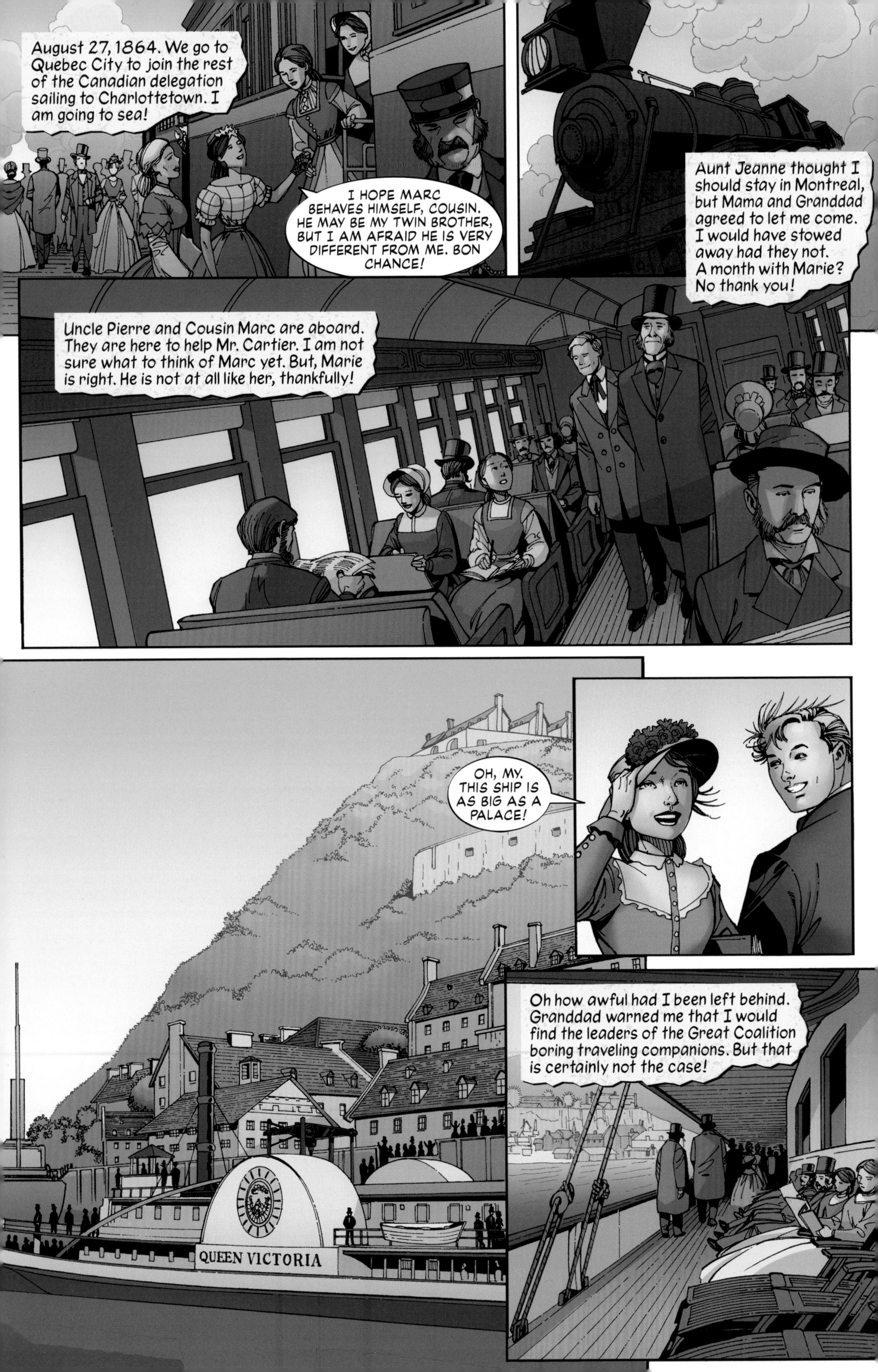

August 27, 1864. We go to Quebec City to join the rest of the Canadian delegation sailing to Charlottetown. I am going to sea!
I HOPE MARC BEHAVES HIMSELF, COUSIN. HE MAY BE MY TWIN BROTHER, BUT I AM AFRAID HE IS VERY DIFFERENT FROM ME. BON CHANCE!
Aunt Jeanne thought I should stay in Montreal, but Mama and Granddad agreed to let me come. I would have stowed away had they not. A month with Marie? No thank you!
Uncle Pierre and Cousin Marc are aboard. They are here to help Mr. Cartier. I am not sure what to think of Marc yet. But, Marie is right. He is not at all like her, thankfully!
QUEEN VICTORIA
OH, MY. THIS SHIP IS AS BIG AS A PALACE!
Oh how awful had I been left behind. Granddad warned me that I would find the leaders of the Great Coalition boring traveling companions. But that is certainly not the case!

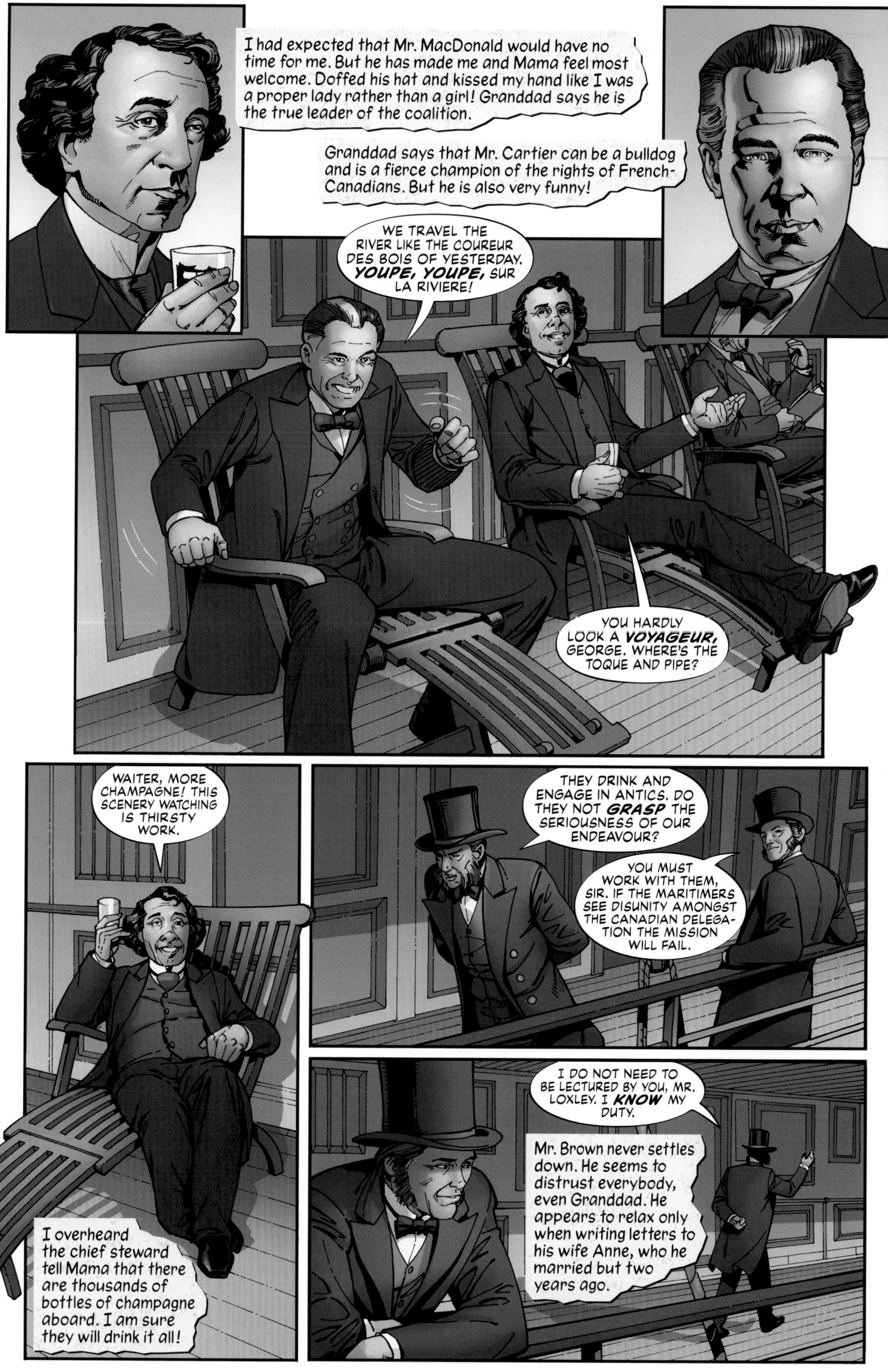
I had expected that Mr. MacDonald would have no time for me. But he has made me and Mama feel most welcome. Doffed his hat and kissed my hand like I was a proper lady rather than a girl! Granddad says he is the true leader of the coalition.
Granddad says that Mr. Cartier can be a bulldog and is a fierce champion of the rights of French-Canadians. But he is also very funny!
WE TRAVEL THE RIVER LIKE THE COUREUR DES BOIS OF YESTERDAY. YOUPE, YOUPE, SUR LA RIVIERE!
YOU HARDLY LOOK A VOYAGEUR, GEORGE. WHERE'S THE TOQUE AND PIPE?
WAITER, MORE CHAMPAGNE! THIS SCENERY WATCHING IS THIRSTY WORK.
I overheard the chief steward tell Mama that there are thousands of bottles of champagne aboard. I am sure they will drink it all!
THEY DRINK AND ENGAGE IN ANTICS. DO THEY NOT GRASP THE SERIOUSNESS OF OUR ENDEAVOUR?
YOU MUST WORK WITH THEM, SIR. IF THE MARITIMERS SEE DISUNITY AMONGST THE CANADIAN DELEGATION THE MISSION WILL FAIL.
I DO NOT NEED TO BE LECTURED BY YOU, MR. LOXLEY. I KNOW MY DUTY.
Mr. Brown never settles down. He seems to distrust everybody, even Granddad. He appears to relax only when writing letters to his wife Anne, who he married but two years ago.

Granddad says that Brown is smart and dedicated. So he takes sound advice more than he would ever admit.

WHAT WONDERS DO YOU WRITE ABOUT TODAY, COUSIN?

DIARIES ARE *PRIVATE*, COUSIN. I WRITE ABOUT WHAT I SEE--

--MY *DIARY!*

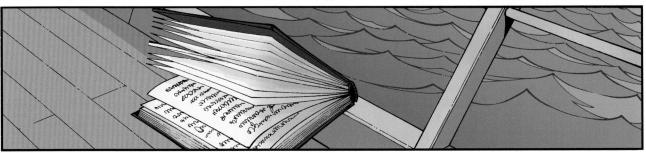

MY WHOLE *WORLD* IS IN THAT DIARY!

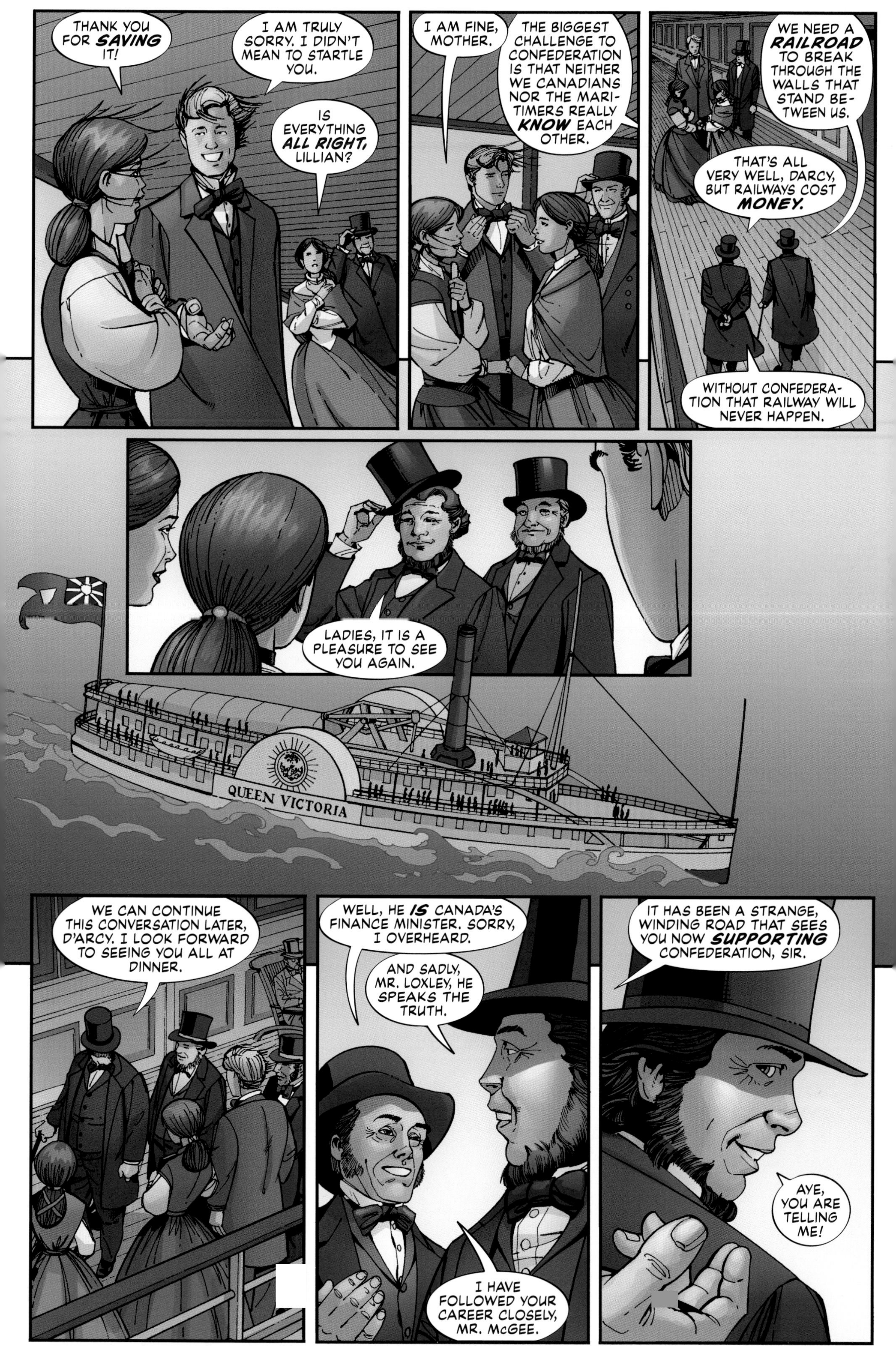
THANK YOU FOR SAVING IT!
I AM TRULY SORRY. I DIDN'T MEAN TO STARTLE YOU.
IS EVERYTHING ALL RIGHT, LILLIAN?
I AM FINE, MOTHER.
THE BIGGEST CHALLENGE TO CONFEDERATION IS THAT NEITHER WE CANADIANS NOR THE MARI-TIMERS REALLY KNOW EACH OTHER.
WE NEED A RAILROAD TO BREAK THROUGH THE WALLS THAT STAND BE-TWEEN US.
THAT'S ALL VERY WELL, DARCY, BUT RAILWAYS COST MONEY.
WITHOUT CONFEDERA-TION THAT RAILWAY WILL NEVER HAPPEN.
LADIES, IT IS A PLEASURE TO SEE YOU AGAIN.
QUEEN VICTORIA
WE CAN CONTINUE THIS CONVERSATION LATER, D'ARCY. I LOOK FORWARD TO SEEING YOU ALL AT DINNER.
WELL, HE IS CANADA'S FINANCE MINISTER. SORRY, I OVERHEARD.
AND SADLY, MR. LOXLEY, HE SPEAKS THE TRUTH.
I HAVE FOLLOWED YOUR CAREER CLOSELY, MR. McGEE.
IT HAS BEEN A STRANGE, WINDING ROAD THAT SEES YOU NOW SUPPORTING CONFEDERATION, SIR.
AYE, YOU ARE TELLING ME!

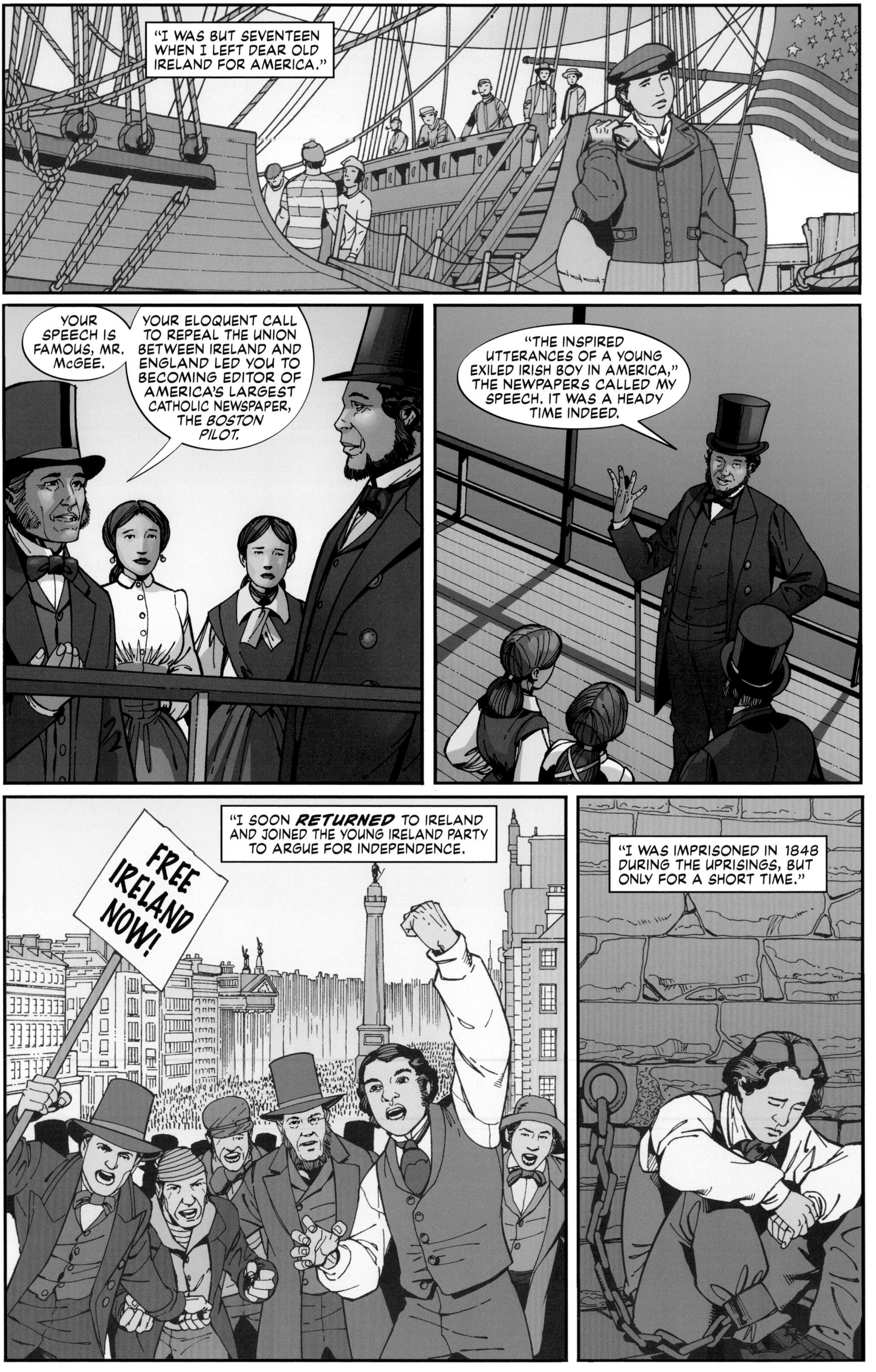
"I WAS BUT SEVENTEEN WHEN I LEFT DEAR OLD IRELAND FOR AMERICA."
YOUR SPEECH IS FAMOUS, MR. McGEE.
YOUR ELOQUENT CALL TO REPEAL THE UNION BETWEEN IRELAND AND ENGLAND LED YOU TO BECOMING EDITOR OF AMERICA'S LARGEST CATHOLIC NEWSPAPER, THE *BOSTON PILOT*.
"THE INSPIRED UTTERANCES OF A YOUNG EXILED IRISH BOY IN AMERICA," THE NEWSPAPERS CALLED MY SPEECH. IT WAS A HEADY TIME INDEED.
"I SOON ***RETURNED*** TO IRELAND AND JOINED THE YOUNG IRELAND PARTY TO ARGUE FOR INDEPENDENCE.
FREE IRELAND NOW!
"I WAS IMPRISONED IN 1848 DURING THE UPRISINGS, BUT ONLY FOR A SHORT TIME."

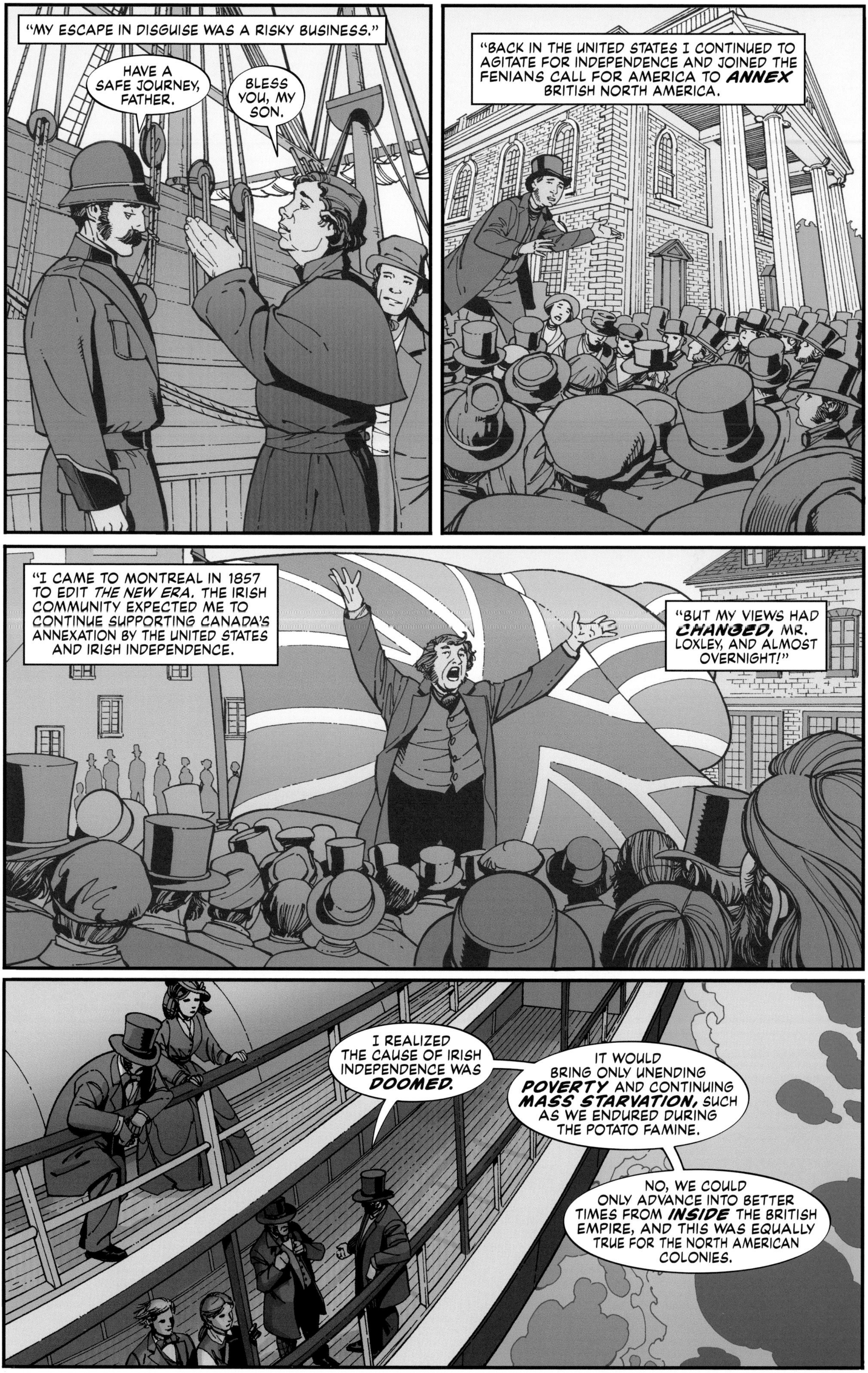
"MY ESCAPE IN DISGUISE WAS A RISKY BUSINESS."
HAVE A SAFE JOURNEY, FATHER.
BLESS YOU, MY SON.
"BACK IN THE UNITED STATES I CONTINUED TO AGITATE FOR INDEPENDENCE AND JOINED THE FENIANS CALL FOR AMERICA TO ***ANNEX*** BRITISH NORTH AMERICA.
"I CAME TO MONTREAL IN 1857 TO EDIT *THE NEW ERA*. THE IRISH COMMUNITY EXPECTED ME TO CONTINUE SUPPORTING CANADA'S ANNEXATION BY THE UNITED STATES AND IRISH INDEPENDENCE.
"BUT MY VIEWS HAD ***CHANGED,*** MR. LOXLEY, AND ALMOST OVERNIGHT!"
I REALIZED THE CAUSE OF IRISH INDEPENDENCE WAS ***DOOMED.***
IT WOULD BRING ONLY UNENDING ***POVERTY*** AND CONTINUING ***MASS STARVATION,*** SUCH AS WE ENDURED DURING THE POTATO FAMINE.
NO, WE COULD ONLY ADVANCE INTO BETTER TIMES FROM ***INSIDE*** THE BRITISH EMPIRE, AND THIS WAS EQUALLY TRUE FOR THE NORTH AMERICAN COLONIES.

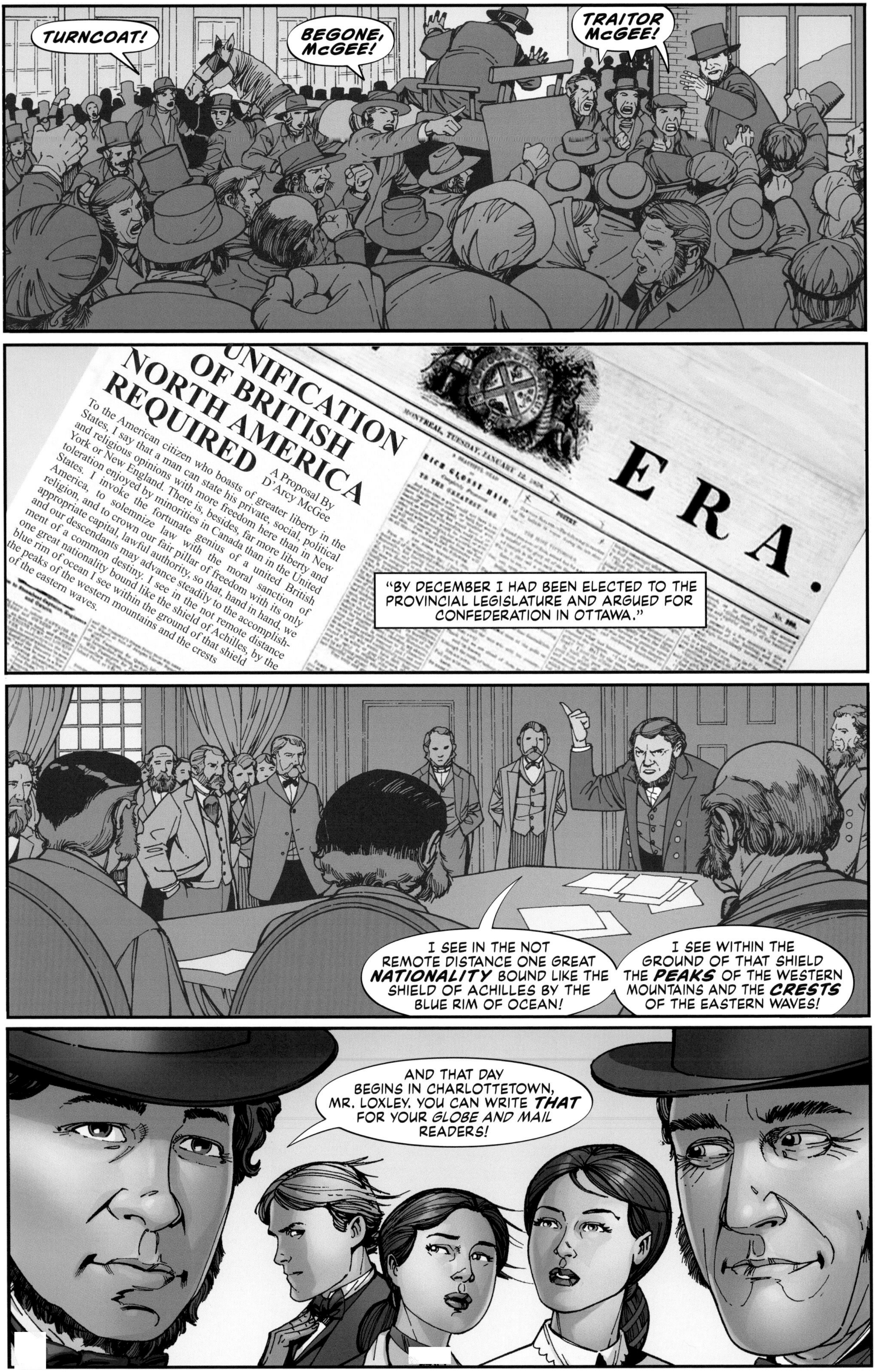

TURNCOAT!
BEGONE, McGEE!
TRAITOR McGEE!
UNIFICATION OF BRITISH NORTH AMERICA REQUIRED
A Proposal By D'Arcy McGee
To the American citizen who boasts of greater liberty in the States, I say that a man can state his private, social, political and religious opinions with more freedom here than in New York or New England. There is, besides, far more liberty and toleration enjoyed by minorities in Canada than in the United States. I invoke the fortunate genius of a united British America, to solemnize law with the moral sanction of religion, and to crown our fair pillar of freedom with its only appropriate capital, lawful authority, so that, hand in hand, we and our descendants may advance steadily to the accomplishment of a common destiny. I see in the not remote distance one great nationality bound like the shield of Achilles, by the blue rim of ocean I see within the ground of that shield the peaks of the western mountains and the crests of the eastern waves.
ERA.
"BY DECEMBER I HAD BEEN ELECTED TO THE PROVINCIAL LEGISLATURE AND ARGUED FOR CONFEDERATION IN OTTAWA."
I SEE IN THE NOT REMOTE DISTANCE ONE GREAT ***NATIONALITY*** BOUND LIKE THE SHIELD OF ACHILLES BY THE BLUE RIM OF OCEAN!
I SEE WITHIN THE GROUND OF THAT SHIELD THE ***PEAKS*** OF THE WESTERN MOUNTAINS AND THE ***CRESTS*** OF THE EASTERN WAVES!
AND THAT DAY BEGINS IN CHARLOTTETOWN, MR. LOXLEY. YOU CAN WRITE ***THAT*** FOR YOUR *GLOBE AND MAIL* READERS!

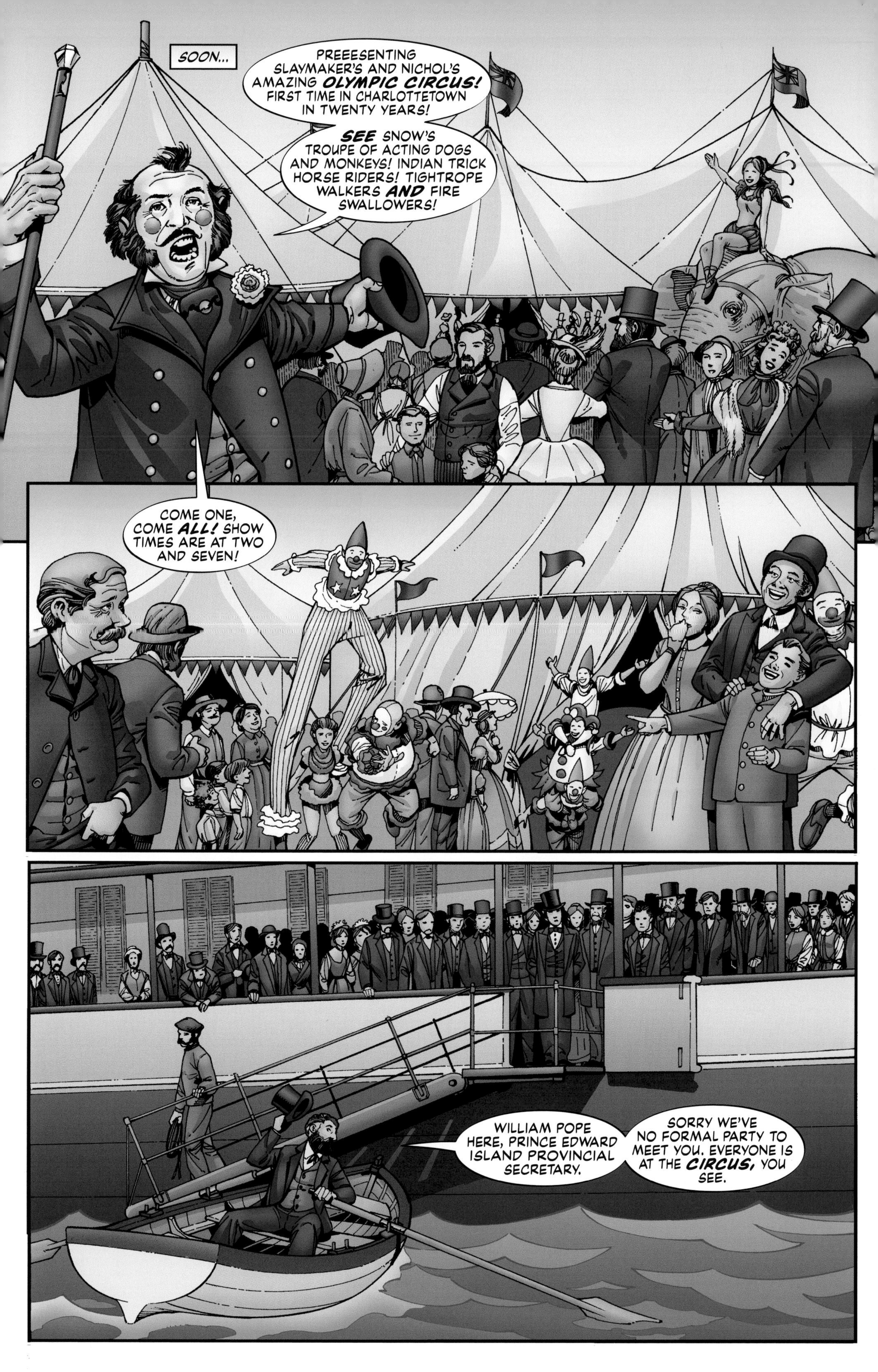
SOON...
PREEESENTING SLAYMAKER'S AND NICHOL'S AMAZING OLYMPIC CIRCUS! FIRST TIME IN CHARLOTTETOWN IN TWENTY YEARS!
SEE SNOW'S TROUPE OF ACTING DOGS AND MONKEYS! INDIAN TRICK HORSE RIDERS! TIGHTROPE WALKERS AND FIRE SWALLOWERS!
COME ONE, COME ALL! SHOW TIMES ARE AT TWO AND SEVEN!
WILLIAM POPE HERE, PRINCE EDWARD ISLAND PROVINCIAL SECRETARY.
SORRY WE'VE NO FORMAL PARTY TO MEET YOU. EVERYONE IS AT THE CIRCUS, YOU SEE.

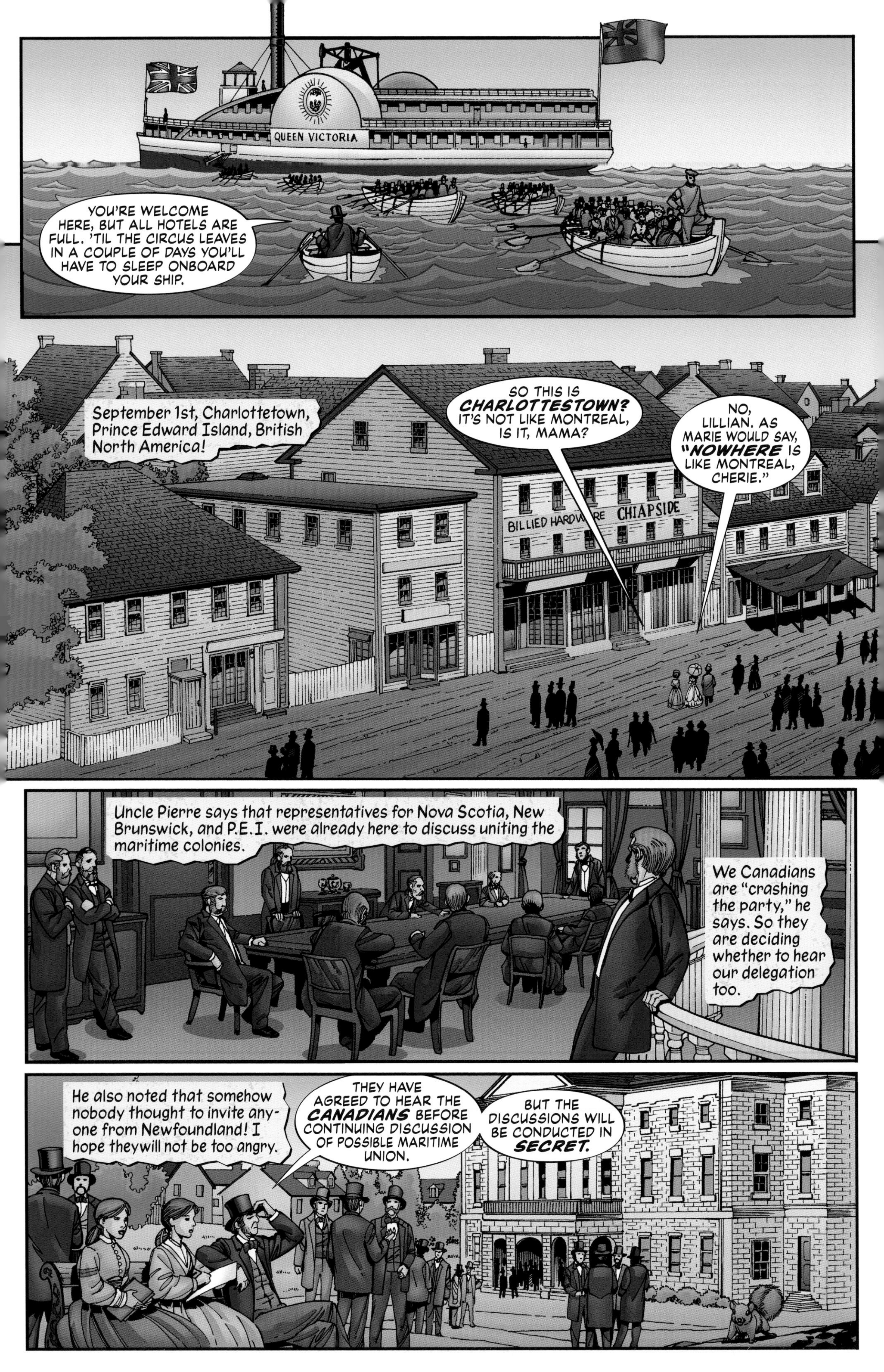

QUEEN VICTORIA
YOU'RE WELCOME HERE, BUT ALL HOTELS ARE FULL. 'TIL THE CIRCUS LEAVES IN A COUPLE OF DAYS YOU'LL HAVE TO SLEEP ONBOARD YOUR SHIP.
September 1st, Charlottetown, Prince Edward Island, British North America!
SO THIS IS CHARLOTTESTOWN? IT'S NOT LIKE MONTREAL, IS IT, MAMA?
NO, LILLIAN. AS MARIE WOULD SAY, "NOWHERE IS LIKE MONTREAL, CHERIE."
BILLIED HARDWARE
CHIAPSIDE
Uncle Pierre says that representatives for Nova Scotia, New Brunswick, and P.E.I. were already here to discuss uniting the maritime colonies.
We Canadians are "crashing the party," he says. So they are deciding whether to hear our delegation too.
He also noted that somehow nobody thought to invite anyone from Newfoundland! I hope theywill not be too angry.
THEY HAVE AGREED TO HEAR THE CANADIANS BEFORE CONTINUING DISCUSSION OF POSSIBLE MARITIME UNION.
BUT THE DISCUSSIONS WILL BE CONDUCTED IN SECRET.

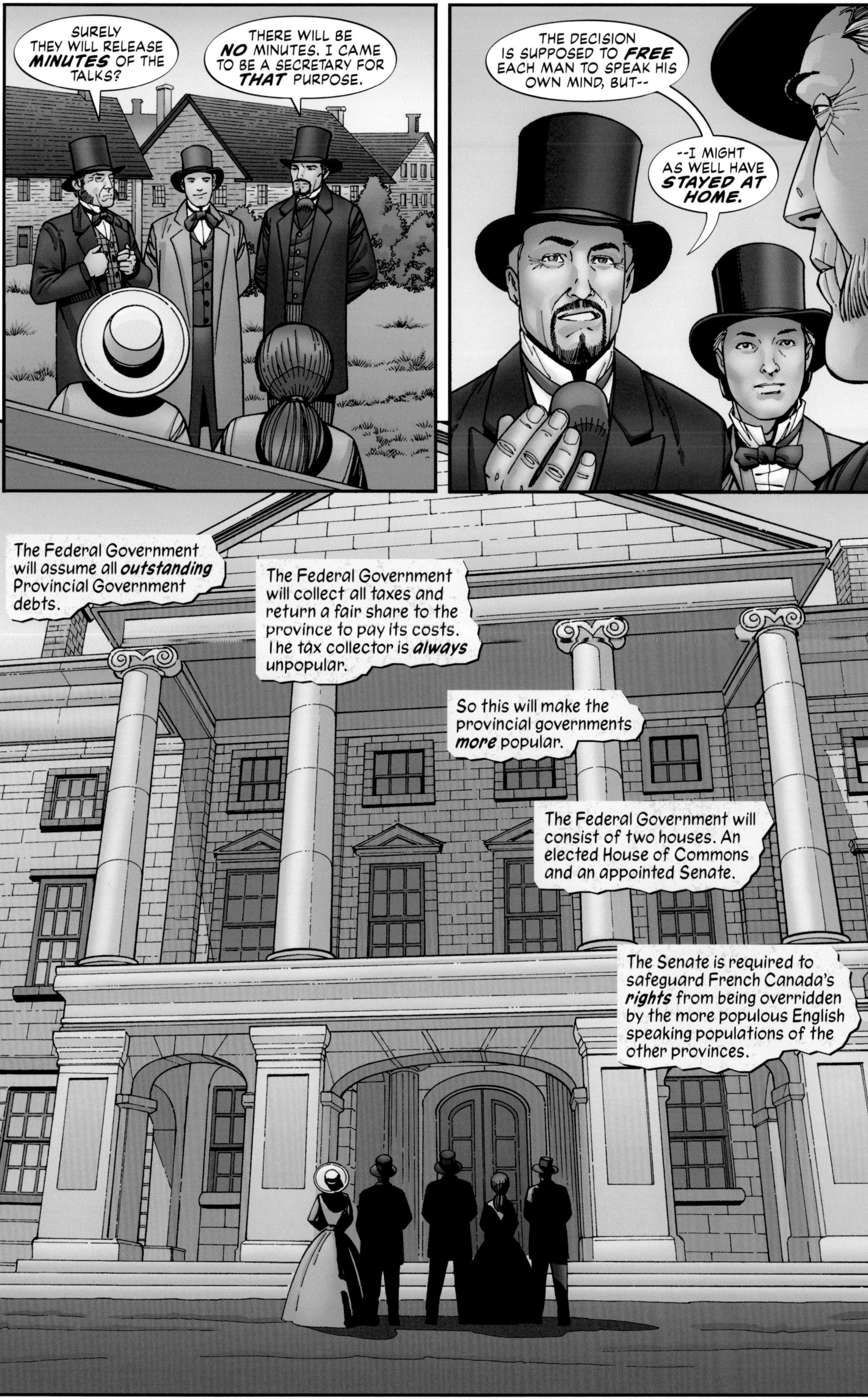
SURELY THEY WILL RELEASE MINUTES OF THE TALKS?
THERE WILL BE NO MINUTES. I CAME TO BE A SECRETARY FOR THAT PURPOSE.
THE DECISION IS SUPPOSED TO FREE EACH MAN TO SPEAK HIS OWN MIND, BUT--
--I MIGHT AS WELL HAVE STAYED AT HOME.
The Federal Government will assume all outstanding Provincial Government debts.
The Federal Government will collect all taxes and return a fair share to the province to pay its costs. The tax collector is always unpopular.
So this will make the provincial governments more popular.
The Federal Government will consist of two houses. An elected House of Commons and an appointed Senate.
The Senate is required to safeguard French Canada's rights from being overridden by the more populous English speaking populations of the other provinces.

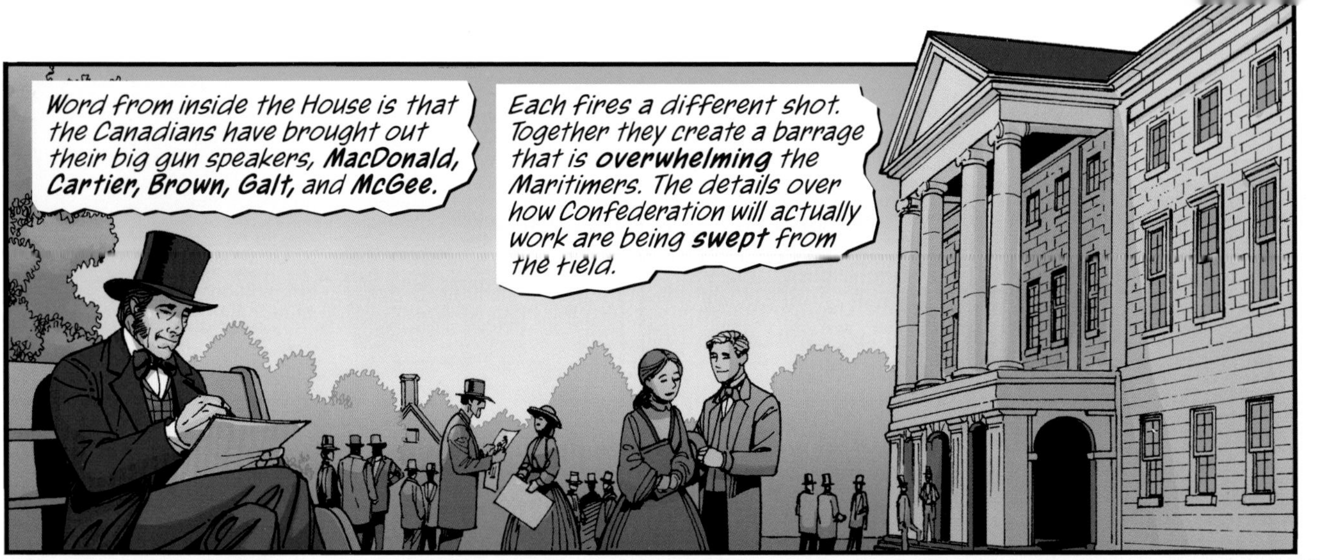
Word from inside the House is that the Canadians have brought out their big gun speakers, **MacDonald, Cartier, Brown, Galt,** and **McGee.**
Each fires a different shot. Together they create a barrage that is **overwhelming** the Maritimers. The details over how Confederation will actually work are being **swept** from the field.

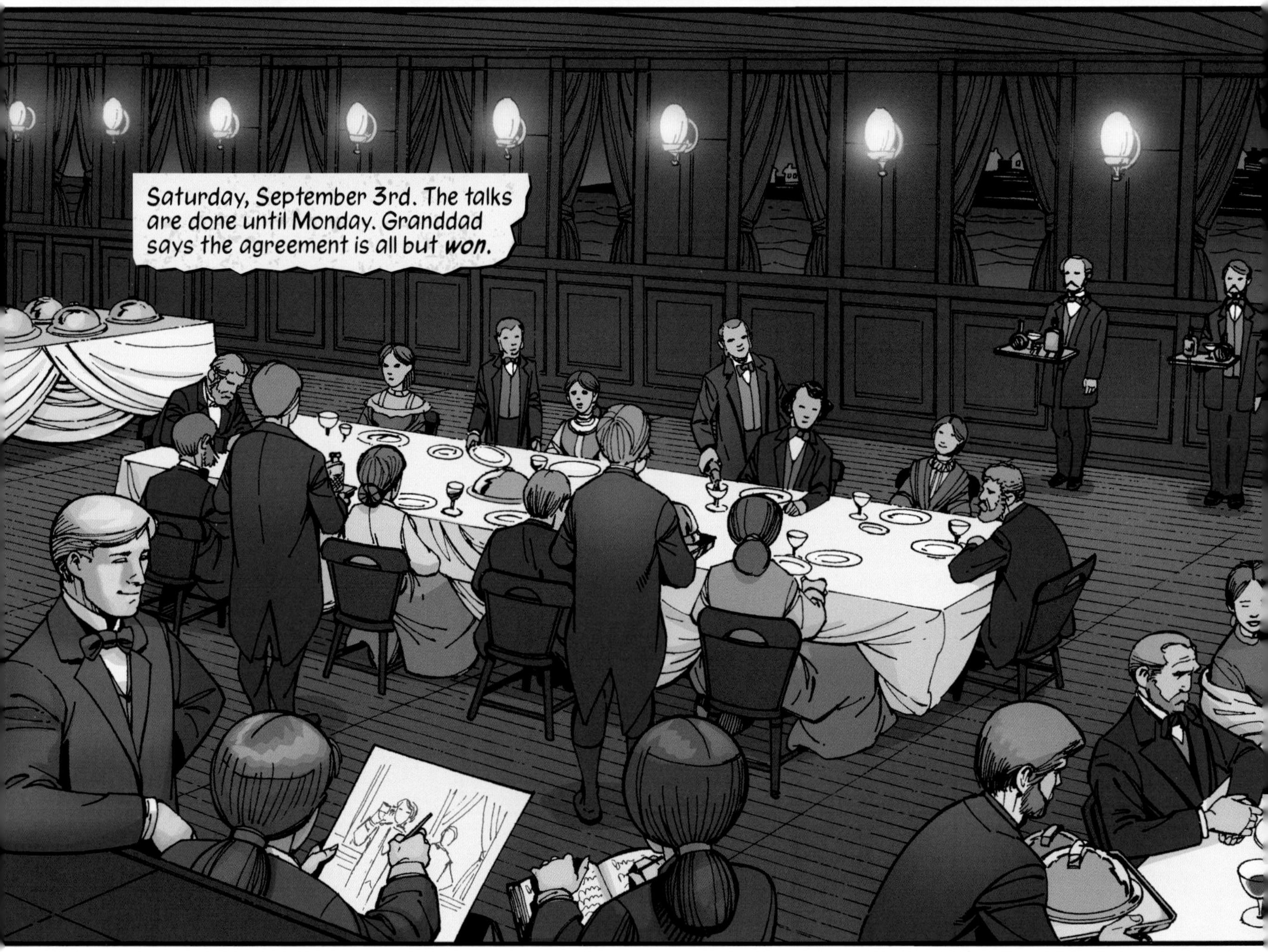
Saturday, September 3rd. The talks are done until Monday. Granddad says the agreement is all but ***won.***

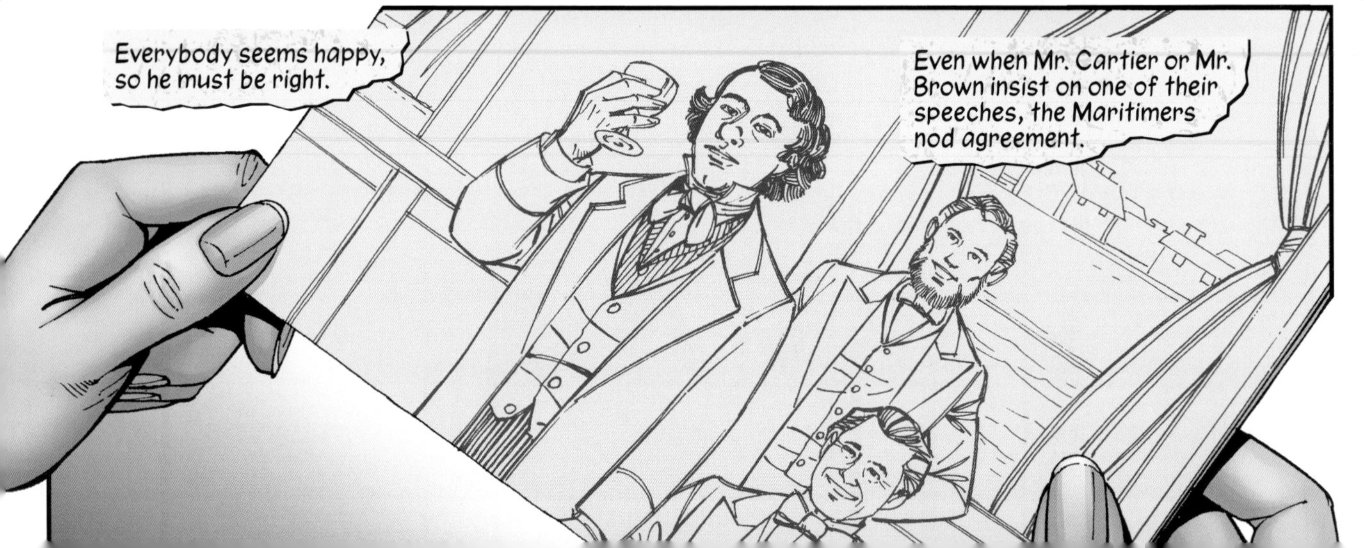
Everybody seems happy, so he must be right.
Even when Mr. Cartier or Mr. Brown insist on one of their speeches, the Maritimers nod agreement.

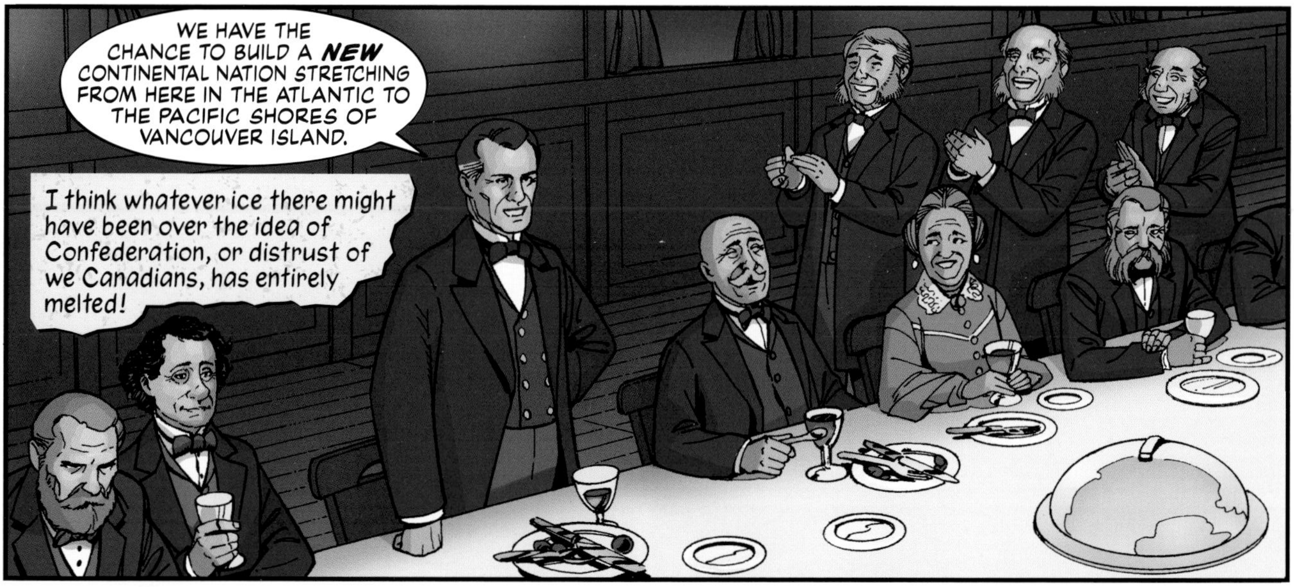
WE HAVE THE CHANCE TO BUILD A ***NEW*** CONTINENTAL NATION STRETCHING FROM HERE IN THE ATLANTIC TO THE PACIFIC SHORES OF VANCOUVER ISLAND.
I think whatever ice there might have been over the idea of Confederation, or distrust of we Canadians, has entirely melted!

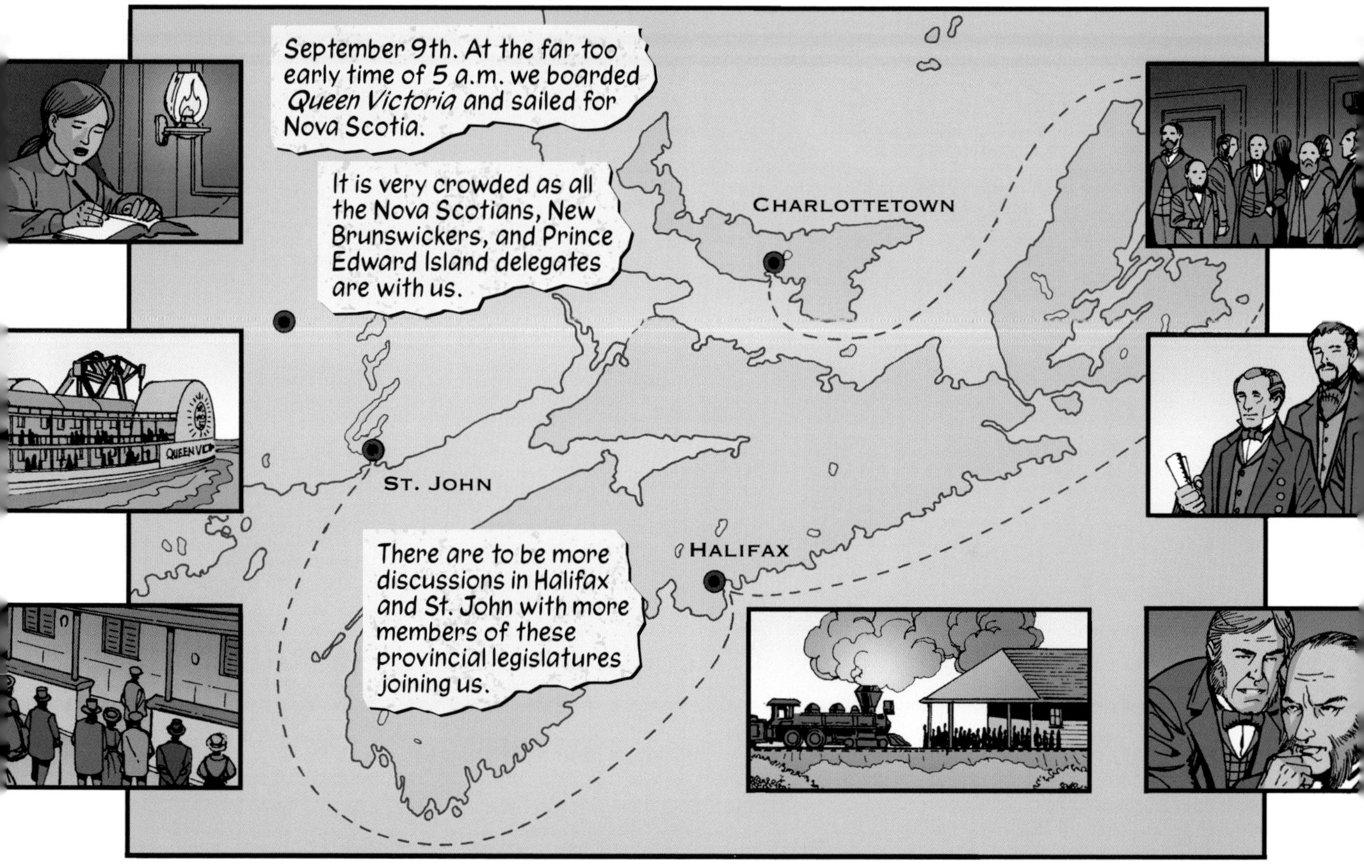
September 9th. At the far too early time of 5 a.m. we boarded *Queen Victoria* and sailed for Nova Scotia.
It is very crowded as all the Nova Scotians, New Brunswickers, and Prince Edward Island delegates are with us.
CHARLOTTETOWN
ST. JOHN
HALIFAX
There are to be more discussions in Halifax and St. John with more members of these provincial legislatures joining us.

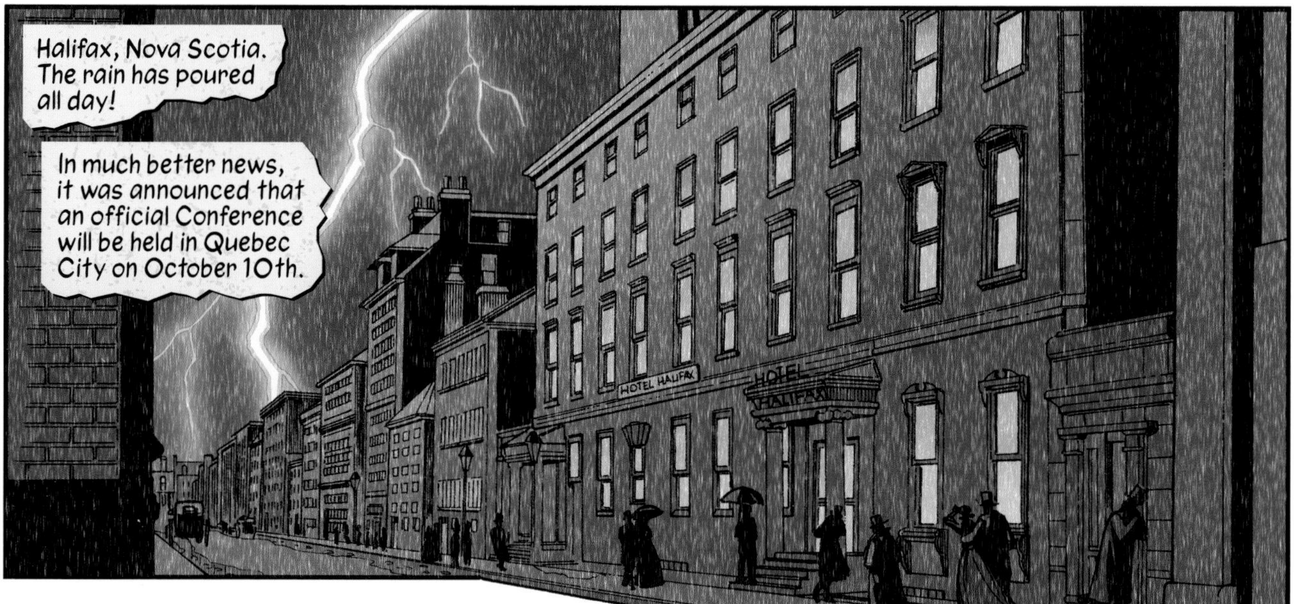
Halifax, Nova Scotia. The rain has poured all day!
In much better news, it was announced that an official Conference will be held in Quebec City on October 10th.
HOTEL HALIFAX
HOTEL HALIFAX

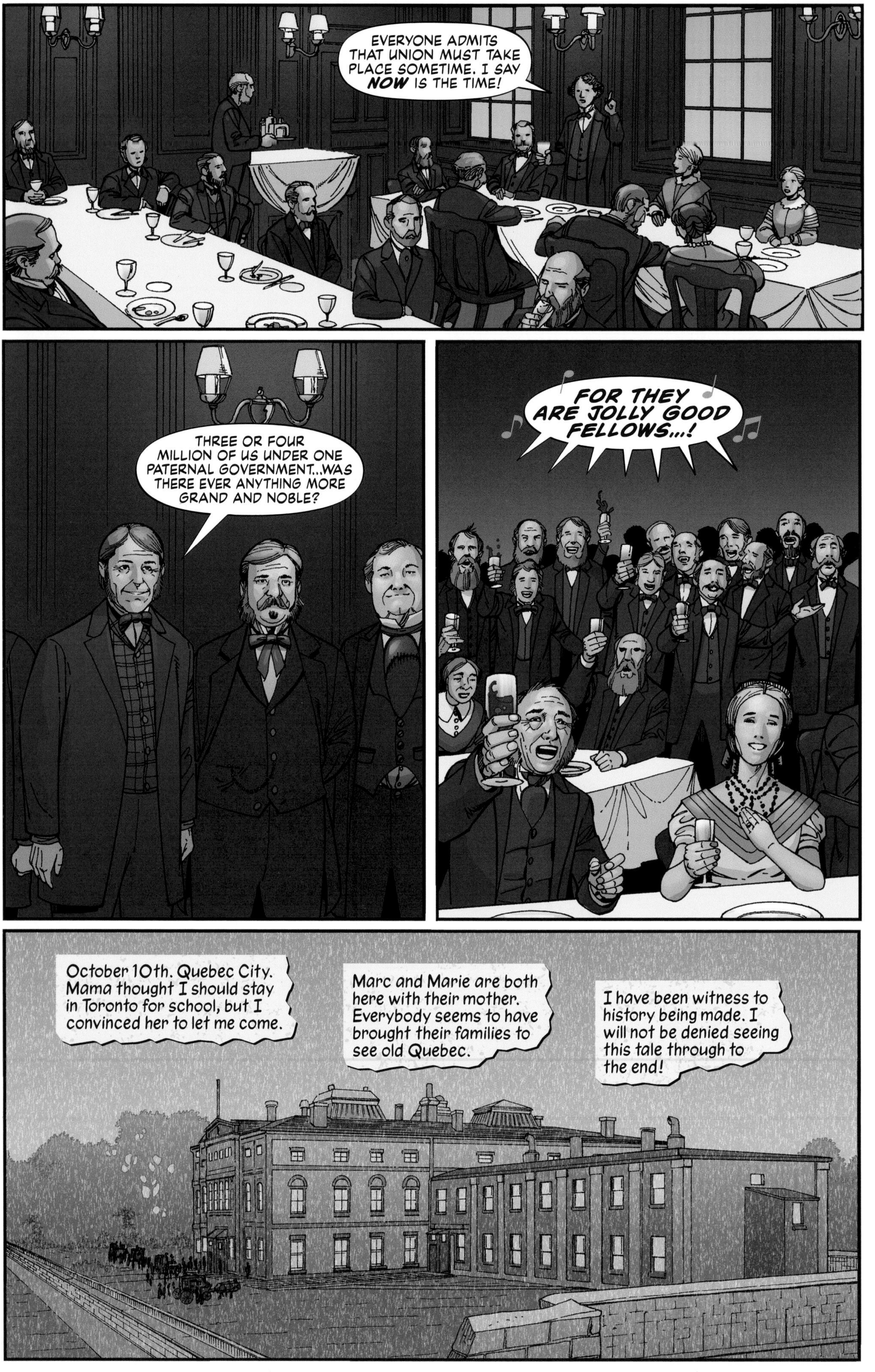
EVERYONE ADMITS THAT UNION MUST TAKE PLACE SOMETIME. I SAY NOW IS THE TIME!
THREE OR FOUR MILLION OF US UNDER ONE PATERNAL GOVERNMENT...WAS THERE EVER ANYTHING MORE GRAND AND NOBLE?
FOR THEY ARE JOLLY GOOD FELLOWS...!
October 10th. Quebec City. Mama thought I should stay in Toronto for school, but I convinced her to let me come.
Marc and Marie are both here with their mother. Everybody seems to have brought their families to see old Quebec.
I have been witness to history being made. I will not be denied seeing this tale through to the end!

Rumours are that the talks have become very complex with disagreement over details of how Confederation will actually work.

Yet there is a will to make it happen.

NOVA SCOTIA PREMIER, CHARLES TUPPER.

I AM A LOYAL NOVA SCOTIAN! EACH OF OUR LITTLE PROVINCES IS A NATION BY ITSELF.

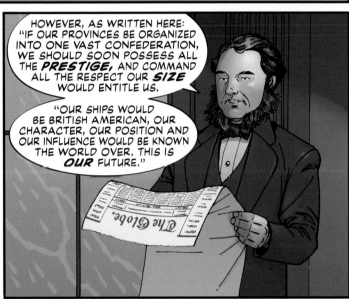

HOWEVER, AS WRITTEN HERE: "IF OUR PROVINCES BE ORGANIZED INTO ONE VAST CONFEDERATION, WE SHOULD SOON POSSESS ALL THE *PRESTIGE*, AND COMMAND ALL THE RESPECT OUR *SIZE* WOULD ENTITLE US.

"OUR SHIPS WOULD BE BRITISH AMERICAN, OUR CHARACTER, OUR POSITION AND OUR INFLUENCE WOULD BE KNOWN THE WORLD OVER. THIS IS *OUR* FUTURE."

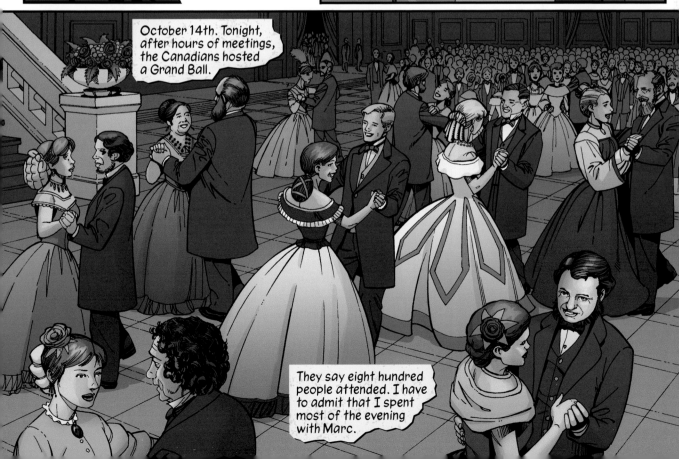

October 14th. Tonight, after hours of meetings, the Canadians hosted a Grand Ball.

They say eight hundred people attended. I have to admit that I spent most of the evening with Marc.

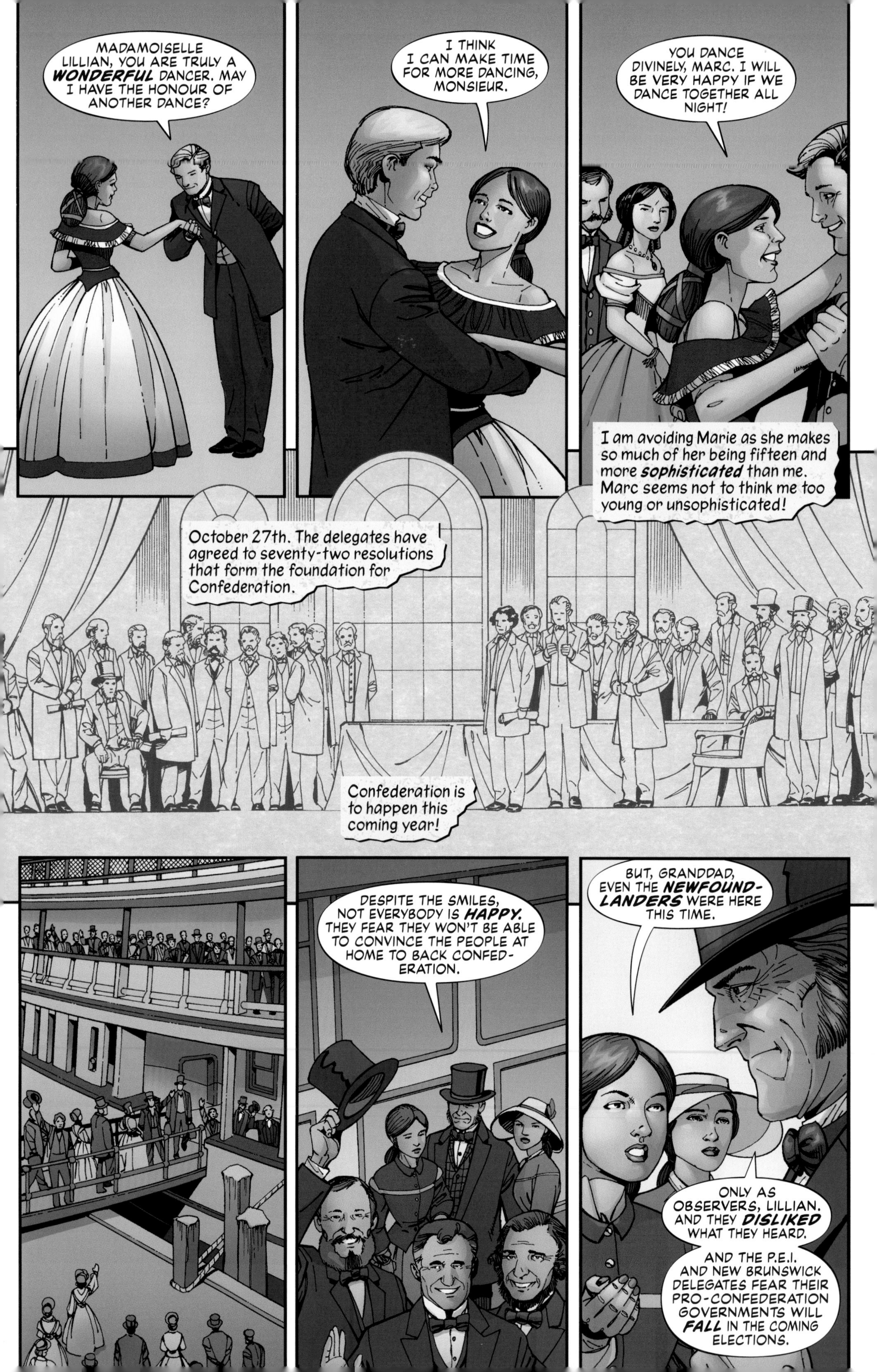
MADAMOISELLE LILLIAN, YOU ARE TRULY A WONDERFUL DANCER. MAY I HAVE THE HONOUR OF ANOTHER DANCE?
I THINK I CAN MAKE TIME FOR MORE DANCING, MONSIEUR.
YOU DANCE DIVINELY, MARC. I WILL BE VERY HAPPY IF WE DANCE TOGETHER ALL NIGHT!
I am avoiding Marie as she makes so much of her being fifteen and more sophisticated than me. Marc seems not to think me too young or unsophisticated!
October 27th. The delegates have agreed to seventy-two resolutions that form the foundation for Confederation.
Confederation is to happen this coming year!
DESPITE THE SMILES, NOT EVERYBODY IS HAPPY. THEY FEAR THEY WON'T BE ABLE TO CONVINCE THE PEOPLE AT HOME TO BACK CONFED-ERATION.
BUT, GRANDDAD, EVEN THE NEWFOUND-LANDERS WERE HERE THIS TIME.
ONLY AS OBSERVERS, LILLIAN. AND THEY DISLIKED WHAT THEY HEARD.
AND THE P.E.I. AND NEW BRUNSWICK DELEGATES FEAR THEIR PRO-CONFEDERATION GOVERNMENTS WILL FALL IN THE COMING ELECTIONS.

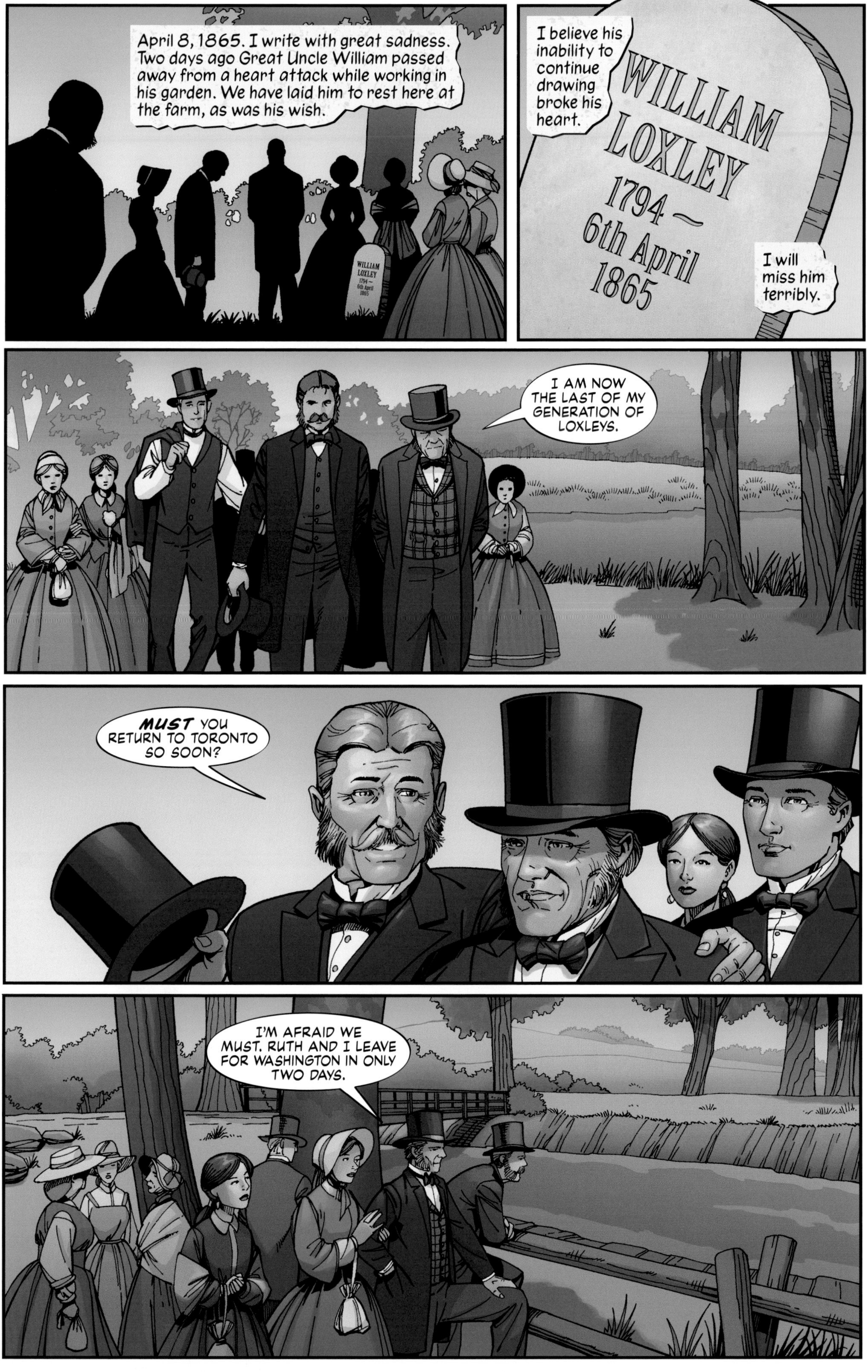
April 8, 1865. I write with great sadness. Two days ago Great Uncle William passed away from a heart attack while working in his garden. We have laid him to rest here at the farm, as was his wish.
WILLIAM LOXLEY 1794 ~ 6th April 1865
I believe his inability to continue drawing broke his heart.
WILLIAM LOXLEY 1794 ~ 6th April 1865
I will miss him terribly.
I AM NOW THE LAST OF MY GENERATION OF LOXLEYS.
MUST YOU RETURN TO TORONTO SO SOON?
I'M AFRAID WE MUST. RUTH AND I LEAVE FOR WASHINGTON IN ONLY TWO DAYS.

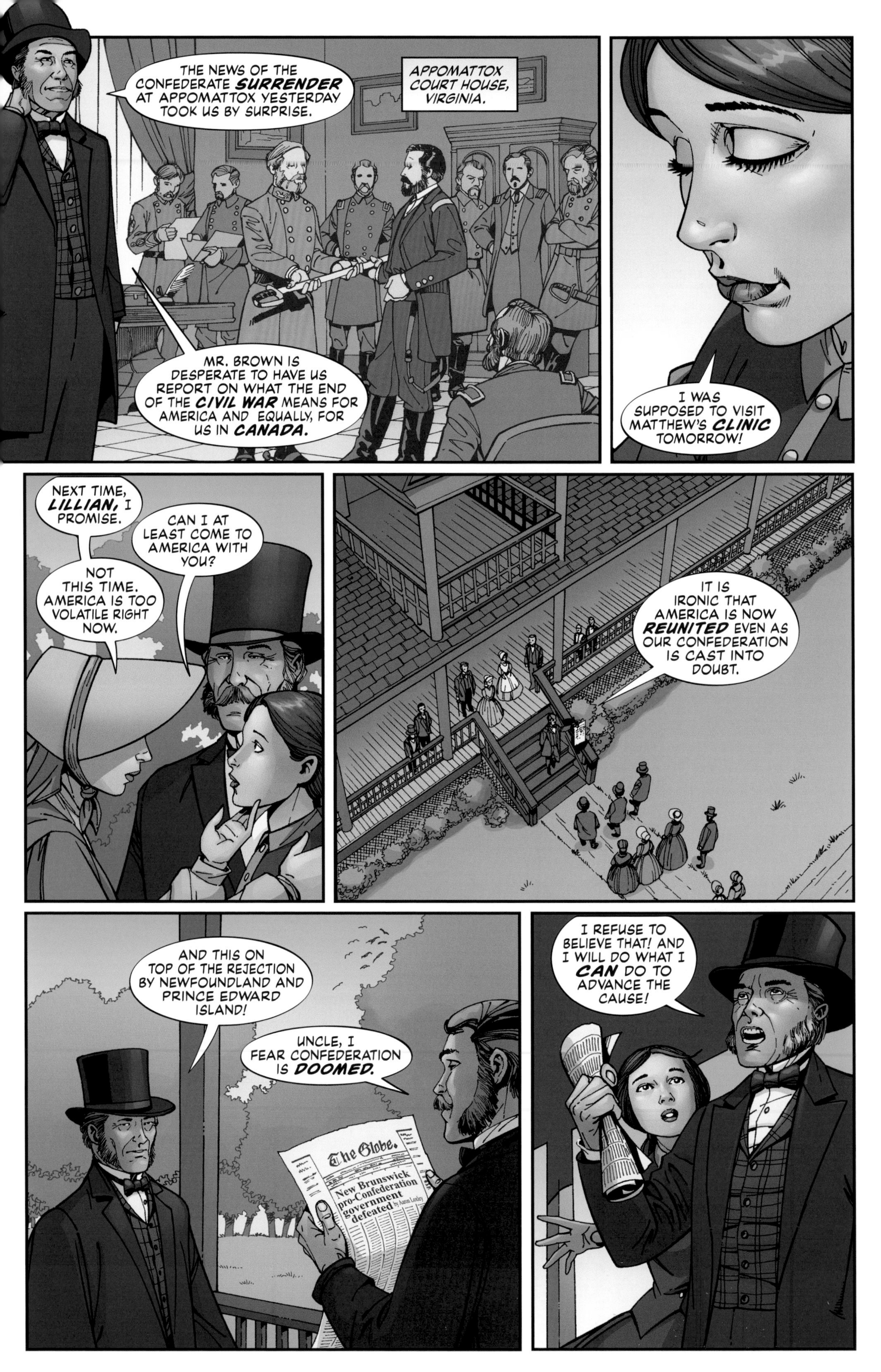
THE NEWS OF THE CONFEDERATE SURRENDER AT APPOMATTOX YESTERDAY TOOK US BY SURPRISE.
APPOMATTOX COURT HOUSE, VIRGINIA.
MR. BROWN IS DESPERATE TO HAVE US REPORT ON WHAT THE END OF THE CIVIL WAR MEANS FOR AMERICA AND EQUALLY, FOR US IN CANADA.
I WAS SUPPOSED TO VISIT MATTHEW'S CLINIC TOMORROW!
CAN I AT LEAST COME TO AMERICA WITH YOU?
NOT THIS TIME. AMERICA IS TOO VOLATILE RIGHT NOW.
NEXT TIME, LILLIAN, I PROMISE.
IT IS IRONIC THAT AMERICA IS NOW REUNITED EVEN AS OUR CONFEDERATION IS CAST INTO DOUBT.
AND THIS ON TOP OF THE REJECTION BY NEWFOUNDLAND AND PRINCE EDWARD ISLAND!
UNCLE, I FEAR CONFEDERATION IS DOOMED.
The Globe.
New Brunswick pro-Confederation government defeated by Aaron Lexley
I REFUSE TO BELIEVE THAT! AND I WILL DO WHAT I CAN DO TO ADVANCE THE CAUSE!

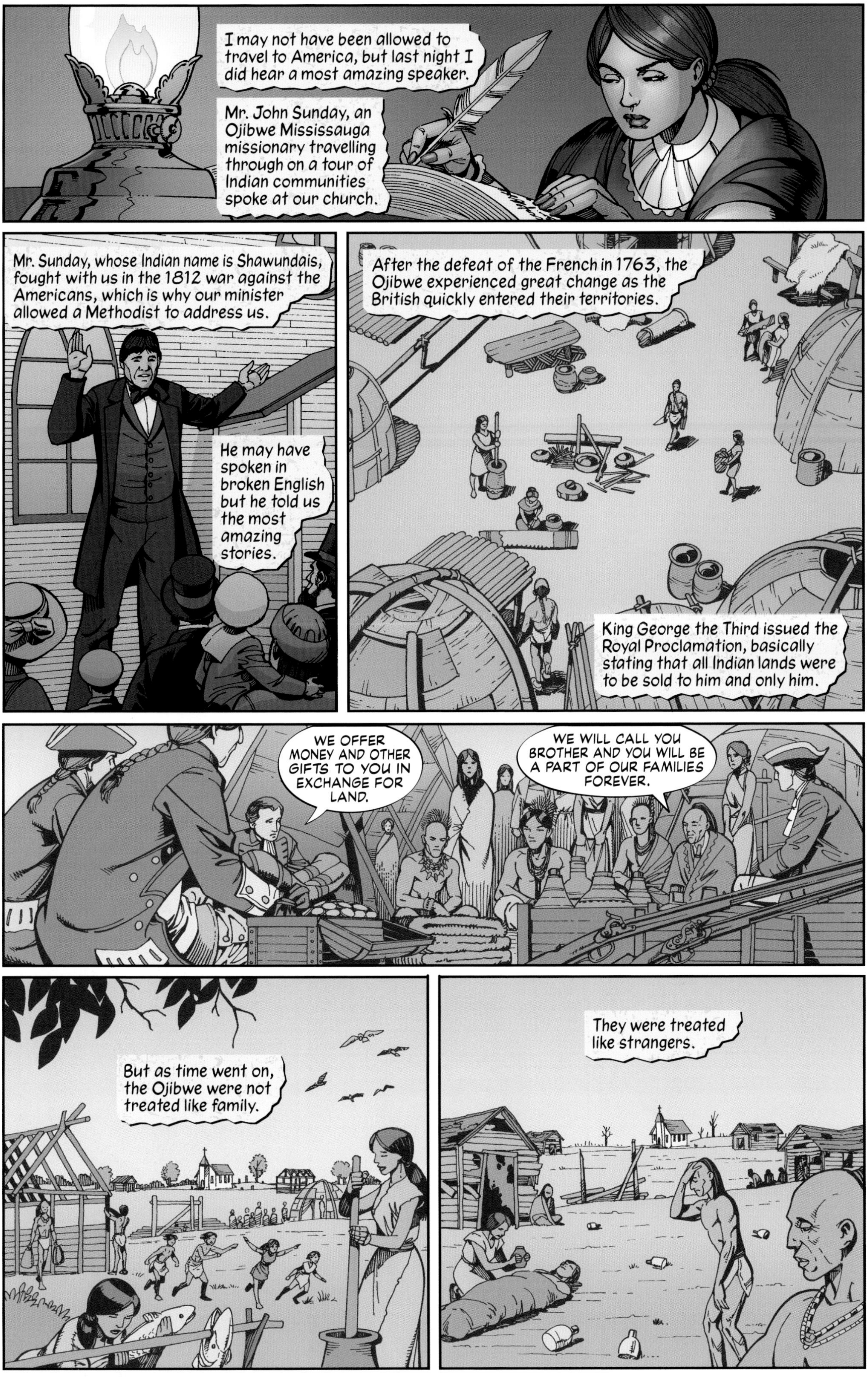
I may not have been allowed to travel to America, but last night I did hear a most amazing speaker.
Mr. John Sunday, an Ojibwe Mississauga missionary travelling through on a tour of Indian communities spoke at our church.
Mr. Sunday, whose Indian name is Shawundais, fought with us in the 1812 war against the Americans, which is why our minister allowed a Methodist to address us.
He may have spoken in broken English but he told us the most amazing stories.
After the defeat of the French in 1763, the Ojibwe experienced great change as the British quickly entered their territories.
King George the Third issued the Royal Proclamation, basically stating that all Indian lands were to be sold to him and only him.
WE OFFER MONEY AND OTHER GIFTS TO YOU IN EXCHANGE FOR LAND.
WE WILL CALL YOU BROTHER AND YOU WILL BE A PART OF OUR FAMILIES FOREVER.
But as time went on, the Ojibwe were not treated like family.
They were treated like strangers.

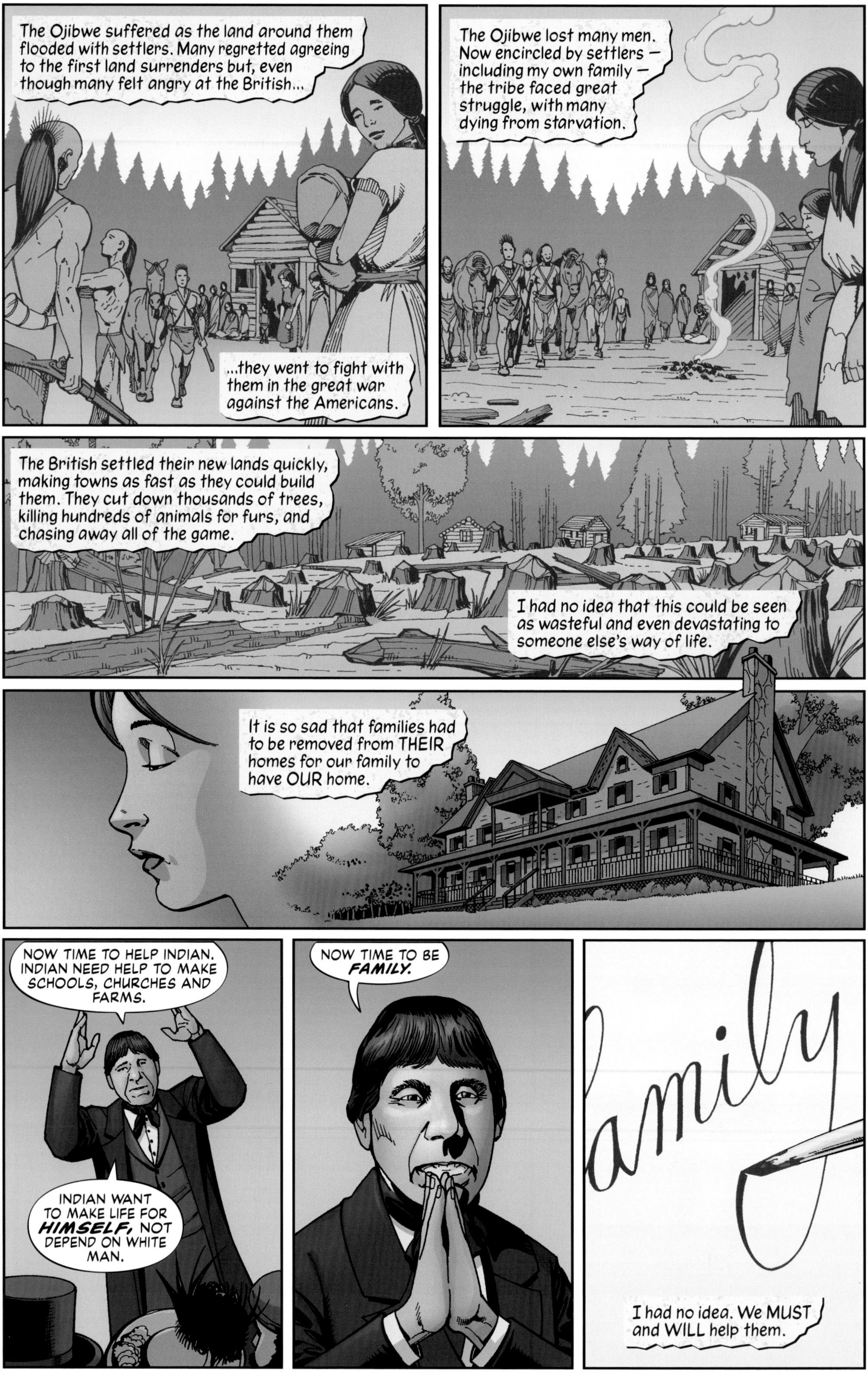
The Ojibwe suffered as the land around them flooded with settlers. Many regretted agreeing to the first land surrenders but, even though many felt angry at the British...
...they went to fight with them in the great war against the Americans.
The Ojibwe lost many men. Now encircled by settlers — including my own family — the tribe faced great struggle, with many dying from starvation.
The British settled their new lands quickly, making towns as fast as they could build them. They cut down thousands of trees, killing hundreds of animals for furs, and chasing away all of the game.
I had no idea that this could be seen as wasteful and even devastating to someone else's way of life.
It is so sad that families had to be removed from THEIR homes for our family to have OUR home.
NOW TIME TO HELP INDIAN. INDIAN NEED HELP TO MAKE SCHOOLS, CHURCHES AND FARMS.
INDIAN WANT TO MAKE LIFE FOR HIMSELF, NOT DEPEND ON WHITE MAN.
NOW TIME TO BE FAMILY.
amily
I had no idea. We MUST and WILL help them.

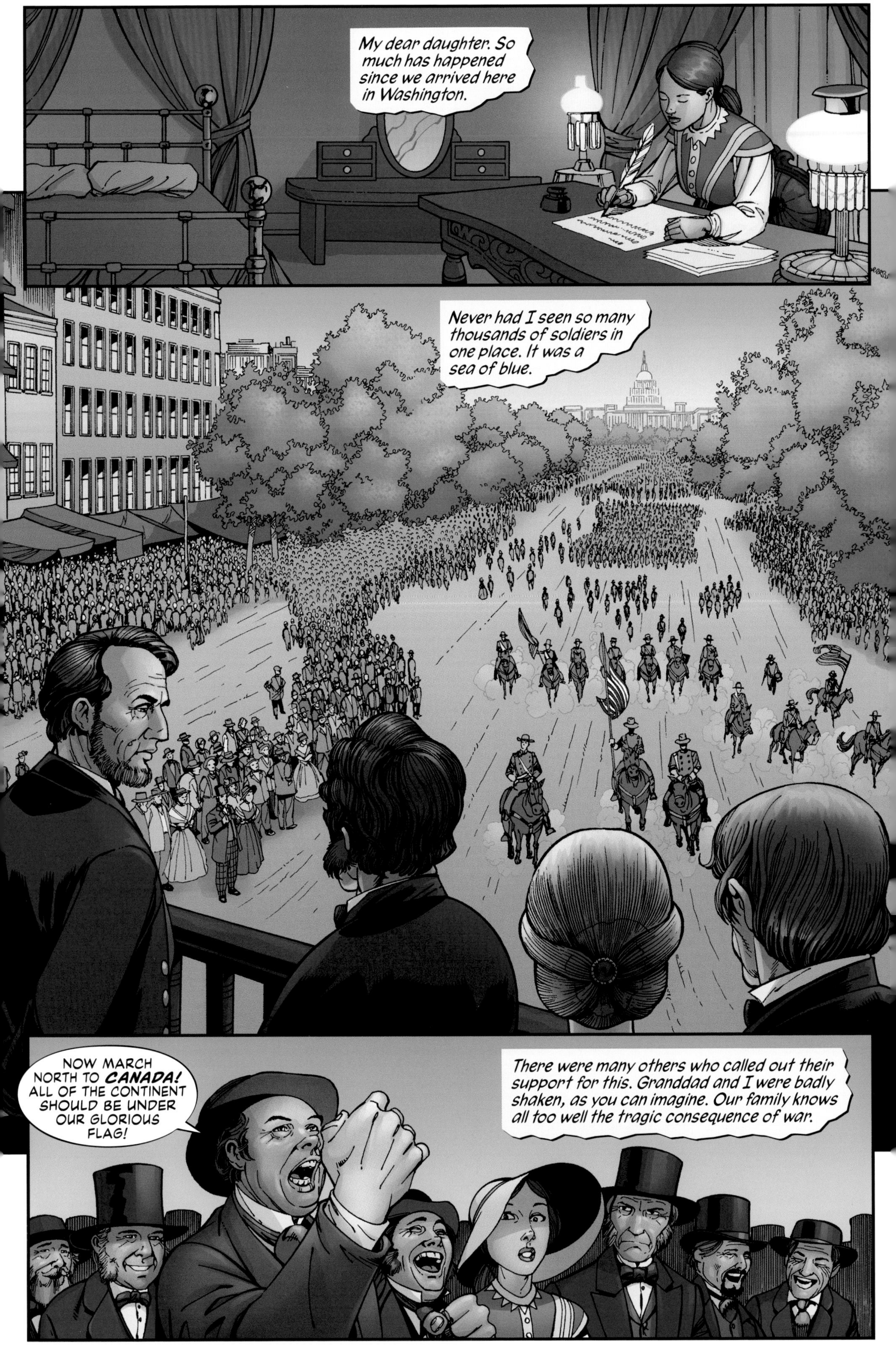
My dear daughter. So much has happened since we arrived here in Washington.
Never had I seen so many thousands of soldiers in one place. It was a sea of blue.
NOW MARCH NORTH TO **CANADA!** ALL OF THE CONTINENT SHOULD BE UNDER OUR GLORIOUS FLAG!
There were many others who called out their support for this. Granddad and I were badly shaken, as you can imagine. Our family knows all too well the tragic consequence of war.

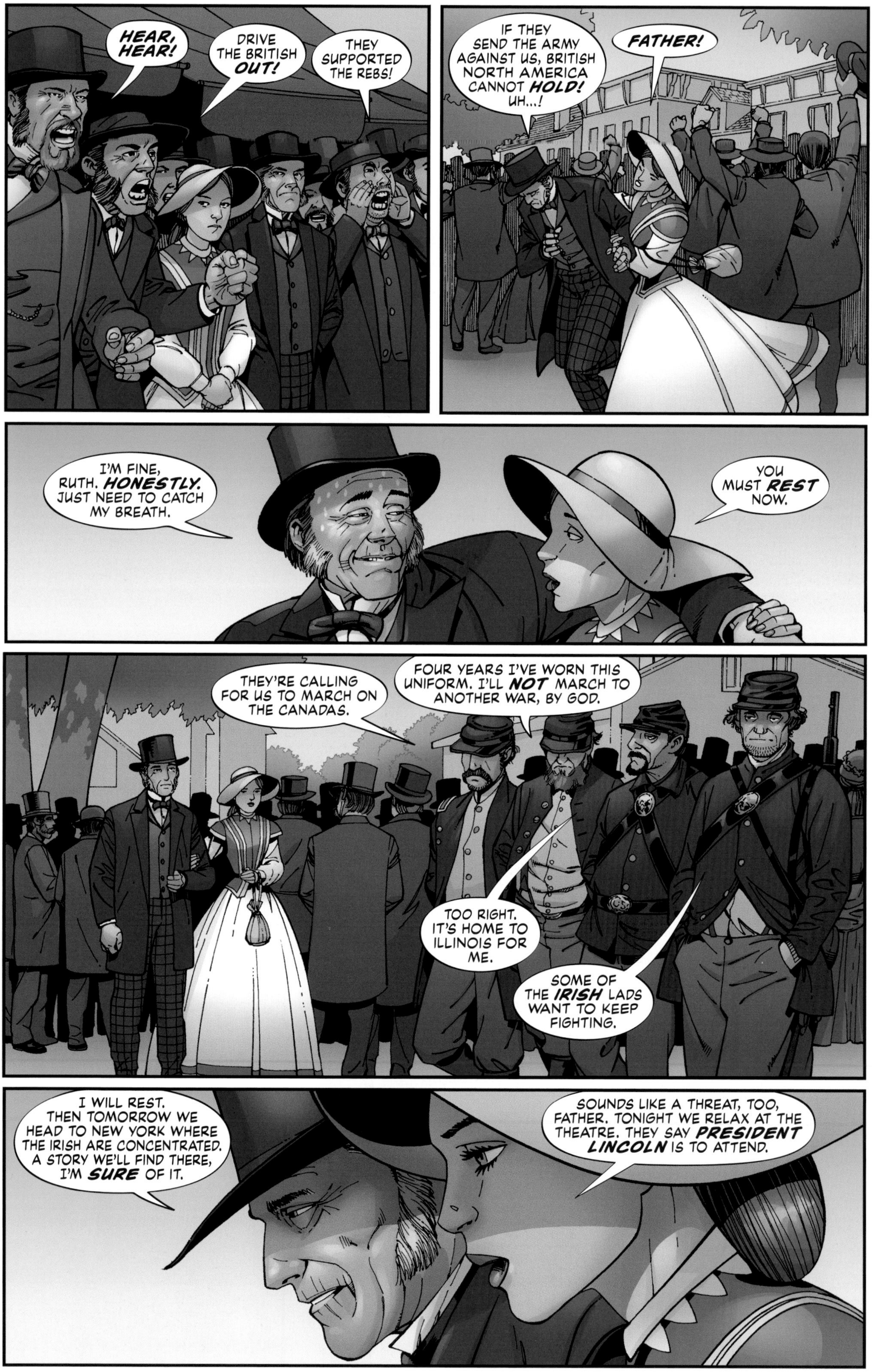
HEAR, HEAR!
DRIVE THE BRITISH OUT!
THEY SUPPORTED THE REBS!
IF THEY SEND THE ARMY AGAINST US, BRITISH NORTH AMERICA CANNOT HOLD! UH...!
FATHER!
I'M FINE, RUTH. HONESTLY. JUST NEED TO CATCH MY BREATH.
YOU MUST REST NOW.
THEY'RE CALLING FOR US TO MARCH ON THE CANADAS.
FOUR YEARS I'VE WORN THIS UNIFORM. I'LL NOT MARCH TO ANOTHER WAR, BY GOD.
TOO RIGHT. IT'S HOME TO ILLINOIS FOR ME.
SOME OF THE IRISH LADS WANT TO KEEP FIGHTING.
I WILL REST. THEN TOMORROW WE HEAD TO NEW YORK WHERE THE IRISH ARE CONCENTRATED. A STORY WE'LL FIND THERE, I'M SURE OF IT.
SOUNDS LIKE A THREAT, TOO, FATHER. TONIGHT WE RELAX AT THE THEATRE. THEY SAY PRESIDENT LINCOLN IS TO ATTEND.

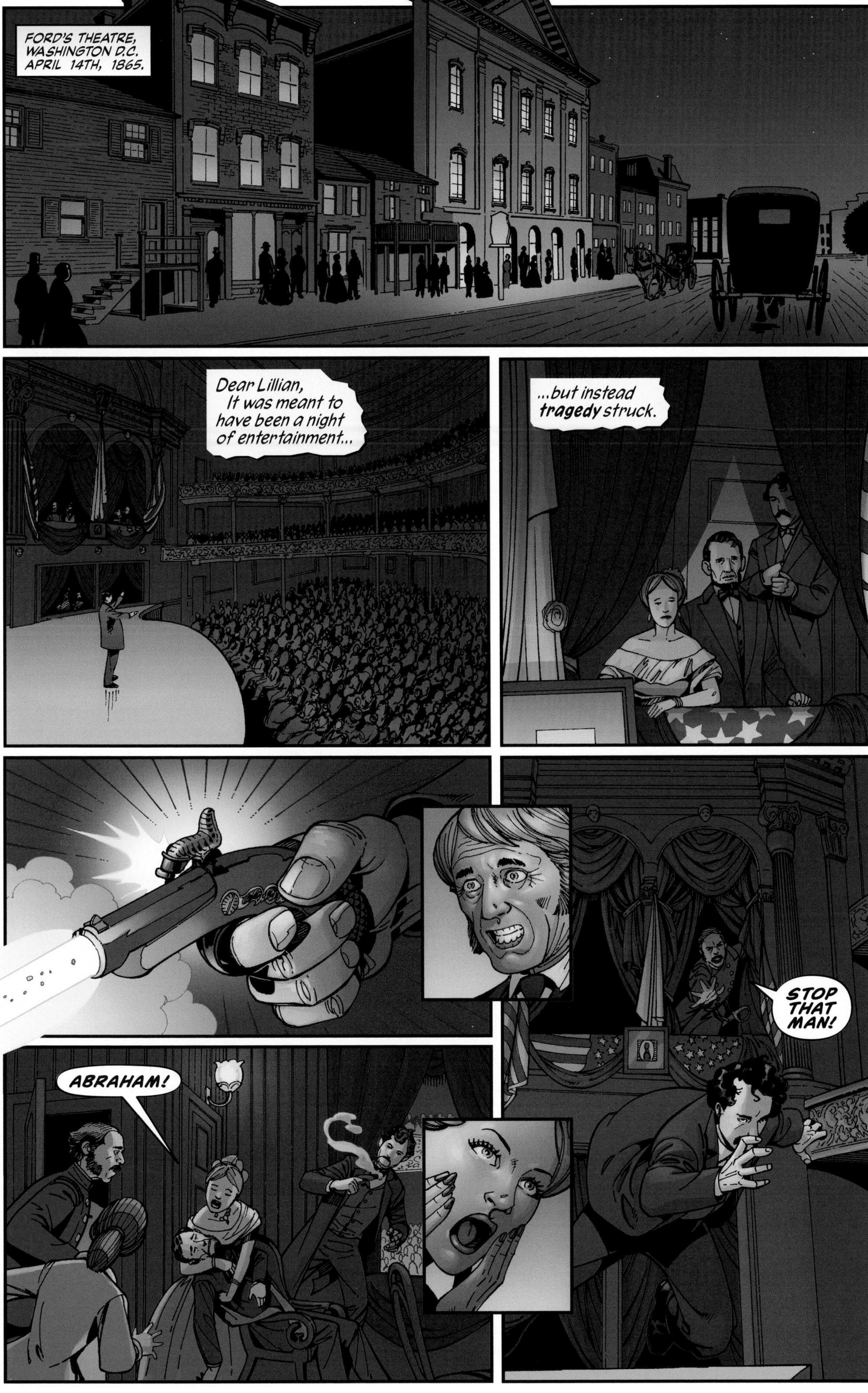
FORD'S THEATRE, WASHINGTON D.C. APRIL 14TH, 1865.
Dear Lillian, It was meant to have been a night of entertainment...
...but instead tragedy struck.
STOP THAT MAN!
ABRAHAM!

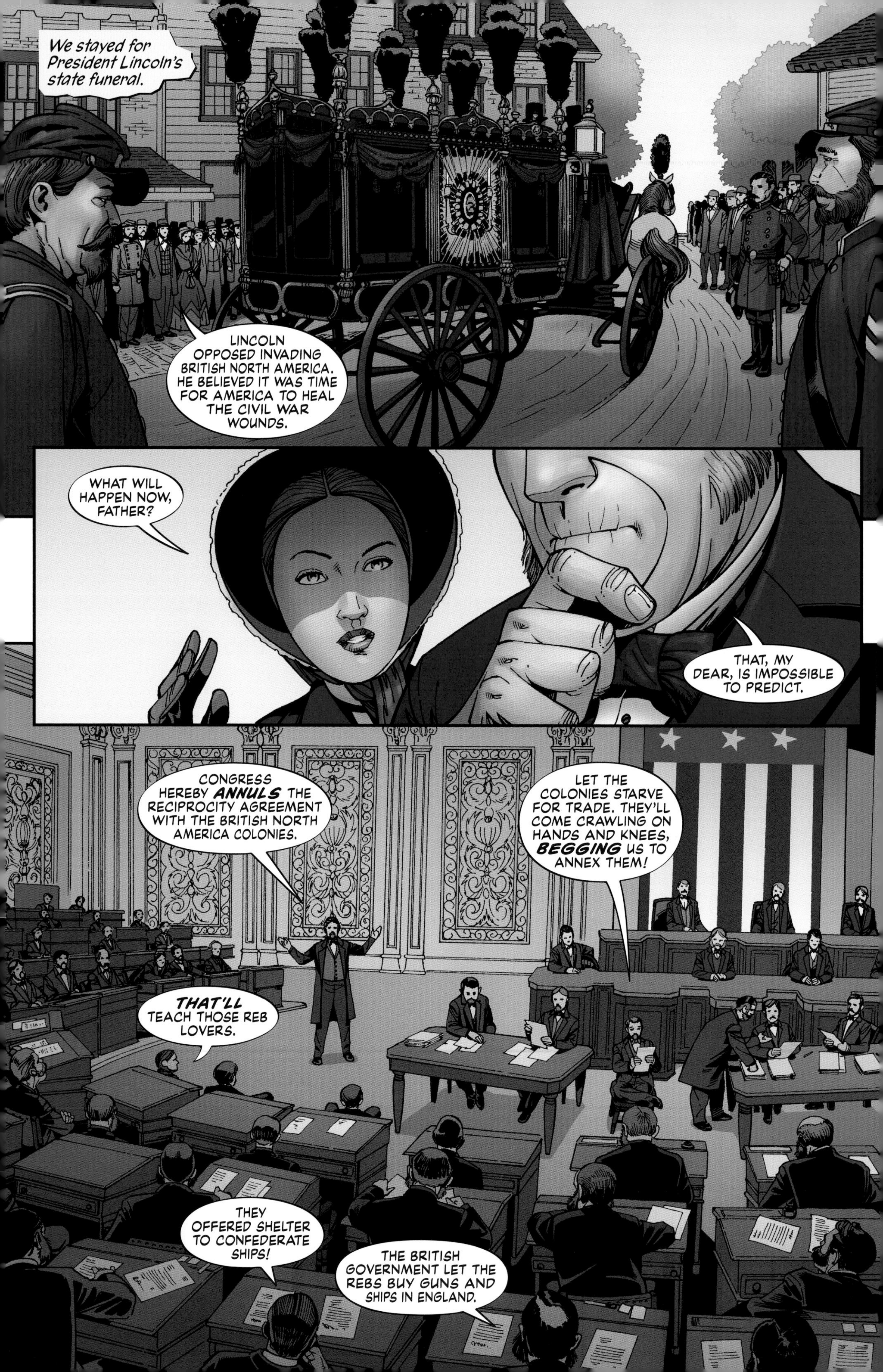
We stayed for President Lincoln's state funeral.
LINCOLN OPPOSED INVADING BRITISH NORTH AMERICA. HE BELIEVED IT WAS TIME FOR AMERICA TO HEAL THE CIVIL WAR WOUNDS.
WHAT WILL HAPPEN NOW, FATHER?
THAT, MY DEAR, IS IMPOSSIBLE TO PREDICT.
CONGRESS HEREBY ANNULS THE RECIPROCITY AGREEMENT WITH THE BRITISH NORTH AMERICA COLONIES.
LET THE COLONIES STARVE FOR TRADE. THEY'LL COME CRAWLING ON HANDS AND KNEES, BEGGING US TO ANNEX THEM!
THAT'LL TEACH THOSE REB LOVERS.
THEY OFFERED SHELTER TO CONFEDERATE SHIPS!
THE BRITISH GOVERNMENT LET THE REBS BUY GUNS AND SHIPS IN ENGLAND.

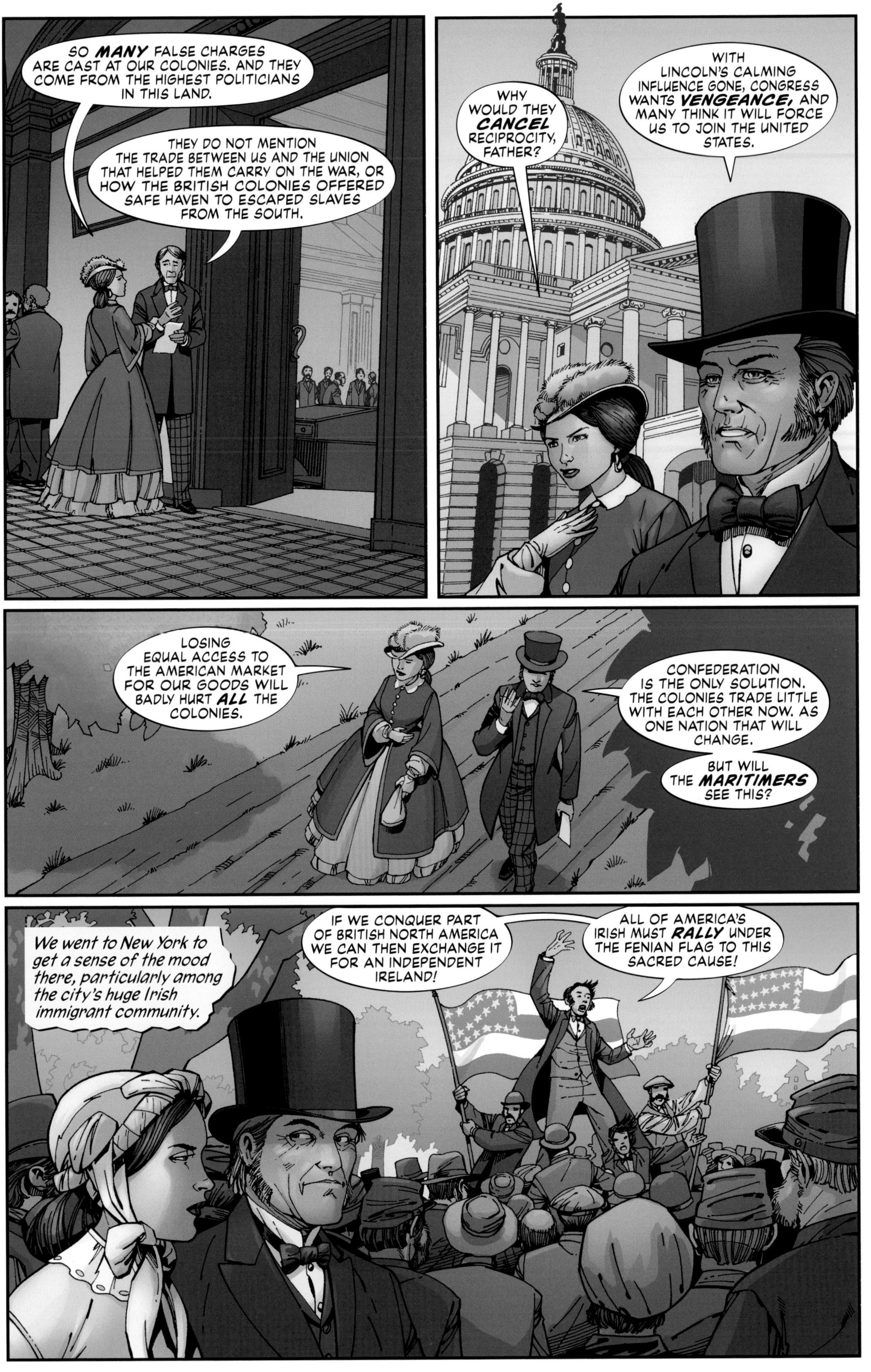
SO MANY FALSE CHARGES ARE CAST AT OUR COLONIES. AND THEY COME FROM THE HIGHEST POLITICIANS IN THIS LAND.
THEY DO NOT MENTION THE TRADE BETWEEN US AND THE UNION THAT HELPED THEM CARRY ON THE WAR, OR HOW THE BRITISH COLONIES OFFERED SAFE HAVEN TO ESCAPED SLAVES FROM THE SOUTH.
WHY WOULD THEY CANCEL RECIPROCITY, FATHER?
WITH LINCOLN'S CALMING INFLUENCE GONE, CONGRESS WANTS VENGEANCE, AND MANY THINK IT WILL FORCE US TO JOIN THE UNITED STATES.
LOSING EQUAL ACCESS TO THE AMERICAN MARKET FOR OUR GOODS WILL BADLY HURT ALL THE COLONIES.
CONFEDERATION IS THE ONLY SOLUTION. THE COLONIES TRADE LITTLE WITH EACH OTHER NOW. AS ONE NATION THAT WILL CHANGE.
BUT WILL THE MARITIMERS SEE THIS?
We went to New York to get a sense of the mood there, particularly among the city's huge Irish immigrant community.
IF WE CONQUER PART OF BRITISH NORTH AMERICA WE CAN THEN EXCHANGE IT FOR AN INDEPENDENT IRELAND!
ALL OF AMERICA'S IRISH MUST RALLY UNDER THE FENIAN FLAG TO THIS SACRED CAUSE!

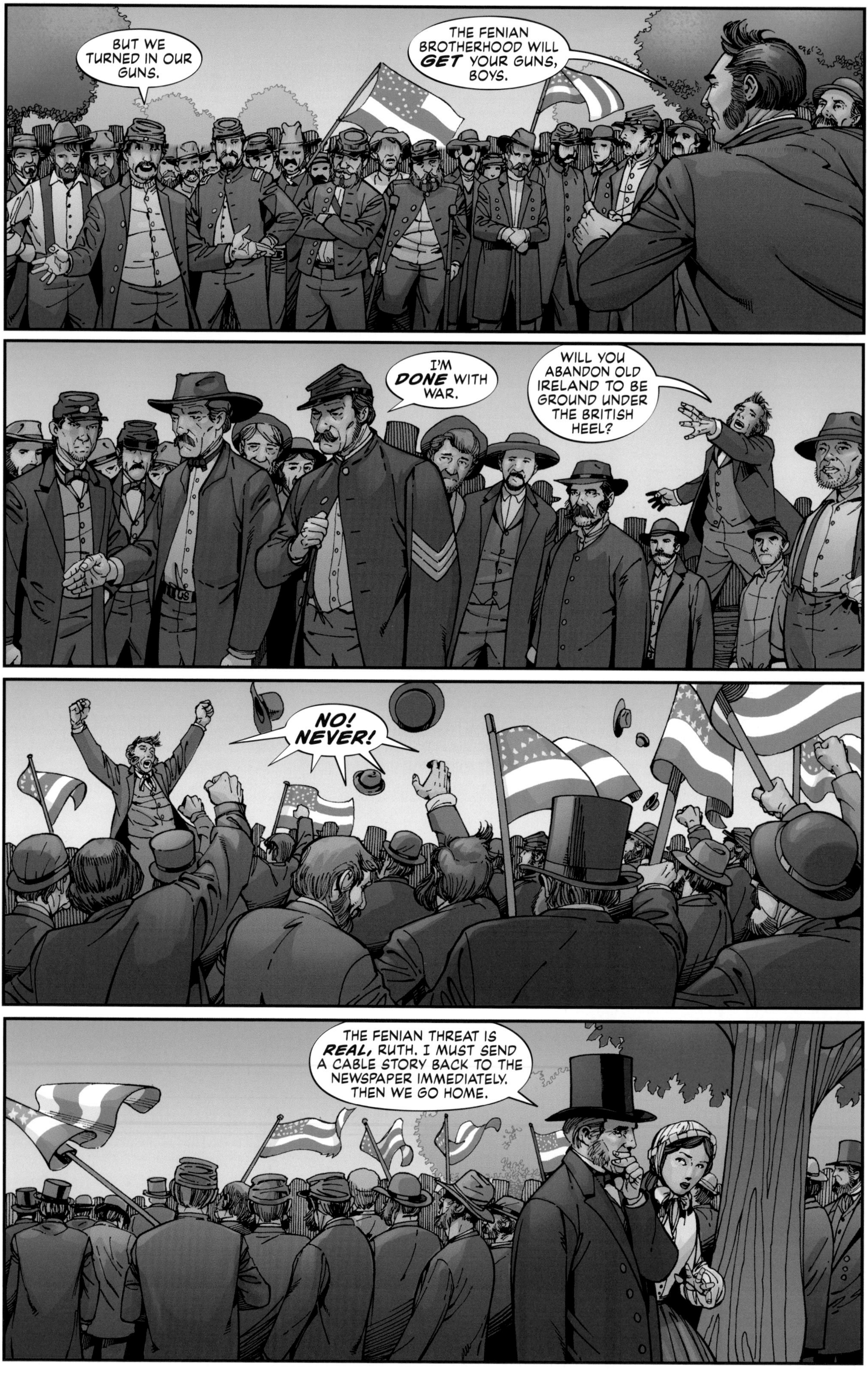
BUT WE TURNED IN OUR GUNS.
THE FENIAN BROTHERHOOD WILL GET YOUR GUNS, BOYS.
I'M DONE WITH WAR.
WILL YOU ABANDON OLD IRELAND TO BE GROUND UNDER THE BRITISH HEEL?
NO! NEVER!
THE FENIAN THREAT IS REAL, RUTH. I MUST SEND A CABLE STORY BACK TO THE NEWSPAPER IMMEDIATELY. THEN WE GO HOME.

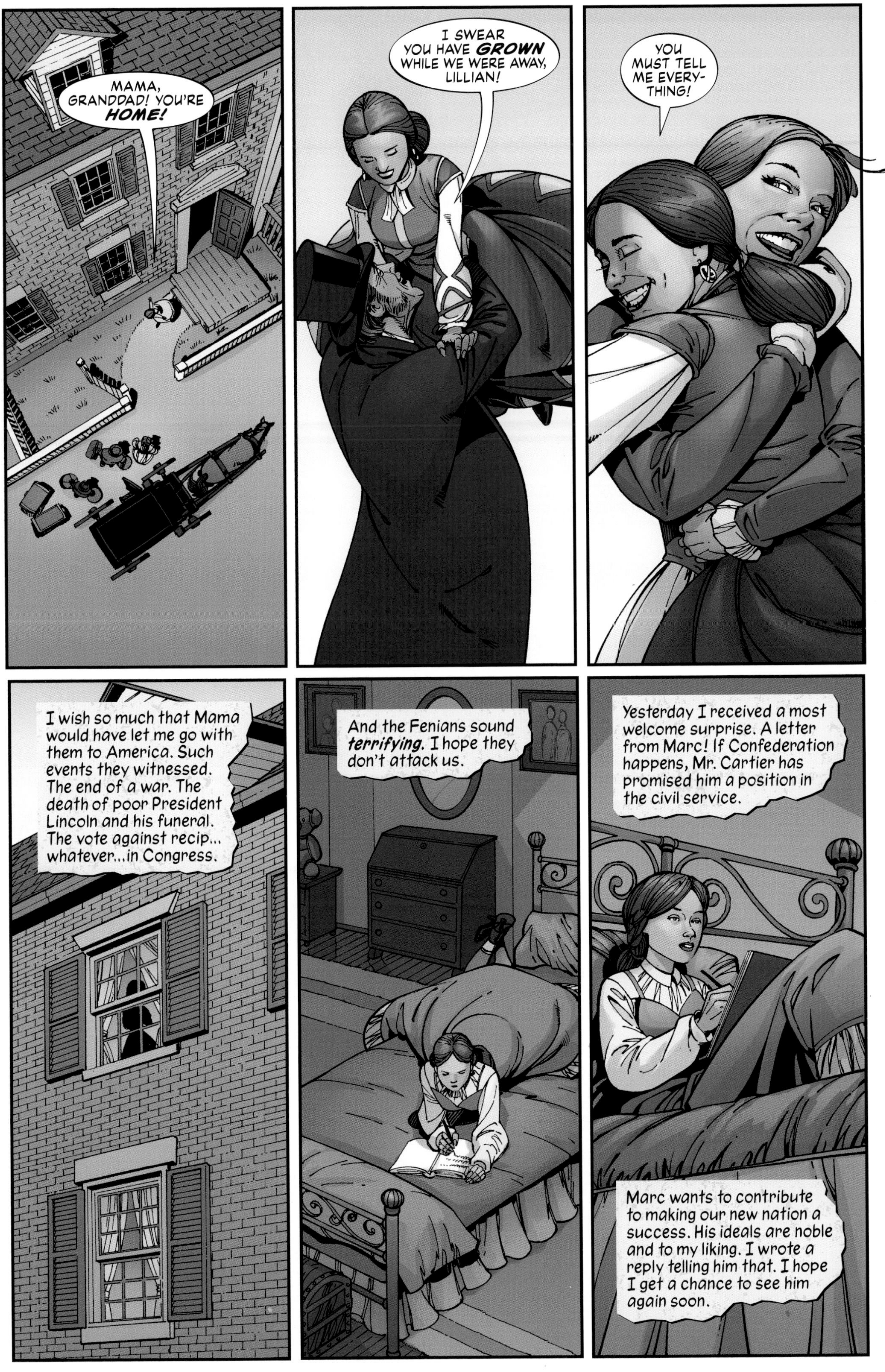
MAMA, GRANDDAD! YOU'RE *HOME!*
I SWEAR YOU HAVE *GROWN* WHILE WE WERE AWAY, LILLIAN!
YOU MUST TELL ME EVERY-THING!
I wish so much that Mama would have let me go with them to America. Such events they witnessed. The end of a war. The death of poor President Lincoln and his funeral. The vote against recip... whatever...in Congress.
And the Fenians sound *terrifying*. I hope they don't attack us.
Yesterday I received a most welcome surprise. A letter from Marc! If Confederation happens, Mr. Cartier has promised him a position in the civil service.
Marc wants to contribute to making our new nation a success. His ideals are noble and to my liking. I wrote a reply telling him that. I hope I get a chance to see him again soon.

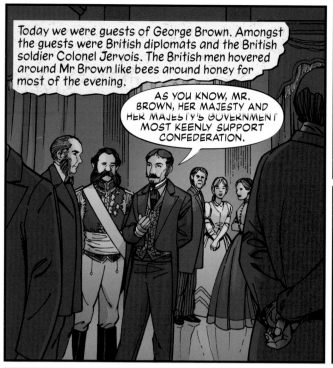

Today we were guests of George Brown. Amongst the guests were British diplomats and the British soldier Colonel Jervois. The British men hovered around Mr Brown like bees around honey for most of the evening.

AS YOU KNOW, MR. BROWN, HER MAJESTY AND HER MAJESTY'S GOVERNMENT MOST KEENLY SUPPORT CONFEDERATION.

FOR YEARS HER MAJESTY'S GOVERNMENT HAS SHOWN ONLY *INDIFFERENCE* TO THE PROBLEMS FACING BRITISH NORTH AMERICA. I FIND THE SUDDEN INTEREST SURPRISING.

NOW SIR, WE ARE LED BY CONCERN FOR HOW BEST TO *DEFEND* THE COLONIES FROM THE THREAT BY THE UNITED STATES.

"I HAVE TOURED THE BORDER BETWEEN OUR COLONIES AND THE UNITED STATES. IF A UNITED CANADA BUILT A NETWORK OF SMALL FORTIFICATIONS ALONG THE BORDER ANY AMERICAN INVASION COULD BE DEFEATED."

AT GETTYSBURG JERVOIS SAID WE COULD NOT HOPE TO DEFEAT AN AMERICAN INVASION. THIS IS A *SHAM*. BUT IT DOES ADD ANOTHER ARGUMENT IN FAVOUR OF CONFEDERATION, AND THAT IS HIS INTENT.

I UNDERSTAND NOTHING OF DEFENSE AND NEITHER DO MOST CANADIANS NOR MARITIMERS, SIR. SO THE ADVICE OF A MILITARY EXPERT IS *MOST* WELCOME!

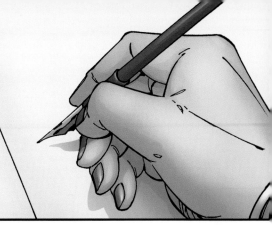

April 1, 1866. The Fenian threat is all the news this spring. The Canadian militia is training with fear that an attack is imminent.

I have heard that in New Brunswick and Nova Scotia, every able-bodied man has been called up for militia training. These are anxious times indeed.

Once again Mama and Granddad have gone off on assignment and left me behind. I am a little cross and very disappointed. I could easily have seen to my studies while traveling. I am just months from being fifteen. Hardly a child!

I correspond regularly with Marc now too, so get all the news about the push for Confederation.

HALIFAX, PREMIER CHARLES TUPPER ADDRESSES THE LEGISLATURE.

THE RESOLUTION IS PASSED. IT IS A SCHEME OF UNION WHICH WILL EFFECTIVELY ENSURE JUST PROVISION FOR THE RIGHTS AND INTERESTS OF THE PROVINCE.

NOVA SCOTIA NOW ENDORSES CONFEDERATION!

HE PUSHED THIS THROUGH IN THE DEAD OF NIGHT WHEN A MAN CAN HARDLY *THINK* STRAIGHT!

EFFECTIVE APRIL 18, 1866, I HEREBY COMMIT NOVA SCOTIA TO PURSUING CONFEDERATION WITH THE *OTHER* BRITISH COLONIES.

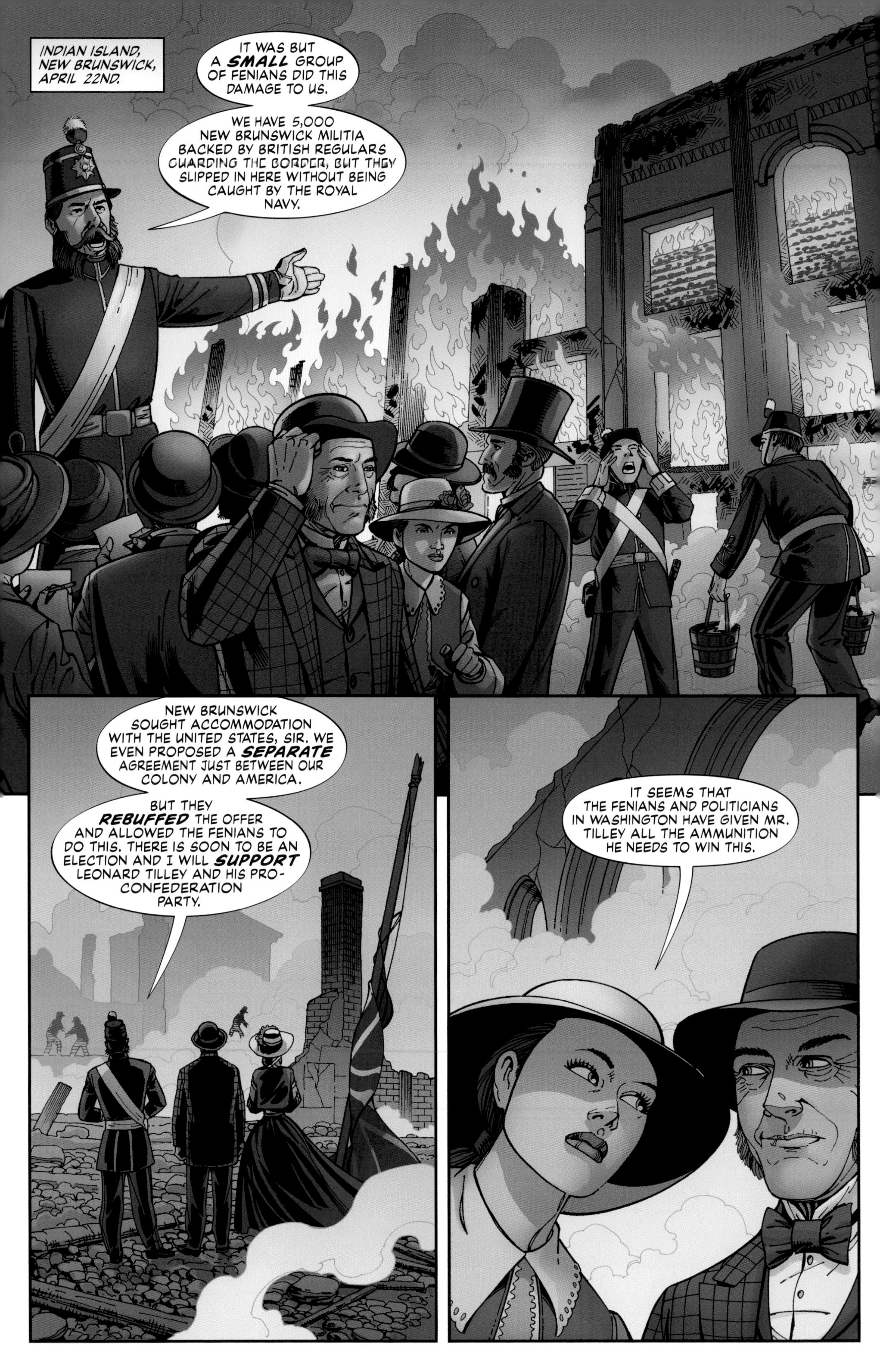
INDIAN ISLAND, NEW BRUNSWICK, APRIL 22ND.
IT WAS BUT A SMALL GROUP OF FENIANS DID THIS DAMAGE TO US.
WE HAVE 5,000 NEW BRUNSWICK MILITIA BACKED BY BRITISH REGULARS GUARDING THE BORDER, BUT THEY SLIPPED IN HERE WITHOUT BEING CAUGHT BY THE ROYAL NAVY.
NEW BRUNSWICK SOUGHT ACCOMMODATION WITH THE UNITED STATES, SIR. WE EVEN PROPOSED A SEPARATE AGREEMENT JUST BETWEEN OUR COLONY AND AMERICA.
BUT THEY REBUFFED THE OFFER AND ALLOWED THE FENIANS TO DO THIS. THERE IS SOON TO BE AN ELECTION AND I WILL SUPPORT LEONARD TILLEY AND HIS PRO-CONFEDERATION PARTY.
IT SEEMS THAT THE FENIANS AND POLITICIANS IN WASHINGTON HAVE GIVEN MR. TILLEY ALL THE AMMUNITION HE NEEDS TO WIN THIS.

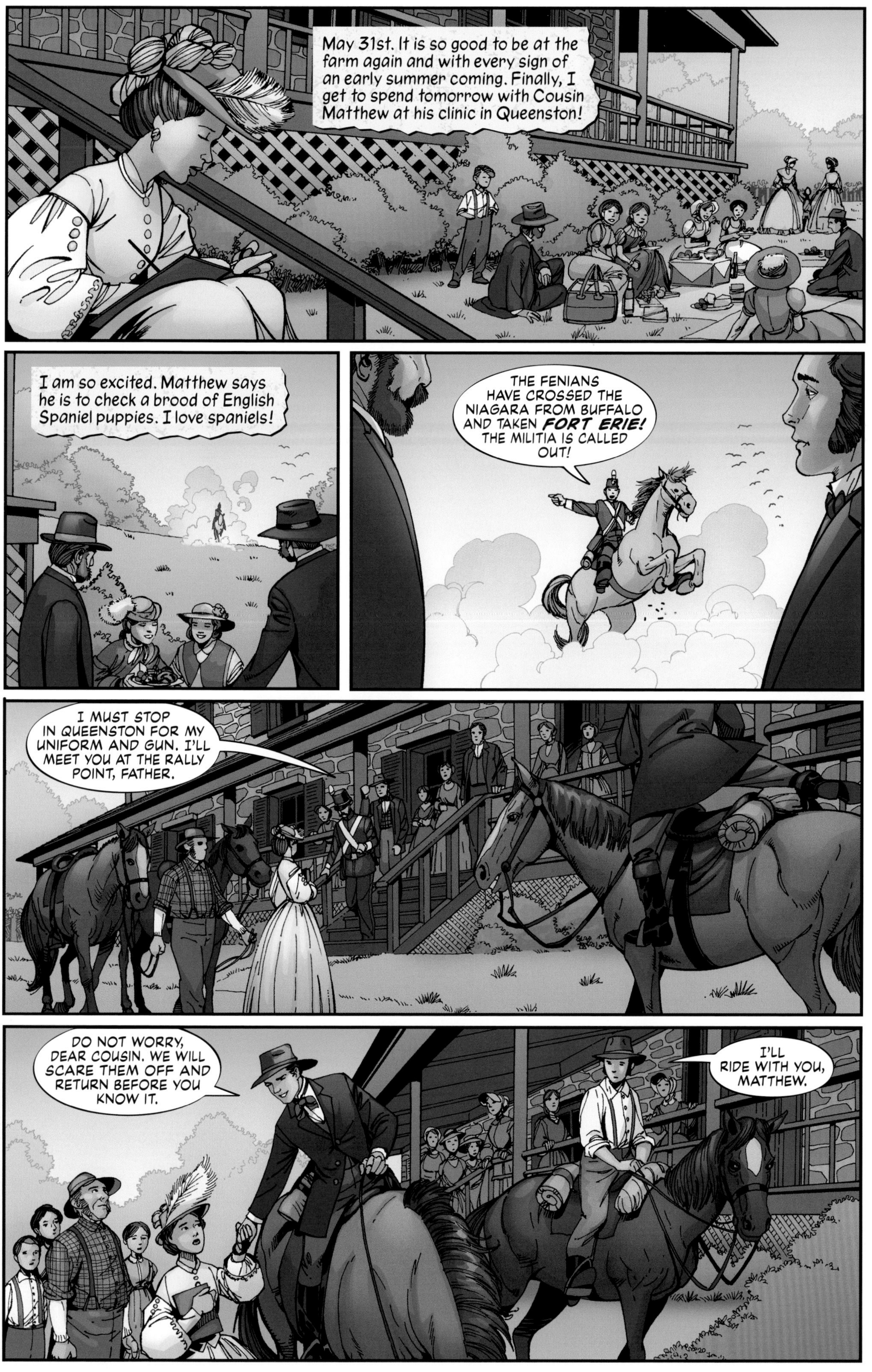
May 31st. It is so good to be at the farm again and with every sign of an early summer coming. Finally, I get to spend tomorrow with Cousin Matthew at his clinic in Queenston!
I am so excited. Matthew says he is to check a brood of English Spaniel puppies. I love spaniels!
THE FENIANS HAVE CROSSED THE NIAGARA FROM BUFFALO AND TAKEN FORT ERIE! THE MILITIA IS CALLED OUT!
I MUST STOP IN QUEENSTON FOR MY UNIFORM AND GUN. I'LL MEET YOU AT THE RALLY POINT, FATHER.
DO NOT WORRY, DEAR COUSIN. WE WILL SCARE THEM OFF AND RETURN BEFORE YOU KNOW IT.
I'LL RIDE WITH YOU, MATTHEW.

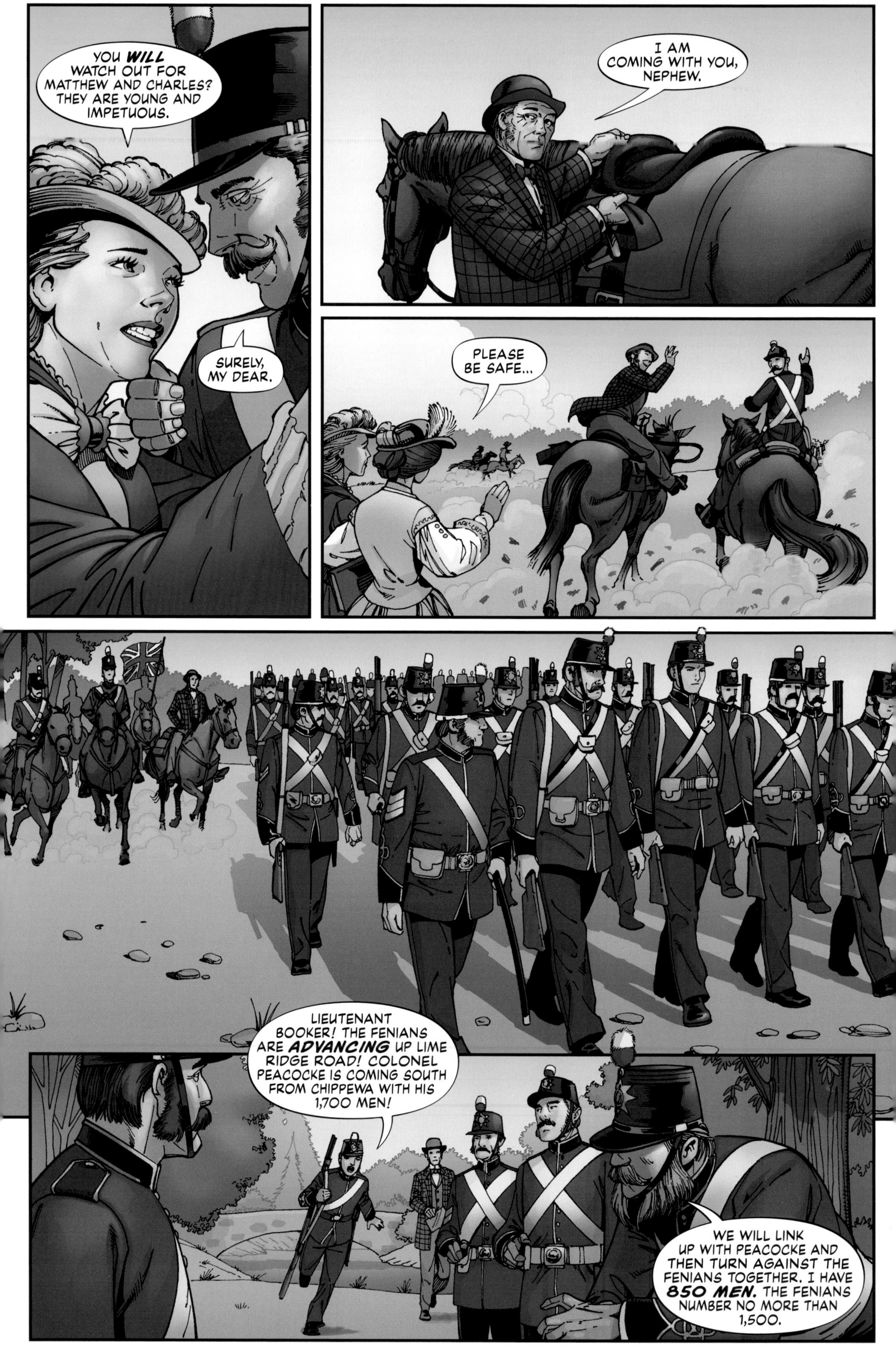
YOU WILL WATCH OUT FOR MATTHEW AND CHARLES? THEY ARE YOUNG AND IMPETUOUS.
SURELY, MY DEAR.
I AM COMING WITH YOU, NEPHEW.
PLEASE BE SAFE...
LIEUTENANT BOOKER! THE FENIANS ARE ADVANCING UP LIME RIDGE ROAD! COLONEL PEACOCKE IS COMING SOUTH FROM CHIPPEWA WITH HIS 1,700 MEN!
WE WILL LINK UP WITH PEACOCKE AND THEN TURN AGAINST THE FENIANS TOGETHER. I HAVE 850 MEN. THE FENIANS NUMBER NO MORE THAN 1,500.

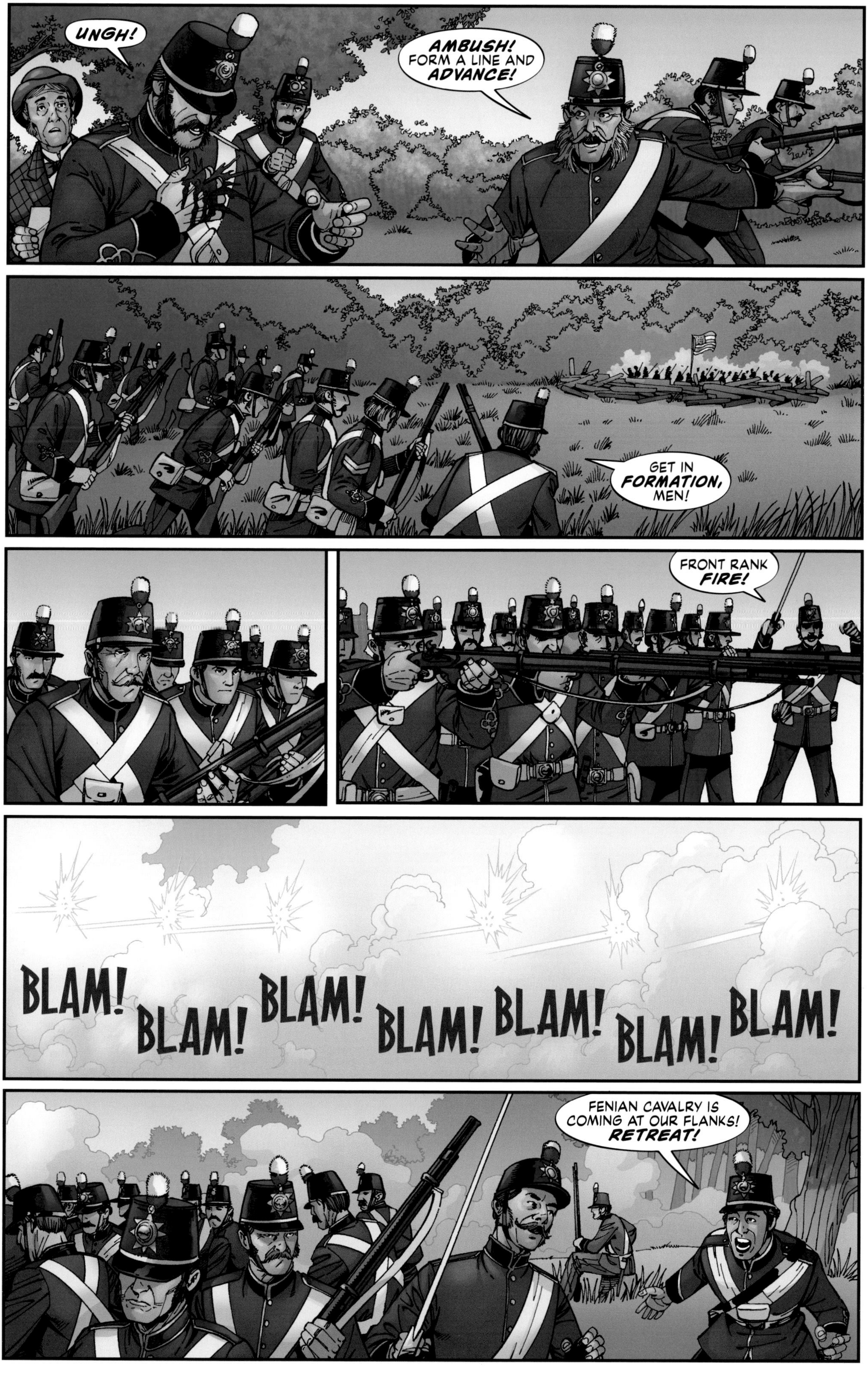
UNGH!
AMBUSH! FORM A LINE AND ADVANCE!
GET IN FORMATION, MEN!
FRONT RANK FIRE!
BLAM! BLAM! BLAM! BLAM! BLAM! BLAM! BLAM!
FENIAN CAVALRY IS COMING AT OUR FLANKS! RETREAT!

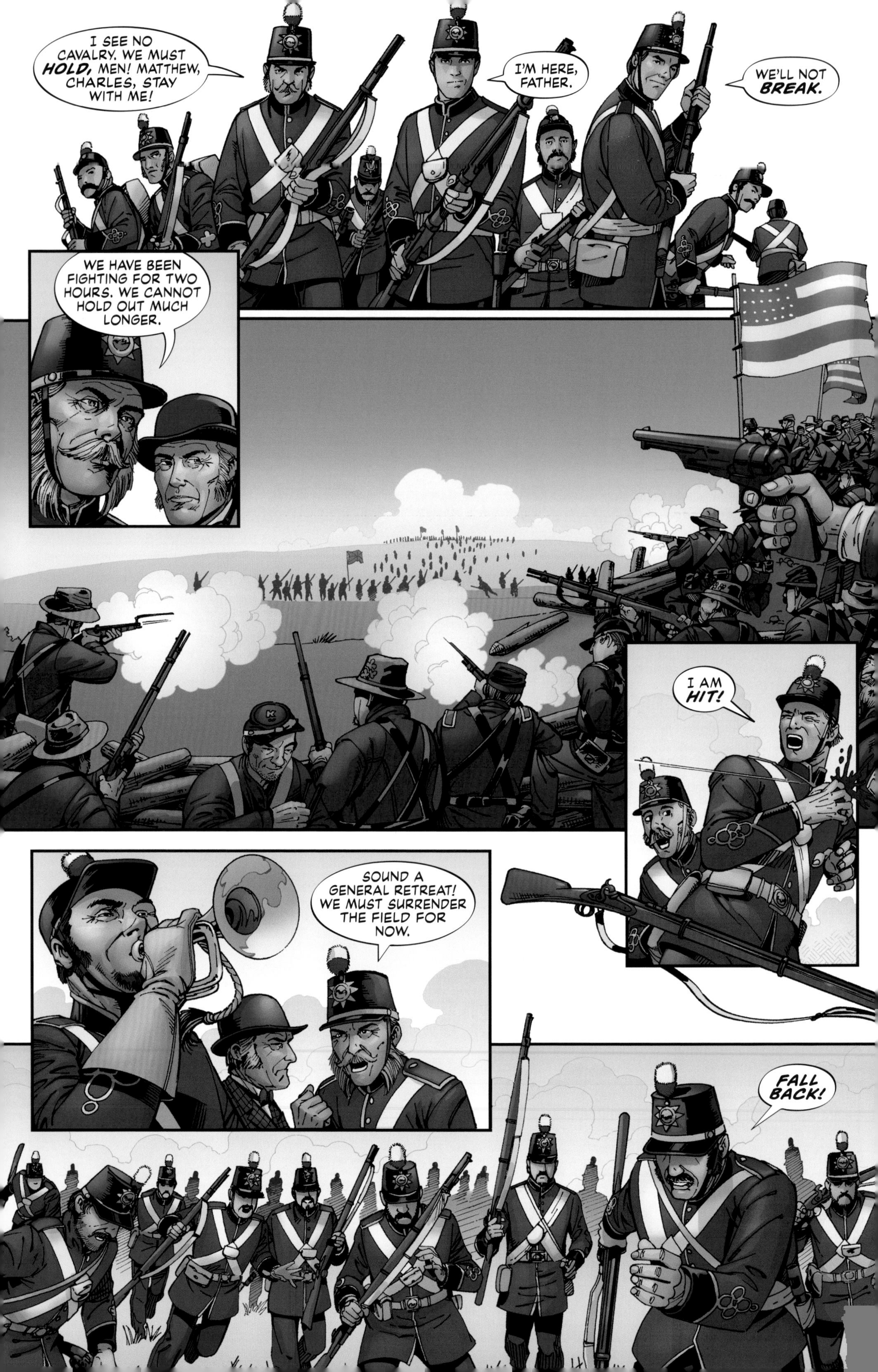
I SEE NO CAVALRY. WE MUST HOLD, MEN! MATTHEW, CHARLES, STAY WITH ME!
I'M HERE, FATHER.
WE'LL NOT BREAK.
WE HAVE BEEN FIGHTING FOR TWO HOURS. WE CANNOT HOLD OUT MUCH LONGER.
I AM HIT!
SOUND A GENERAL RETREAT! WE MUST SURRENDER THE FIELD FOR NOW.
FALL BACK!

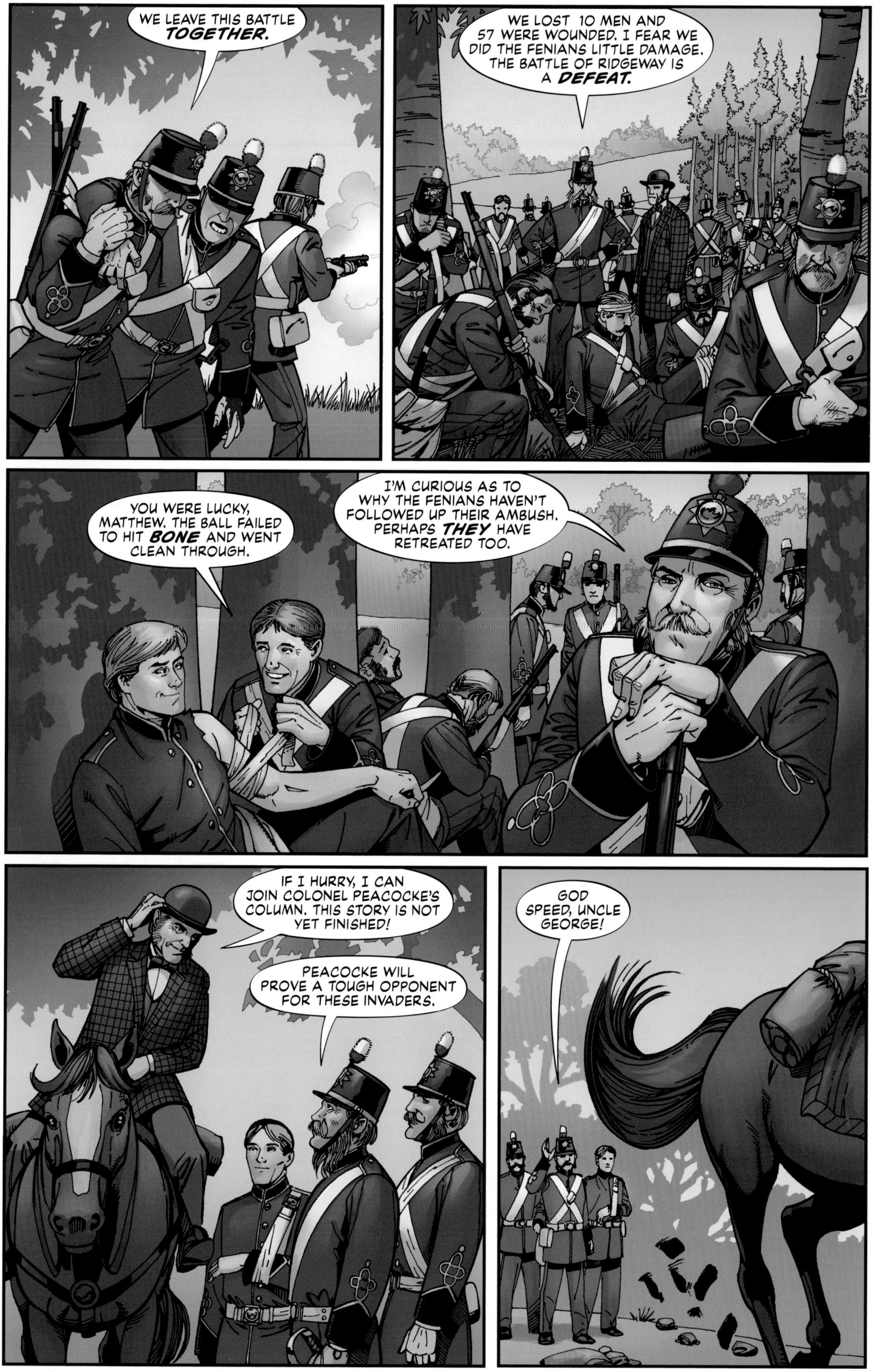
WE LEAVE THIS BATTLE TOGETHER.
WE LOST 10 MEN AND 57 WERE WOUNDED. I FEAR WE DID THE FENIANS LITTLE DAMAGE. THE BATTLE OF RIDGEWAY IS A DEFEAT.
YOU WERE LUCKY, MATTHEW. THE BALL FAILED TO HIT BONE AND WENT CLEAN THROUGH.
I'M CURIOUS AS TO WHY THE FENIANS HAVEN'T FOLLOWED UP THEIR AMBUSH. PERHAPS THEY HAVE RETREATED TOO.
IF I HURRY, I CAN JOIN COLONEL PEACOCKE'S COLUMN. THIS STORY IS NOT YET FINISHED!
PEACOCKE WILL PROVE A TOUGH OPPONENT FOR THESE INVADERS.
GOD SPEED, UNCLE GEORGE!

I WAS TOO LATE FOR THE RIDGEWAY BATTLE. BOOKER WAS BEATEN?

YES, BUT THE FENIANS RETREATED TOO.

GOOD. I HOPE TO BRING THEM TO BATTLE AT FORT ERIE.

THE FENIANS ARE *ESCAPING*, COLONEL!

TAKE PRISONERS, MEN!

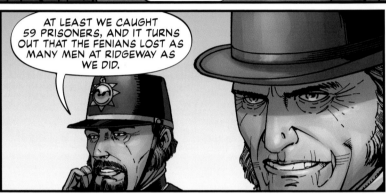

AT LEAST WE CAUGHT 59 PRISONERS, AND IT TURNS OUT THAT THE FENIANS LOST AS MANY MEN AT RIDGEWAY AS WE DID.

"I HOPE WE CAN DECLARE THAT JUNE 2nd SAW THE FENIAN FORCES DEFEATED."

SOON...

THEY'RE *BACK!*

OH, MATTHEW!

FEAR NOT, MOTHER. I'M FINE.

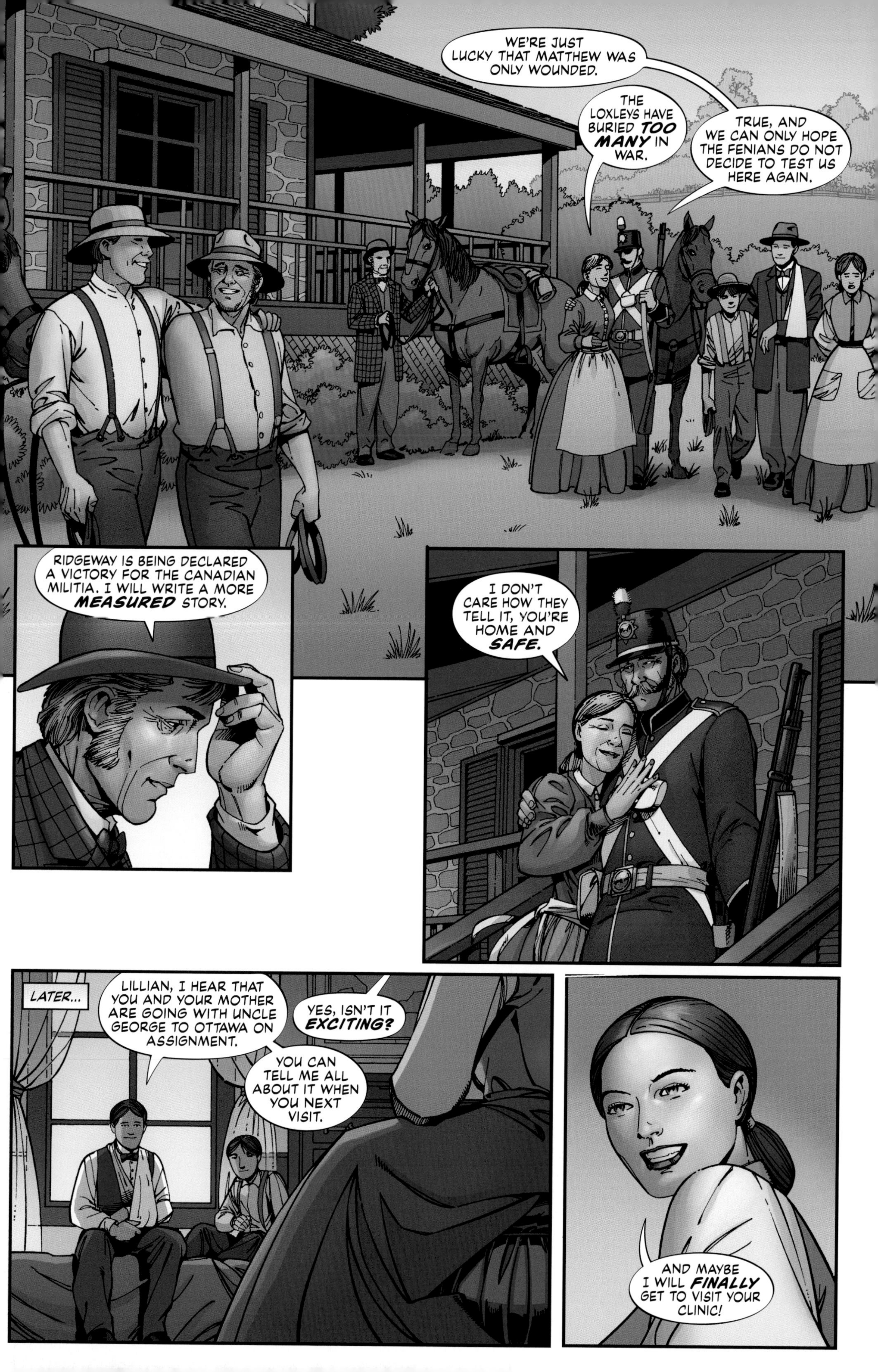
WE'RE JUST LUCKY THAT MATTHEW WAS ONLY WOUNDED.
THE LOXLEYS HAVE BURIED TOO MANY IN WAR.
TRUE, AND WE CAN ONLY HOPE THE FENIANS DO NOT DECIDE TO TEST US HERE AGAIN.
RIDGEWAY IS BEING DECLARED A VICTORY FOR THE CANADIAN MILITIA. I WILL WRITE A MORE MEASURED STORY.
I DON'T CARE HOW THEY TELL IT, YOU'RE HOME AND SAFE.
LATER...
LILLIAN, I HEAR THAT YOU AND YOUR MOTHER ARE GOING WITH UNCLE GEORGE TO OTTAWA ON ASSIGNMENT.
YES, ISN'T IT EXCITING?
YOU CAN TELL ME ALL ABOUT IT WHEN YOU NEXT VISIT.
AND MAYBE I WILL FINALLY GET TO VISIT YOUR CLINIC!

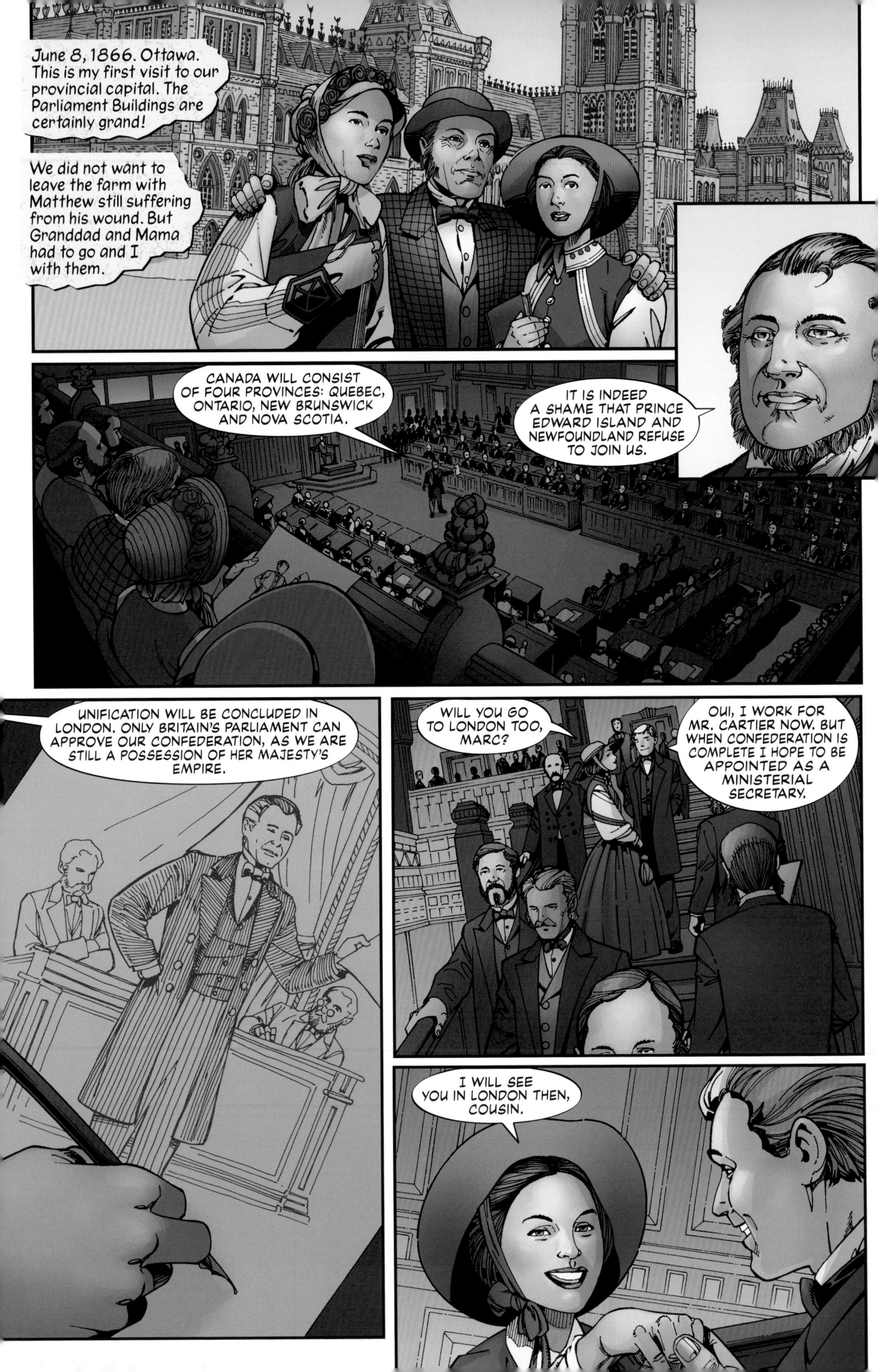
June 8, 1866. Ottawa. This is my first visit to our provincial capital. The Parliament Buildings are certainly grand!
We did not want to leave the farm with Matthew still suffering from his wound. But Granddad and Mama had to go and I with them.
CANADA WILL CONSIST OF FOUR PROVINCES: QUEBEC, ONTARIO, NEW BRUNSWICK AND NOVA SCOTIA.
IT IS INDEED A SHAME THAT PRINCE EDWARD ISLAND AND NEWFOUNDLAND REFUSE TO JOIN US.
UNIFICATION WILL BE CONCLUDED IN LONDON. ONLY BRITAIN'S PARLIAMENT CAN APPROVE OUR CONFEDERATION, AS WE ARE STILL A POSSESSION OF HER MAJESTY'S EMPIRE.
WILL YOU GO TO LONDON TOO, MARC?
OUI, I WORK FOR MR. CARTIER NOW. BUT WHEN CONFEDERATION IS COMPLETE I HOPE TO BE APPOINTED AS A MINISTERIAL SECRETARY.
I WILL SEE YOU IN LONDON THEN, COUSIN.

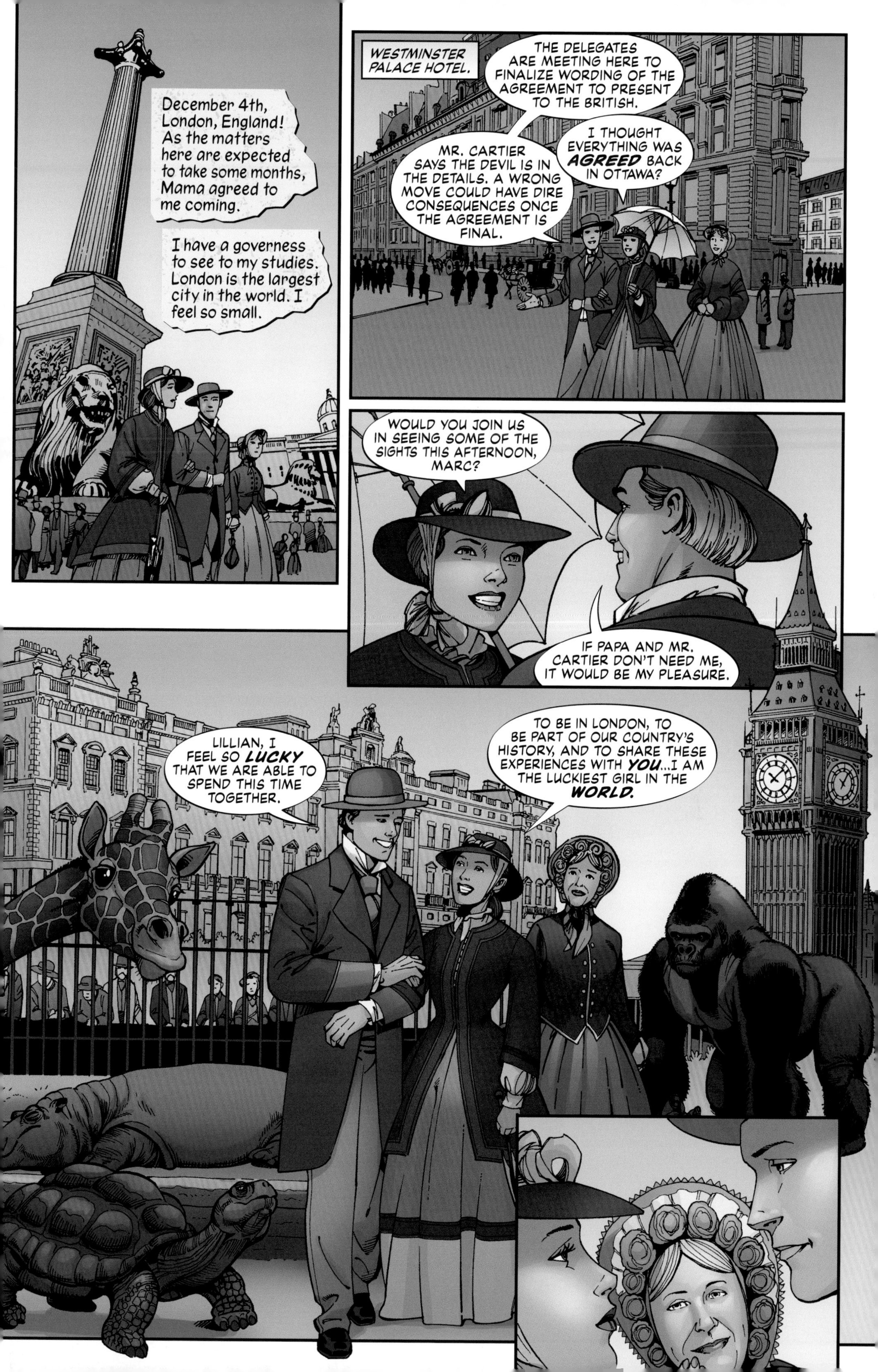
December 4th, London, England! As the matters here are expected to take some months, Mama agreed to me coming.
I have a governess to see to my studies. London is the largest city in the world. I feel so small.
WESTMINSTER PALACE HOTEL.
THE DELEGATES ARE MEETING HERE TO FINALIZE WORDING OF THE AGREEMENT TO PRESENT TO THE BRITISH.
I THOUGHT EVERYTHING WAS AGREED BACK IN OTTAWA?
MR. CARTIER SAYS THE DEVIL IS IN THE DETAILS. A WRONG MOVE COULD HAVE DIRE CONSEQUENCES ONCE THE AGREEMENT IS FINAL.
WOULD YOU JOIN US IN SEEING SOME OF THE SIGHTS THIS AFTERNOON, MARC?
IF PAPA AND MR. CARTIER DON'T NEED ME, IT WOULD BE MY PLEASURE.
LILLIAN, I FEEL SO LUCKY THAT WE ARE ABLE TO SPEND THIS TIME TOGETHER.
TO BE IN LONDON, TO BE PART OF OUR COUNTRY'S HISTORY, AND TO SHARE THESE EXPERIENCES WITH YOU...I AM THE LUCKIEST GIRL IN THE WORLD.

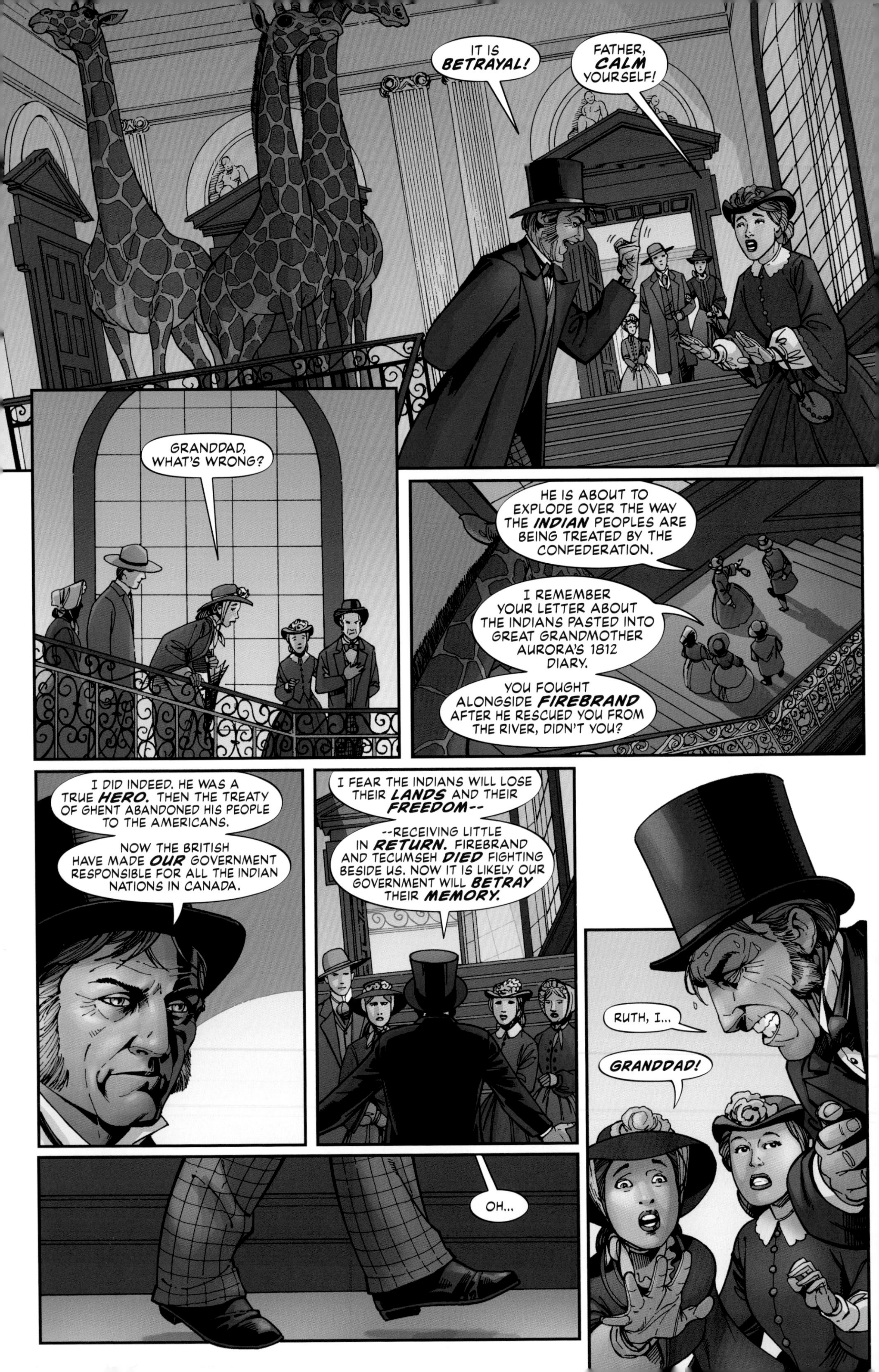
IT IS BETRAYAL!
FATHER, CALM YOURSELF!
GRANDDAD, WHAT'S WRONG?
HE IS ABOUT TO EXPLODE OVER THE WAY THE INDIAN PEOPLES ARE BEING TREATED BY THE CONFEDERATION.
I REMEMBER YOUR LETTER ABOUT THE INDIANS PASTED INTO GREAT GRANDMOTHER AURORA'S 1812 DIARY.
YOU FOUGHT ALONGSIDE FIREBRAND AFTER HE RESCUED YOU FROM THE RIVER, DIDN'T YOU?
I DID INDEED. HE WAS A TRUE HERO. THEN THE TREATY OF GHENT ABANDONED HIS PEOPLE TO THE AMERICANS.
NOW THE BRITISH HAVE MADE OUR GOVERNMENT RESPONSIBLE FOR ALL THE INDIAN NATIONS IN CANADA.
I FEAR THE INDIANS WILL LOSE THEIR LANDS AND THEIR FREEDOM--
--RECEIVING LITTLE IN RETURN. FIREBRAND AND TECUMSEH DIED FIGHTING BESIDE US. NOW IT IS LIKELY OUR GOVERNMENT WILL BETRAY THEIR MEMORY.
RUTH, I...
GRANDDAD!
OH...

THE DOCTOR SAYS IT WAS A MILD HEART ATTACK.

HE ADVISES *REST* AND AVOIDING EXCITEMENT.

AVOID EXCITEMENT INDEED! I AM AS GOOD AS EVER.

GRANDDAD, *PLEASE.* YOU MUST BE CAREFUL.

MY DEAREST LILLIAN. I *WILL,* I PROMISE YOU.

ENOUGH TALK OF MY HEALTH. ISN'T THERE A *CHRISTMAS FEAST* WE'RE MEANT TO BE ENJOYING?

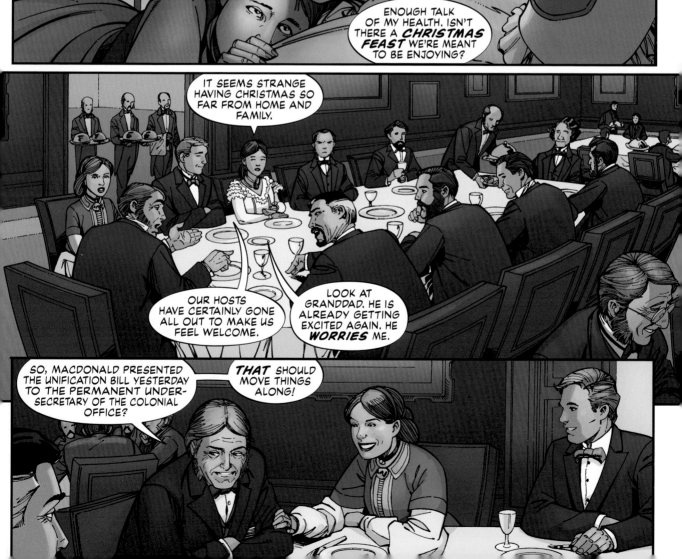

IT SEEMS STRANGE HAVING CHRISTMAS SO FAR FROM HOME AND FAMILY.

OUR HOSTS HAVE CERTAINLY GONE ALL OUT TO MAKE US FEEL WELCOME.

LOOK AT GRANDDAD. HE IS ALREADY GETTING EXCITED AGAIN. HE *WORRIES* ME.

SO, MACDONALD PRESENTED THE UNIFICATION BILL YESTERDAY TO THE PERMANENT UNDER-SECRETARY OF THE COLONIAL OFFICE?

THAT SHOULD MOVE THINGS ALONG!

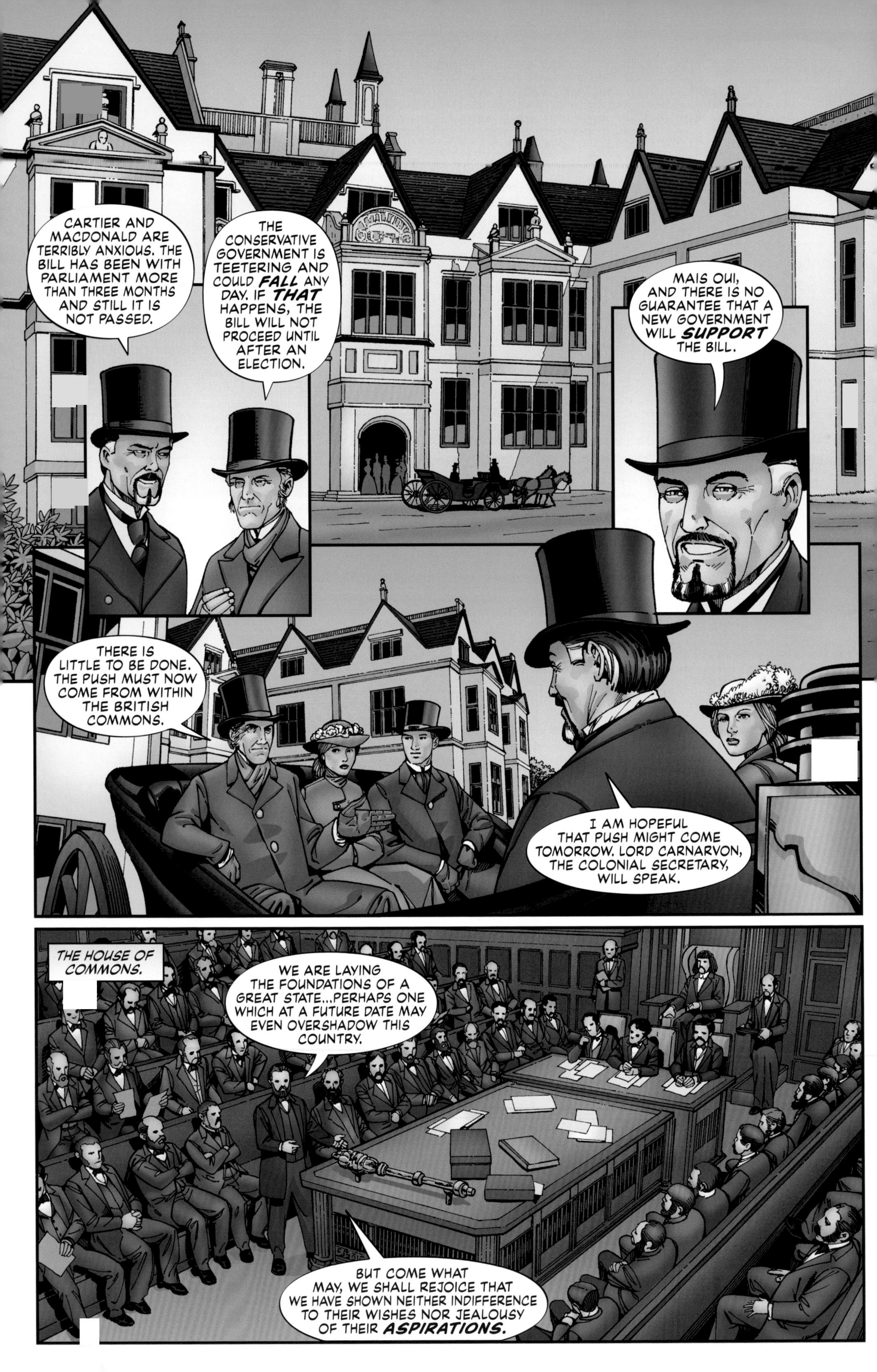
CARTIER AND MACDONALD ARE TERRIBLY ANXIOUS. THE BILL HAS BEEN WITH PARLIAMENT MORE THAN THREE MONTHS AND STILL IT IS NOT PASSED.
THE CONSERVATIVE GOVERNMENT IS TEETERING AND COULD FALL ANY DAY. IF THAT HAPPENS, THE BILL WILL NOT PROCEED UNTIL AFTER AN ELECTION.
MAIS OUI, AND THERE IS NO GUARANTEE THAT A NEW GOVERNMENT WILL SUPPORT THE BILL.
THERE IS LITTLE TO BE DONE. THE PUSH MUST NOW COME FROM WITHIN THE BRITISH COMMONS.
I AM HOPEFUL THAT PUSH MIGHT COME TOMORROW. LORD CARNARVON, THE COLONIAL SECRETARY, WILL SPEAK.
THE HOUSE OF COMMONS.
WE ARE LAYING THE FOUNDATIONS OF A GREAT STATE...PERHAPS ONE WHICH AT A FUTURE DATE MAY EVEN OVERSHADOW THIS COUNTRY.
BUT COME WHAT MAY, WE SHALL REJOICE THAT WE HAVE SHOWN NEITHER INDIFFERENCE TO THEIR WISHES NOR JEALOUSY OF THEIR ASPIRATIONS.

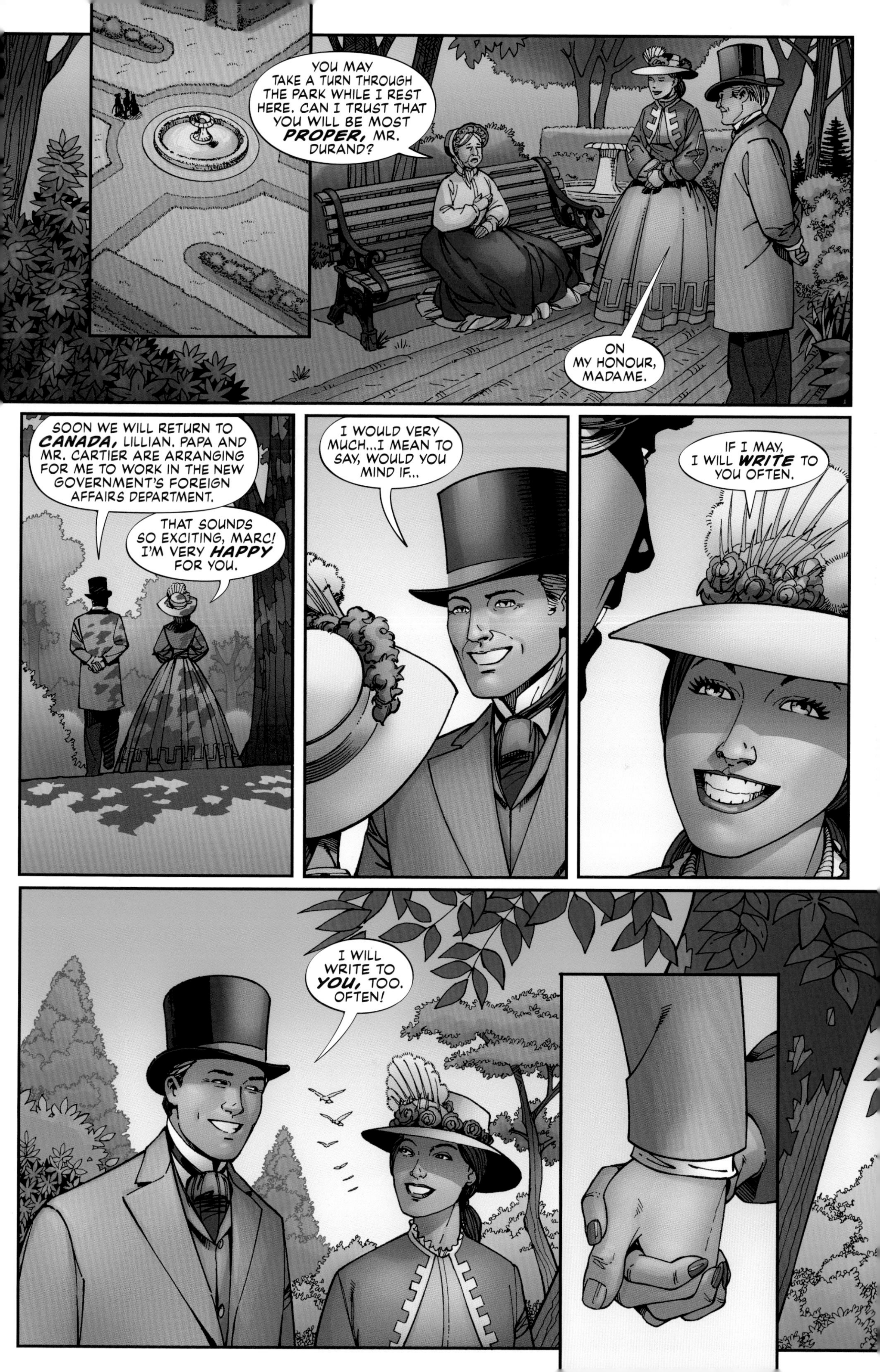
YOU MAY TAKE A TURN THROUGH THE PARK WHILE I REST HERE. CAN I TRUST THAT YOU WILL BE MOST PROPER, MR. DURAND?
ON MY HONOUR, MADAME.
SOON WE WILL RETURN TO CANADA, LILLIAN. PAPA AND MR. CARTIER ARE ARRANGING FOR ME TO WORK IN THE NEW GOVERNMENT'S FOREIGN AFFAIRS DEPARTMENT.
THAT SOUNDS SO EXCITING, MARC! I'M VERY HAPPY FOR YOU.
I WOULD VERY MUCH...I MEAN TO SAY, WOULD YOU MIND IF...
IF I MAY, I WILL WRITE TO YOU OFTEN.
I WILL WRITE TO YOU, TOO. OFTEN!

IT IS **DONE!** IT REMAINS ONLY FOR THE QUEEN TO SIGN THE BILL INTO LAW!

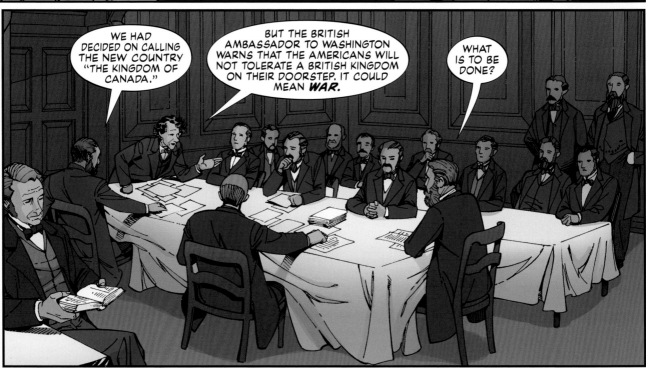

WE HAD DECIDED ON CALLING THE NEW COUNTRY "THE KINGDOM OF CANADA."

BUT THE BRITISH AMBASSADOR TO WASHINGTON WARNS THAT THE AMERICANS WILL NOT TOLERATE A BRITISH KINGDOM ON THEIR DOORSTEP. IT COULD MEAN **WAR.**

WHAT IS TO BE DONE?

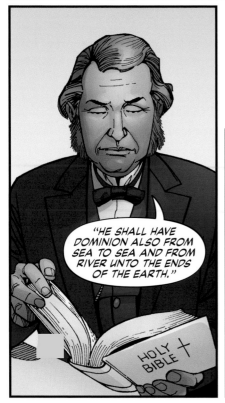

"HE SHALL HAVE DOMINION ALSO FROM SEA TO SEA AND FROM RIVER UNTO THE ENDS OF THE EARTH."

DOES THAT NOT DESCRIBE THE **CANADA** WE ALL ENVISION FOR THE FUTURE?

I SAY WE DECLARE OUR NATION THE DOMINION OF CANADA!

THE **DOMINION OF CANADA** IT **SHALL BE!**

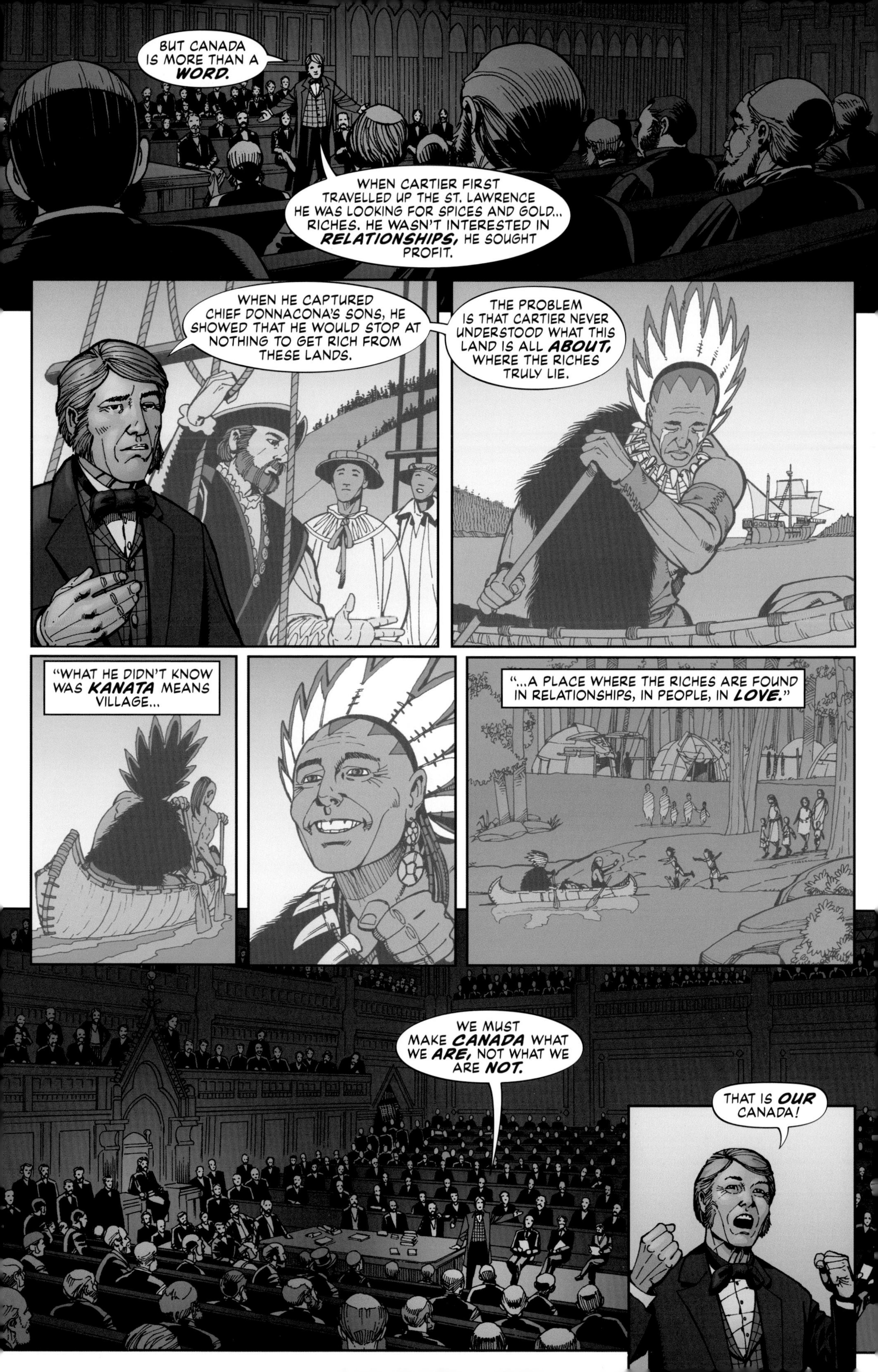
BUT CANADA IS MORE THAN A WORD.
WHEN CARTIER FIRST TRAVELLED UP THE ST. LAWRENCE HE WAS LOOKING FOR SPICES AND GOLD... RICHES. HE WASN'T INTERESTED IN RELATIONSHIPS, HE SOUGHT PROFIT.
WHEN HE CAPTURED CHIEF DONNACONA'S SONS, HE SHOWED THAT HE WOULD STOP AT NOTHING TO GET RICH FROM THESE LANDS.
THE PROBLEM IS THAT CARTIER NEVER UNDERSTOOD WHAT THIS LAND IS ALL ABOUT, WHERE THE RICHES TRULY LIE.
"WHAT HE DIDN'T KNOW WAS KANATA MEANS VILLAGE...
"...A PLACE WHERE THE RICHES ARE FOUND IN RELATIONSHIPS, IN PEOPLE, IN LOVE."
WE MUST MAKE CANADA WHAT WE ARE, NOT WHAT WE ARE NOT.
THAT IS OUR CANADA!

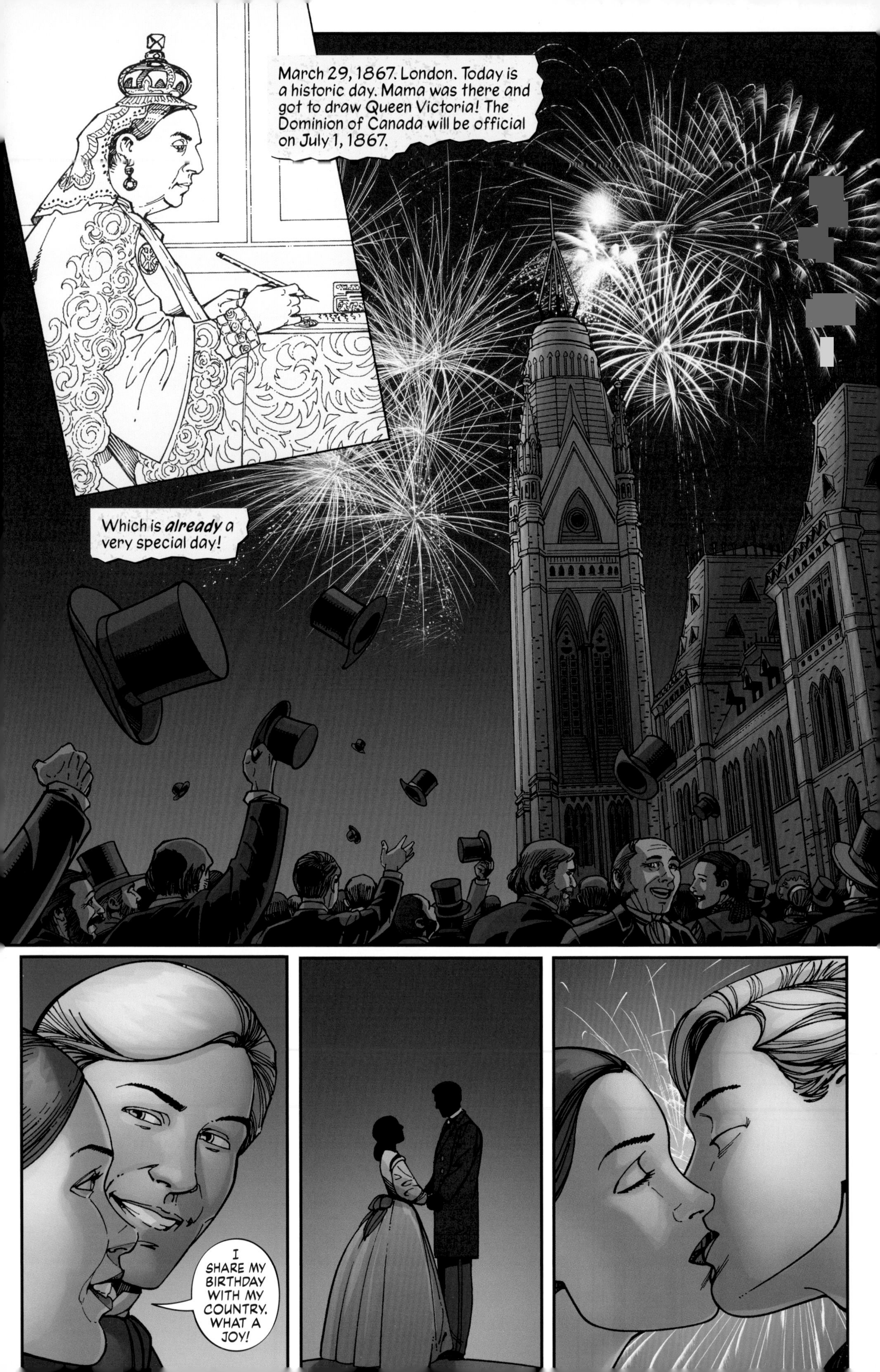

March 29, 1867. London. Today is a historic day. Mama was there and got to draw Queen Victoria! The Dominion of Canada will be official on July 1, 1867.
Which is *already* a very special day!
I SHARE MY BIRTHDAY WITH MY COUNTRY. WHAT A JOY!

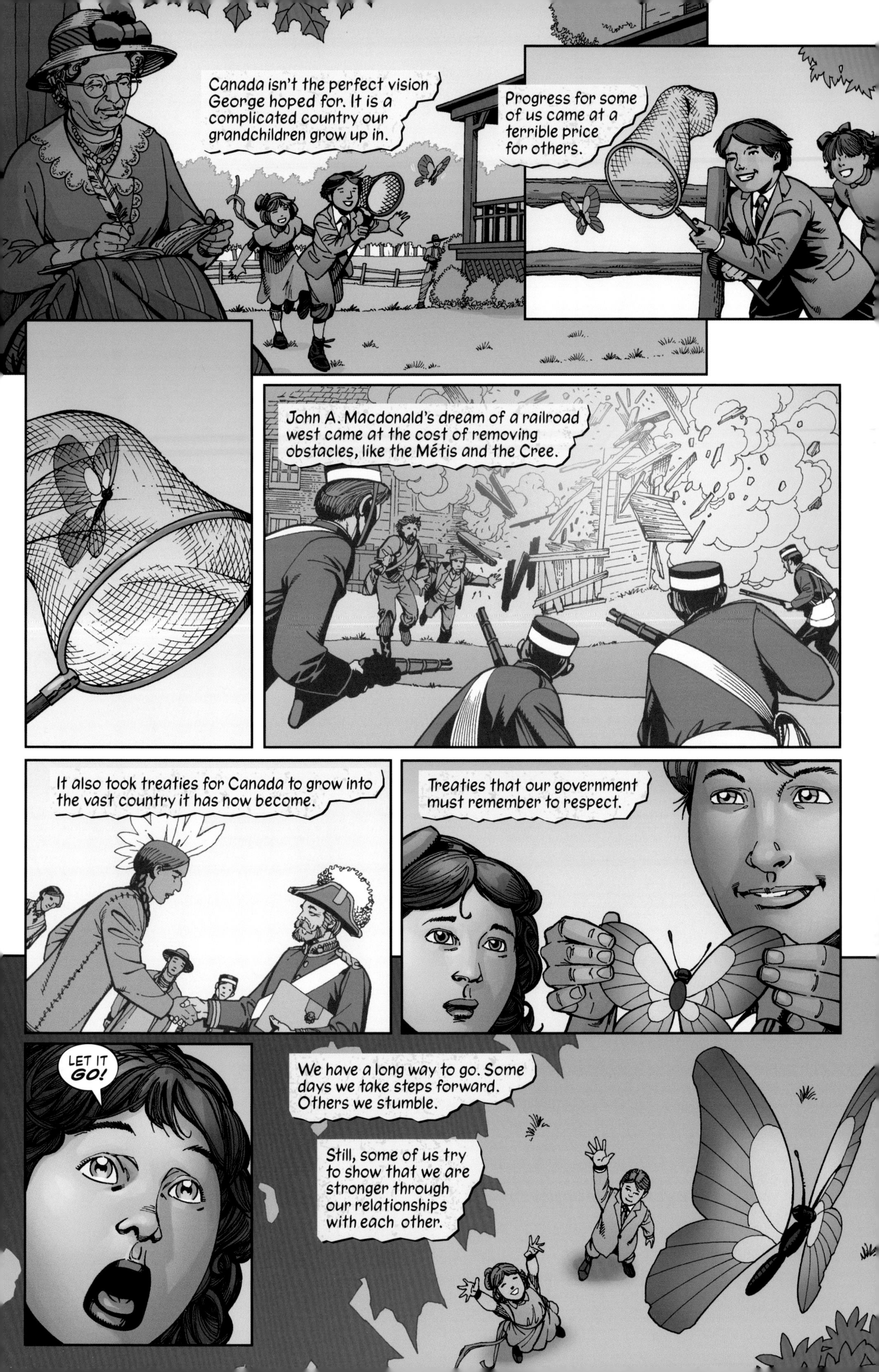

Canada isn't the perfect vision George hoped for. It is a complicated country our grandchildren grow up in.
Progress for some of us came at a terrible price for others.
John A. Macdonald's dream of a railroad west came at the cost of removing obstacles, like the Métis and the Cree.
It also took treaties for Canada to grow into the vast country it has now become.
Treaties that our government must remember to respect.
LET IT GO!
We have a long way to go. Some days we take steps forward. Others we stumble.
Still, some of us try to show that we are stronger through our relationships with each other.

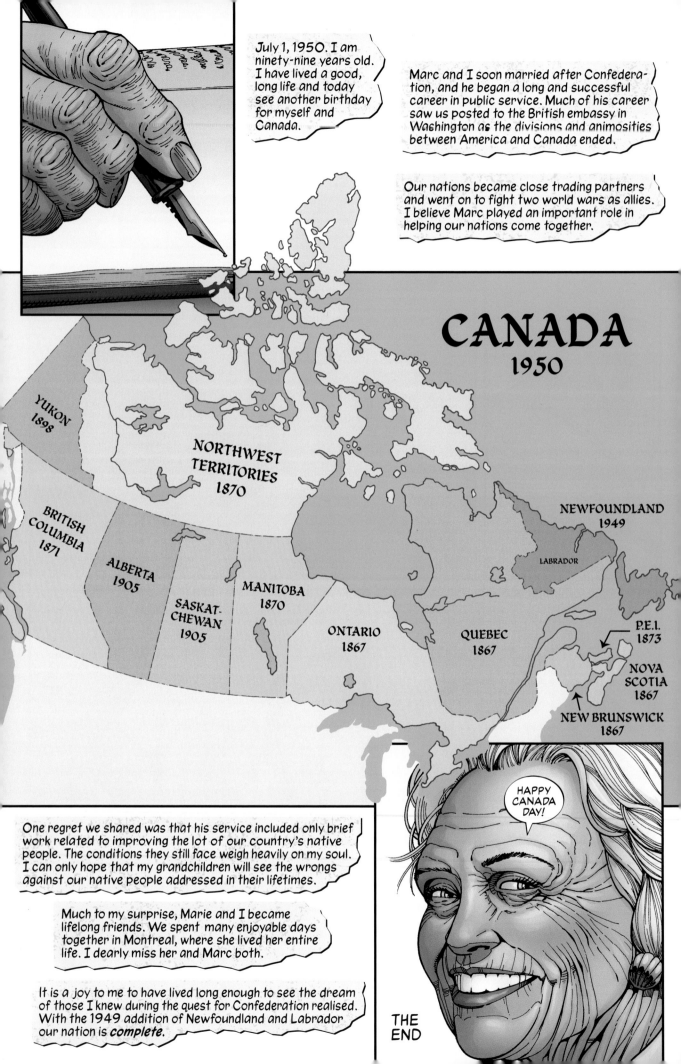

July 1, 1950. I am ninety-nine years old. I have lived a good, long life and today see another birthday for myself and Canada.

Marc and I soon married after Confederation, and he began a long and successful career in public service. Much of his career saw us posted to the British embassy in Washington as the divisions and animosities between America and Canada ended.

Our nations became close trading partners and went on to fight two world wars as allies. I believe Marc played an important role in helping our nations come together.

CANADA
1950

YUKON
1898

NORTHWEST TERRITORIES
1870

BRITISH COLUMBIA
1871

ALBERTA
1905

SASKAT-CHEWAN
1905

MANITOBA
1870

ONTARIO
1867

QUEBEC
1867

NEWFOUNDLAND
1949

LABRADOR

P.E.I.
1873

NOVA SCOTIA
1867

NEW BRUNSWICK
1867

One regret we shared was that his service included only brief work related to improving the lot of our country's native people. The conditions they still face weigh heavily on my soul. I can only hope that my grandchildren will see the wrongs against our native people addressed in their lifetimes.

Much to my surprise, Marie and I became lifelong friends. We spent many enjoyable days together in Montreal, where she lived her entire life. I dearly miss her and Marc both.

It is a joy to me to have lived long enough to see the dream of those I knew during the quest for Confederation realised. With the 1949 addition of Newfoundland and Labrador our nation is **complete**.

HAPPY CANADA DAY!

THE END

From the Diary of Lillian Stock

1867

September 1st, 1867

It has been two months to the day since the Dominion of Canada was created.

What a wonderful celebration in Ottawa. I had never seen such fireworks!

The morning after, I decided to find out more about some of the issues that either helped or hindered Confederation. Having witnessed most of what led to this great event, I wanted to understand it as fully as possible and record it here for future Canadians. As my country and I share a birthday, I rather feel like a Daughter of Confederation.

I clearly remember Grandad and the others talking on the Loxley Farm about how the end of reciprocity threatened the livelihood of many in British North America, and might even force all the colonies to join the United States. At the time the issue seemed rather complex, but it proved simpler than I thought.

The Reciprocity Treaty was signed by British North America and the United States on June 6th, 1854. The treaty gave American and Maritime fishermen the right to fish in certain waters under control of the other. More important for Ontario and Quebec (then called Upper and Lower Canada) it allowed free trade on most goods and products, or set only very limited tariffs. So the Loxleys could send wheat and other farm products to America, and Americans could send likewise to British North America. The treaty benefited us all.

By 1865 however, relations between British North America and America were poor, largely because the Americans in the Northern States thought we supported the rebels in the Confederate Southern States. There was little truth to this. But, as Grandad likes to say, truth is often to one person entirely the opposite of what it appears to be to another. So the American federal government gave notice that the treaty would be ended on March 17th, 1866. No argument by our delegations to Washington could reverse this.

Loss of free trade with the United States did have one positive effect. It caused many people in Ontario and Quebec to realise the need for new markets for our agricultural and other goods. The obvious market was the rest of British North America. With reciprocity, Ontario traded mostly with Ohio, Illinois, and Michigan. Quebec was tied to New York and Vermont, and the Maritimes were linked to Maine and Massachusetts. The only possible way to replace these markets was to increase trade between the colonies. Confederation made this easier because there was no need to negotiate treaties.

Canada, of course, still hopes one day the Americans will change their minds and reciprocity can be restored. But we are learning that each province has many things that the other provinces lack. As we build railways that connect us together this trade will become simpler and less expensive to conduct. Already Great Uncle Aaron reports he now ships some Loxley Farm goods to Montreal. Imagine! Marie's beloved baguette or morning croissant may be baked from our family's flour!

September 3rd, 1867

It seems the Americans have never truly accepted British North America's right to exist. During the American Revolutionary War of 1774 to 1776, they repeatedly invaded Lower Canada. Had their long siege of Quebec City succeeded, it is said the British colonies would have certainly fallen under their control and I would today be an American. But Quebec held out and the war ended with the Thirteen Colonies independent of the British Empire. About 50,000 people, called United Empire Loyalists, took refuge in Lower Canada and Nova Scotia rather than stay in the new country.

In the years following the revolution the United States and Britain could not get along. The Americans complained that Britain violated the new country's freedom of the seas by boarding and searching their ships for Royal Navy deserters and contraband goods. Meanwhile, American settlers pushed ever westward and made war on the Indians whose territory they claimed.

Many Americans believed British North America aided the Indians in fighting them by providing weapons and military advice. Grandad has always said this was not true. But combined with the sea issue, which was called impressment, it provided their politicians the excuse they needed to attack us in 1812. For three years the war raged and repeated attacks were driven off before the Americans agreed to a peace treaty. My family, like so many other Canadian families, paid a dreadful price for our freedom from American conquest.

The Treaty of Ghent, signed on Christmas Eve of 1814, restored the situation that existed between British North America and the United States in 1812. So the Americans won nothing from their war. The relationship between British North America and the United States slowly improved. The reciprocity agreement was a sign of that.

But then the Civil War broke out in 1861 when most southern states sought to break away from the United States and create a nation called the Confederate States of America. The war raged until 1865 and more than 620,000 people died. Mama says that when she and Grandad went to Washington that year to report on the war's end they were both frightened by how many Americans wanted to send the vast Union Army north to conquer our colonies and drive the British off the continent for good. Thankfully poor President Lincoln had no interest in this plan and wanted instead for Americans to concentrate on healing the wounds the war had opened in their own country. After his assassination, the U.S. government soon disbanded the army and the threat of invasion ceased.

This did not stop an Irish-American group, called the Fenians, from leading attacks into Canada and some people say, that the American government secretly supported the Fenians and encouraged them to take the British colonies by force. Thankfully the Fenian attacks seem to have ended without too many dying. The shoulder wound that Cousin Matthew suffered at Ridgeway has entirely healed and he continues his veterinarian work. I consider myself fortunate to have been able to spend time with him helping the animals. I shall always treasure those memories.

What does the future hold for relations between our new Dominion and the United States? Dear Marc (I can call him that in these most secret of pages) says Canada is certain to expand over the next few years. All the Maritime Colonies, the vast expanses of Rupert's Land, and the far distant colony of British Columbia on the shores of the Pacific Ocean, he says will surely join us. Once our country extends from sea to sea, Marc says, we will have a defined border between ourselves and America. Canada will consist of all the land north of that border and the United States will extend across all the land to its south.

I don't know if he is right, for just this past March the United States purchased from Russia the vast territory of Alaska. But I doubt that we Canadians will greatly miss losing a half million or more miles of ice and snow. If the Hudson's Bay Company turns Rupert's Land over to us we shall have more than enough ice and snow of our own!

I think most Canadians believe the time when we must fear being invaded by America is past. And as our boundaries become more settled relations between our two nations will improve. The old animosities, I hope, can be set aside and our two countries (which really have more in common than not) can live in harmony.

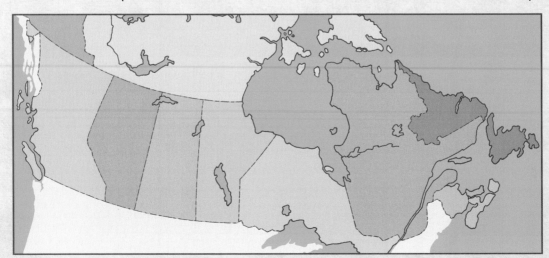

September 7th, 1867

Enough about Americans!

I will write now about the issues that threatened Confederation's success. If I sound like a school teacher, I'm sorry! Hopefully this will be useful information one day.

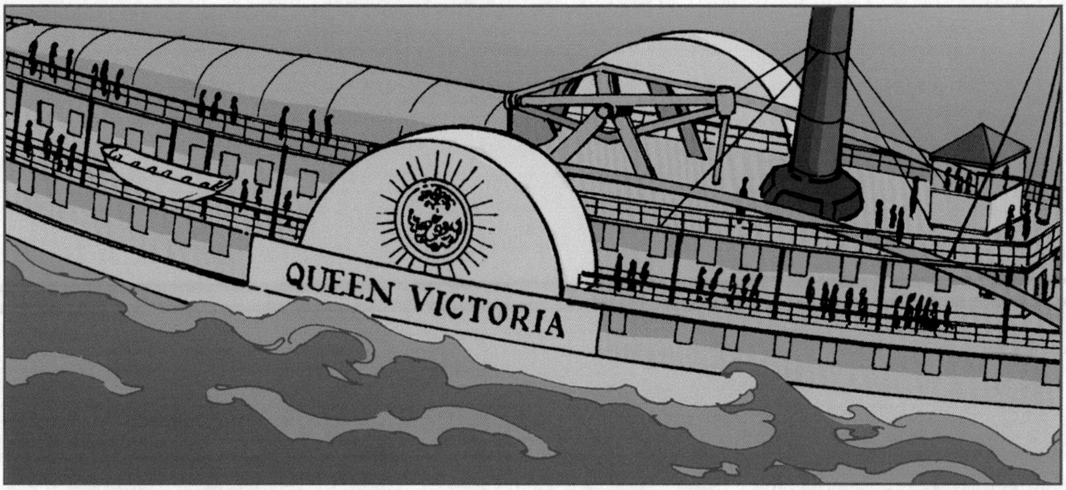
QUEEN VICTORIA

I remember aboard the Queen of Victoria how Mr. Brown once went on at length about the great differences between us Protestants in Ontario and the French-Canadian Catholics of Quebec. He believed these differences threatened Confederation. Mr. Brown made it clear that he did not like Catholics, whether they were French-Canadian, Irish, or otherwise, and most supporters of his Reform Party in Ontario were of like mind. We Loxleys have never understood this distrust and dislike of Catholics. Grandad says it is rooted in ignorance. While it is true that for centuries Catholics and Protestants slaughtered each other in Europe, it seems there is no reason to continue these hatreds. People are people no matter their faith. My Great Aunt Ellen married the French-Canadian Pierre Durand. It was a great tragedy for our family when he was killed in battle in 1814. Then, Great Aunt Ellen married a friend of his and moved to Montreal. This continued the French-Canadian side of the Loxleys.

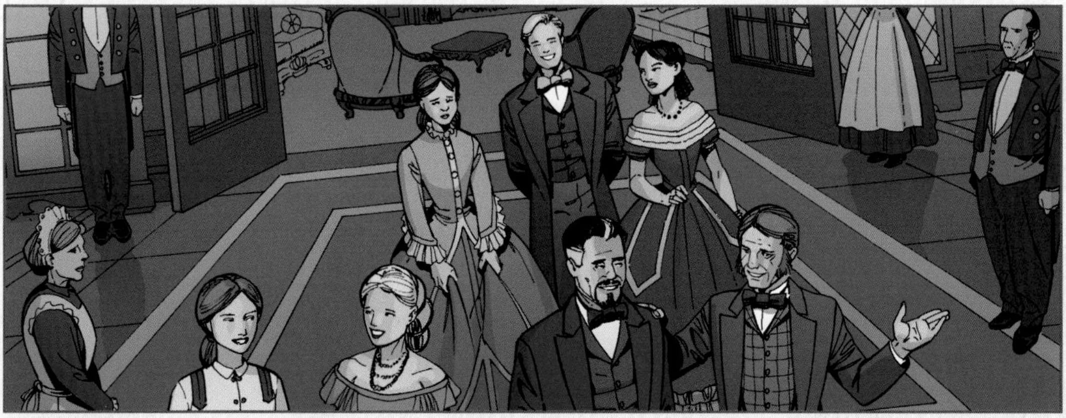

Of course there are Catholics who dislike Protestants too. The delegates from both religions at the talks feared that the other wanted to use Confederation to weaken the other. But it was the Catholics who had most to fear. The 1851 census had revealed that Ontario's population was now greater than that of Quebec. By 1867, Ontario's population was far, far larger and certain to continue growing.

Because Ontario had more people, Mr. Brown and his Reformers (sometimes called Clear Grits for reasons that escape me) demanded that the new country elect its government on the basis of what is called representation by population. Or "Rep by Pop" as it is known.

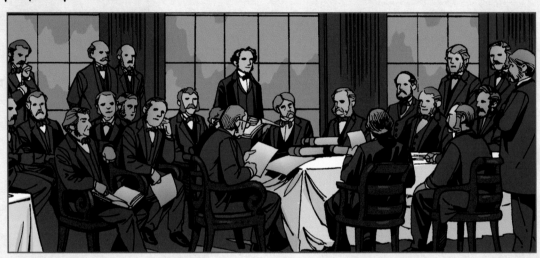

Mr. Cartier and other French-Canadian delegates responded that such an approach would place their people at the mercy of the British and Protestant majority. We have seen what happens to minorities at the hands of a majority in how the Americans have treated the Indians. They have been mercilessly driven from their lands. For a short time during the war, Grandad lived and fought alongside the Iroquois people after they rescued him when he became lost in the wilderness. In just a few years after the war's end they lost all their territory south of our colonies. Those that survive have taken refuge in Ontario and Quebec. Was it unreasonable that French-Canadians feared a similar fate at the hands of Mr. Brown's majority?

The response was that the rights of the majority must prevail, but that any majority would not unfairly treat a minority group. I overheard Mr. McGee's response to Mr. Brown aboard the Queen of Victoria when he advanced that claim.

"Would you truly have us believe, sir, that any majority would not tread roughly on the rights of a minority?" Mr. Brown talked on, but it seemed to me even he found his arguments unconvincing.

A solution was eventually found and it seems quite clever. The government consists of two houses, the House of Commons and the Senate. The seats in the House of Commons are subject to representation by population size. But there was a condition that helped ensure that Ontario could not impose its will on the French-Canadian population. Quebec was guaranteed sixty-five seats of the initial one hundred and eighty one, which as Mr. Cartier said meant that if the French-Canadians voted as a block they "could make and unmake governments."

It is different for those who sit in the Senate, as they are appointed rather than elected. Ontario and Quebec can each appoint twenty-four senators while New Brunswick and Nova Scotia have twelve apiece. This provides balance, making it impossible for Ontario's Protestants to mistreat Quebec's French-Canadians. The Maritime provinces were also assured by the creation of the Senate that their rights and interests would not be overridden by Ontario and Quebec.

The creation of the Senate was the first part of the solution. The other key to it was the agreement that all matters directly relating to the culture and life of a province are to be decided by provincial governments rather than the federal government in Ottawa. This was particularly important to the French-Canadians in Quebec.

This federal system differs greatly from the government of the United States and is modelled on that of Britain. It does seem, as Marc says, to ensure that our Dominion of Canada should never fall victim to the "tyranny of the majority" that plagues the Americans and has resulted in their fighting a devastating civil war. I hope to never live through a war in my lifetime. We have created a nation. There will be disputes, but I believe we have set ourselves on a course whereby they can be resolved peacefully.

September 10th, 1867

I was very disappointed when Prince Edward Island decided not to enter into Confederation. During the 1864 Charlottetown Conference I found the island colony most pleasant. I will surely never forget its strong red coloured soil. Her people struck me as very down to earth and straight forward. The kind of people we Loxleys like.

Newfoundland also chose not to join, but the only Newfoundlanders I have ever met were the three delegates to the Quebec conference. They spoke an old form of English that I found very difficult to understand. And they displayed no particular interest in being part of our new country. I can understand this, as their great island colony is separated from us by about 500 miles of stormy Atlantic Ocean. They made it clear that they are extremely self-sufficient and most of their trade and business is conducted directly with Britain to the east. They have no interest in looking westward to our continent.

For the people of Prince Edward Island the decision was less simple. It appears they feared the changes that Confederation might bring. Their own small legislative government would have been preserved as a provincial government, but the fear was that Ottawa would overrule its decisions. The island's population is so small that most everyone knows everybody else. And being on an island they tend to keep very much to themselves. Joining Confederation, it was feared, would eventually undermine their close and small society.

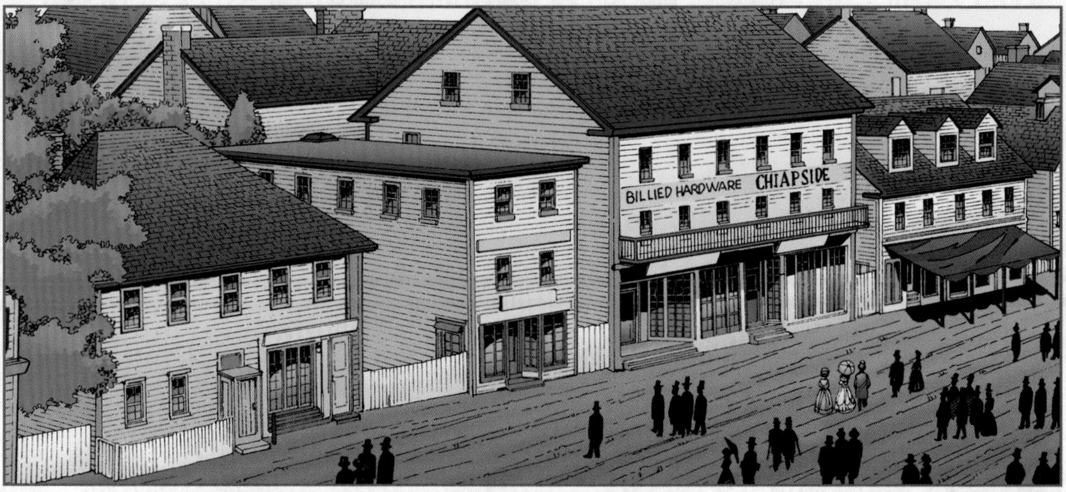
BILLIED HARDWARE
CHIAPSIDE

I hope eventually when the people of PEI see Confederation working so well for the rest of us that their minds will change and they shall seek to join us and be welcomed. I am not confident that Newfoundland will do likewise. But I shall hope they eventually do.

September 14th, 1867

Well, this has been an interesting project these past couple of weeks. I know there are likely issues that I have failed to address. But I think I have considered and investigated the main matters I think are important. One can only study upon things so much!

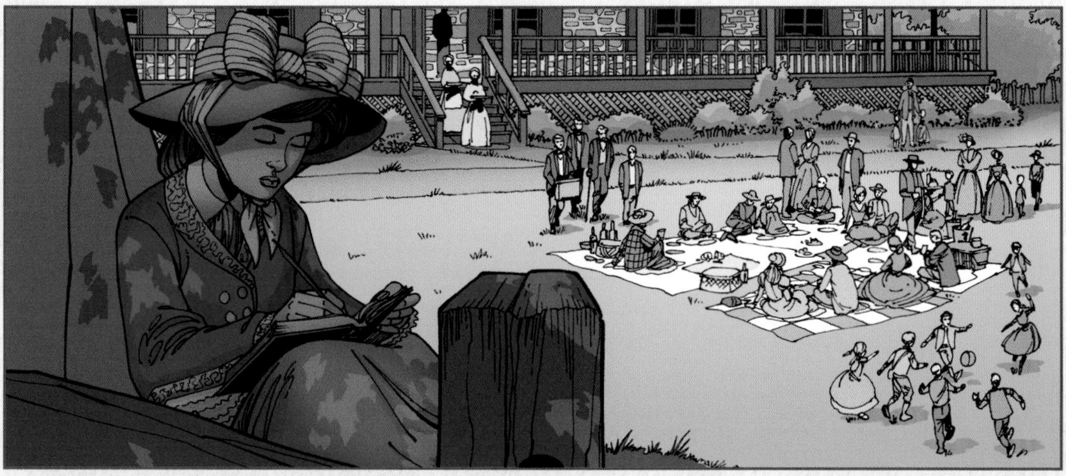

These past few years have been a fascinating adventure for me. I was but thirteen when we set off for Charlottetown and now I am a young woman of sixteen. It is as if I grew up from childhood to adulthood right alongside my country. At Charlottetown the idea of Confederation was barely more than just that, an idea that might or might not be realised. But it has been. I consider it little short of a miracle that a new country could be founded from a group of colonies whose peoples seemed to have so little in common.

Grandad is right to worry about how the native peoples of Canada will fare within our new country. I hope they will be treated fairly and with dignity, though the attitudes of many of the politicians I have met towards them breaks my heart.

Elsewhere, such as in the United States, great forces have pulled peoples apart rather than encouraged them to come together. I believe we Canadians may well be seen around the world as a beacon of hope for those who wish to see humanity live in a state of peace and goodwill for all.

This I fervently hope for.

There is so much to be hopeful about for the future and dearest Marc being not the least! And it is in no small part due to him that I have decided to end further study on the issues surrounding Confederation.

These pages might become increasingly dull at a time when my life is anything but. For yesterday Dearest Marc asked for my hand! And Grandad, standing in for my father, and with Mama's blessing, approved the match. We are to be wed!

And so another adventure now lies before me and I am anxious to set out upon that road.

The End!

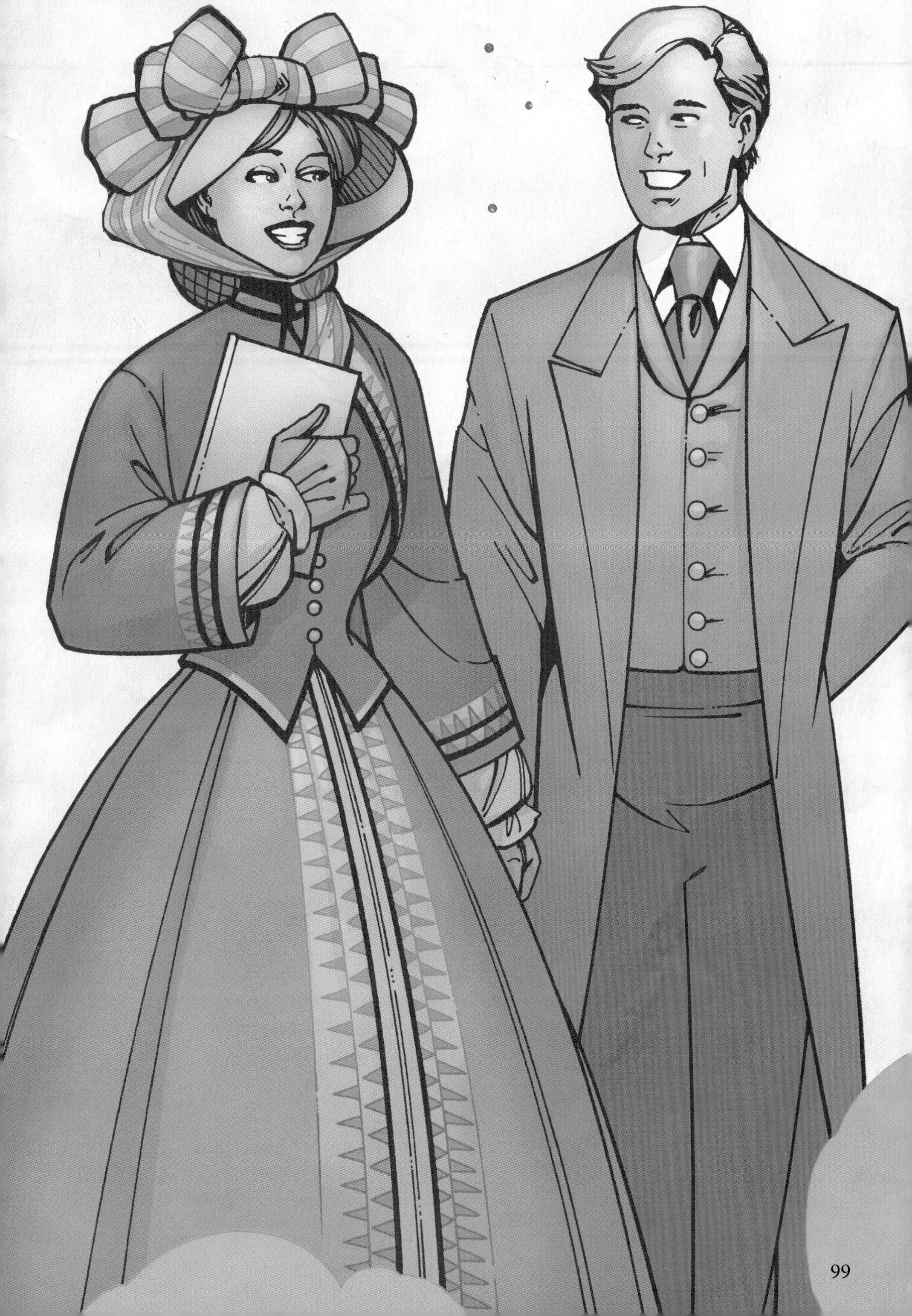

Afterword: Looking for Kanata.

We all travel at some point in our lives, whether to another community, country, or even continent. Human beings like discovering things, people, and places; they encourage and lead us to learn, experience, and tell new stories. Travelling is many things but it is most often exciting; full of the previously unseen, new smells and tastes and the often radically different. This can be both something to look forward to and something to fear – often at the same time.

Those first few moments in a new culture and community are full of incredible intersections of wonder and nervousness. What do you see? How do you act? How different is the food? The people? We're trained to make meaning of what our senses take in and fit the pieces we find into pieces we already have.

When we encounter something new we take what we already know and interpret it through that lens. This often challenges and expands our knowledge and experience as we take what we know and add what we don't. Think of it like a math equation. It's what comes after the equal sign that shapes our next world.

Sometimes our first moments set the stage for a whole series of misunderstandings. Often with very little information, we make decisions on the value and purpose of an entire host of things. Feelings like greed and desire, or ideas found in religious or educational institutions can shape relationships and policies and laws and governments. Impressions lead to choices that impact decades, even centuries of events into the future. Pretty soon we get to some damn confusing places. Contradictory. Conflictual.

Pretty much the Canada we have today.

People have been travelling to and inventing stories about Canada for a long time. The name "Canada" is in fact one grand intersection of competing ideas, misunderstandings, and conflicts – that we have never reconciled. This starts about 500 years ago with a little meeting between two men in 1534.

Turtle Island in the 16th century was a village made up of thousands of villages, a nation of nations. Not perfect by any means, this was a place of large and small governments and communities who worked collaboratively and competitively, trading and warring and sharing and migrating over the seasons and for many reasons. These people were travelling all the time, meeting new people, tasting new tastes, witnessing new ways of being, adopting and changing, and so on.

It was this way for millennia and not one bit of this changed when the Europeans arrived. Europeans were just a knot on an already existing tree, a ring in a long series of rings.

One of the first to arrive was Jacques Cartier, who in May of 1534 came to North America looking for a sailing route to Asia. Cartier was terrible at relationship-building. Reaching the eastern shores of Turtle Island, he first encountered groups of Mi'kmaq and traded furs for metal, the first recorded trade between Europeans and Indigenous peoples this far north. The next day, when more arrived to trade, Jacques commanded his men to shoot at them. Then, he and his men spent a few days shooting over 1000 birds on an island on his way inland.

Cartier was probably the worst house guest anyone could ever have.

On July 24, 1534, Cartier travelled to the mouth of Kaniatarowanenneh, later known as the St. Lawrence River, and set anchor near a village called Stadacona. After a couple of hours he put ashore and did what most Europeans did: claimed everything he saw for his country by planting a 10 metre cross with the engraving "Vive le Roi de France" on it. To him the land was uninhabited, unused, and empty. The problem of course, was he was actually standing in someone else's backyard.

Emerging onto the shoreline was a man named Donnacona, who had witnessed Cartier's arrival. Explaining he was a leader at Stadacona, he asked Cartier what he was doing, gesturing that planting a huge monument without permission was a little disrespectful. Some of his men even started to take the marker down. The Stadaconans clearly had law and it dictated that individuals did not simply walk into someone else's territory and take over the place.

In response, Cartier told Donnacona that he was simply placing the cross so that he could find and return to this place later. Then, he invited Donnacona onto his ship with the promise of trade.

Accompanied by three sons and carrying furs to exchange, Donnacona later arrived on Cartier's ship. He sought from the Frenchmen metallic items and refused trinkets or decorations. Cartier however wanted something else. Seizing the moment, Cartier took two of Donnacona's sons, Dom Agaya and Taignoagny, captive and told the chief they would be returned the following season.

Cartier saw the opportunity to obtain interpreters to achieve the real purpose of his journey: spices and gold. For Cartier, profit and resources was the primary reason he came to the New World, not relationships. Donnacona, likely seeing an opportunity to get a new, exclusive trading partner, let his sons be taken to France, no doubt wondering if he would ever see them again (I have always wondered how he explained this to their mother). After travelling up the coastline, Cartier found no spices or gold so he returned to France. While en route, Cartier demanded to know from his two captives where the riches of North America were. The boys told him that the riches they knew of resided in a place called "Kanata," the "great village." Imagining a place full of resources he could bring back for sale in France, Cartier marked his map with the name "Canada" and vowed to return to fulfill his vision.

Returning the following year, Cartier brought the young men to Stadacona, instructing them to show him Canada. The second the two sons touched land though, they returned to their father's side, for the men had reached their riches: their community, their family, their home.

A furious Cartier, in the meantime, left and continued to look for Canada. The captain hunted long and hard, almost succumbing with his men to a scurvy epidemic. And who saved him? His former captive, Dom Agaya, who returned and fed them cedar tea.

Blinded by dreams of wealth and profit, Cartier could not see Kanata for what it really is: a place of relationships. Of medicine, healing, and life. Of people. Instead, Cartier saw Canada for what he could take, turn into profit, and sell. The truth is that Canada has never really existed. There is only Kanata.

Unfortunately, we still live under Cartier's delusion. Most of the 18th and 19th century, the time covered by the The Loxleys and Confederation, illustrates this repeating cycle. As much as Canada is a place of immense personal and communal struggle by many brave men and women in history, it is also a place where the arrival of commerce and resource exploitation created a foundation for the country we know now.

As much as we can see Canada in these pages I encourage you to see Kanata too, in the moments it could have been, the place it always has been. Our riches lie in the way we interact, the gifts we trade, the stories we share – nothing else. It certainly does not lie in pipelines, corrupted waterways, and failed, genocidal policies like residential schools and the Indian Act. We are a people created by our interactions, good and bad, and the truth we tell about who we truly are.

Our past is covered with a veneer of national pride and patriotic fever surrounding the building of railroads and battles on the frontier, and we too often forget and obscure what had to happen for these moments to occur. We live in a history of removals, countless destructions of communities, and theft of property and ideology – this is the Canada we have to see too. We are also a place of tremendous generosity, bravery, and gift-giving, seen in words like Kanata, cups of cedar tea, and laws and policies like multiculturalism, democracy, and treaties.

Canada was not founded by two nations but hundreds, with French and English bringing food to an already bustling and full feast. Now, textbooks and history teachers may say that the English and French brought more food than they really did – and certainly pushed a lot off the table – but they are just two new members of a great village, where everyone was welcomed.

This is an important narrative all Canadians should know and learn, and was my purpose in participating in this incredible project, The Loxleys and Confederation. I hope I have helped to illustrate a Kanata we can all know the truth about. We will do well to see Kanata for the riches it is rather than the Canada we think we see, for one is real and the other is a fantasy. The more flags and crosses we drive into the earth to divide ourselves, the more we buy into visions of profit instead of people. The more we misunderstand one another, the less we know about ourselves and our history.

The more we fantasize about ourselves as Cartier's Canadians, the less chance we have to reach our fullest potential. Who we really are is a great village, full with the riches of our relationships. The riches of Canada lie not in imaginations of gold and spices, or the policies and stories we create from this vision, but in strong, healthy, equal relationships with people, the land, and the world around us.
That's the Kanata we deserve to tell stories about.

Miigwech,

Niigaanwewidam James Sinclair

Creator Biographies

Mark Zuehlke is an award-winning author generally considered to be Canada's foremost popular military historian. The Loxleys and Confederation is his first graphic novel, following his collaboration with Alan Grant on the award winning The Loxleys and the War of 1812.

His Canadian Battle Series is the most exhaustive recounting of the battles and campaigns fought by any nation during World War II to have been written by a single author. In recognition of his contribution to popularizing Canadian history, Mark was awarded the 2014 Governor General's History Award for Popular Media: The Pierre Berton Award. In 2007, his For Honour's Sake: The War of 1812 and the Brokering of an Uneasy Peace won the Canadian Author's Association Lela Common Award for Canadian History. The Canadian Battle Series Holding Juno captured the City of Victoria Butler Book Prize in 2006. Mark is also an award winning mystery writer, whose popular Elias McCann series has garnered much critical praise in Canada and abroad. Set in storm-swept west Vancouver Island village of Tofino, the series follows the reluctant community coroner Elias McCann. Hands Like Clouds, the debut in this series, won the Crime Writer's of Canada's Arthur Ellis Award for the 2000 Best First Novel and the third instalment, Sweep Lotus, was nominated for the 2004 Arthur Ellis Best Novel.

Claude St-Aubin was born in Matheson, Ontario, of French Canadian parents. He spent his teen and young adult years in Montreal, Quebec where he graduated from college as a graphic designer. He started his career as a comic book artist on Captain Canuck. He has worked for most of the major American publishers on titles including The Green Lantern, X-Files, Superman and Green Arrow. For Renegade, Claude has drawn The Loxleys and the War of 1812, and painted the children's book Jacqueline the Singing Crow.

Alexander Finbow started his career in England making movies, directing the action flick 24 HOURS IN LONDON as well as commercials, music videos and educational films. Now, a resident of Canmore, Alberta, Alexander handles the role of publisher and editor for Renegade. Alexander also writes the comics series SHADES OF GREY and the upcoming graphic novel BLOOD LIGHT with artist Al Davison.

Niigaanwewidam James Sinclair is Anishinaabe (St. Peter's/Little Peguis) and an Associate Professor in the Department of Native Studies at the University of Manitoba. He has written graphic novels for Graphic Classics and is currently at work on a comic called Trickster Reflections. He is also a regular commentator on Indigenous issues nationally on CTV, CBC, and APTN and internationally in The Guardian and Al-Jazeera America. His essays and stories can be found in the pages of The Exile Edition of Native Canadian Fiction and Drama, newspapers like The Globe and Mail and The Winnipeg Free Press, and online with CBC Books: Canada Writes. Niigaan is also the co-editor of the award-winning Manitowapow: Aboriginal Writings from the Land of Water (Highwater Press, 2011) Centering Anishinaabeg Studies: Understanding the World Through Stories (Michigan State University Press, 2013) and The Winter We Danced: The Past, the Future, and the Idle No More Movement (Arbeiter Ring, 2014).

Chris Chuckry is a professional colourist and illustrator, who has had the good fortune to have worked with many wonderful clients--including Renegade Arts Entertainment. You can also find his work in publications by DC Comics and Marvel Entertainment among others. Chris lives by the muddy Red River in Winnipeg, with his wife Cheryl, and two boys, Simon and Julian.

Todd Klein's comics career began in 1977 when he was hired to work in the DC Comics production department. During 10 years on staff there, Todd tried many kinds of freelance work including writing (TALES OF THE GREEN LANTERN CORPS), inking and colouring, but found lettering suited him best, and developed a freelance career as a letterer and logo designer. Through the years he's lettered over 65,000 comics pages and covers and designed over 800 logos. Todd has been presented with 16 Eisner Awards for Best Lettering, as well as 8 Harvey Awards and other honors. Current projects include SANDMAN with Neil Gaiman and J.H. Williams III, MIRACLEMAN with Gaiman and Mark Buckingham, STARSTRUCK with Elaine Lee and Michael Wm. Kaluta, THE LEAGUE OF EXTRAORDINARY GENTLEMEN with Alan Moore and Kevin O'Neill, and many other projects for DC Comics.

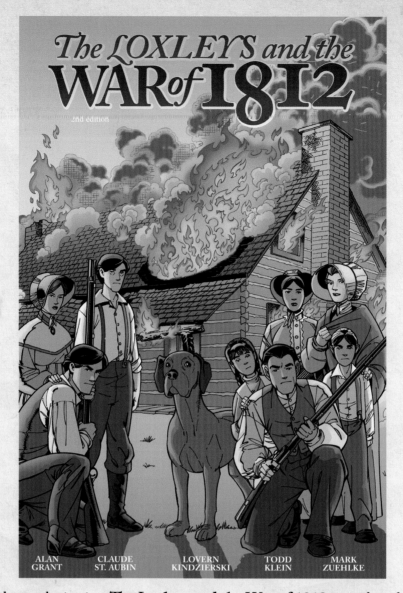

The LOXLEYS and the
WAR of 1812
2nd edition

ALAN
GRANT
CLAUDE
ST. AUBIN
LOVERN
KINDZIERSKI
TODD
KLEIN
MARK
ZUEHLKE

The best-selling and award winning **The Loxleys and the War of 1812** introduced us to the Loxley family in this 176 page, beautiful graphic novel featuring the historically accurate comic strip about a Canadian family caught up in the war. With an accompanying illustrated summary of the war and its implications for Canada and America, written by acclaimed Canadian, military historian Mark Zuehlke, plus maps and illustrations. The story follows the Loxley family living in the Niagara peninsula as they're torn apart by the American invasion of Canada in 1812 and the subsequent war that raged across both countries as British troops, Canadian militia, and First Nation warriors sought to thwart the expansionist plans of the American government. The story follows the characters through key historical events as they deal with the realities of war on their doorstep, their personal losses, setbacks and victories tied into the conflict.